The Streel

The STREEL

A Deadwood Mystery

MARY LOGUE

University of Minnesota Press
Minneapolis * London

Published by the University of Minnesota Press
111 Third Avenue South, Suite 290
Minneapolis, MN 55401-2520
http://www.upress.umn.edu

LIBRARY OF CONGRESS CATALOGING-IN-PUBLICATION DATA
Logue, Mary, author.
The streel / Mary Logue.
Minneapolis : University of Minnesota Press, 2020.
Identifiers: LCCN 2019027192 (print) | ISBN 978-1-5179-0859-1 (hc) | ISBN
    978-1-5179-0860-7 (pb)
Subjects: GSAFD: Mystery fiction.
Classification: LCC PS3562.O456 S77 2020 (print) | DDC 813/.54—dc23
LC record available at https://lccn.loc.gov/2019027192

Printed in the United States of America on acid-free paper

The University of Minnesota is an equal-opportunity educator and employer.

25 24 23 22 21 20   10 9 8 7 6 5 4 3 2 1

streel: from the Irish *straoill,* which means
a slattern, a slovenly woman, a harlot

The Crossing

As we're crossing over the deep to the other side,
Lord of patience, keep hold of our arm.
While we fear the strong wave,
Mary, keep watch for the swell.

—Irish prayer

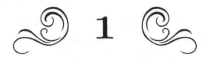

1

Galway, Ireland

May 1877

When I was fifteen and my brother Seamus sixteen, we attended our own wake.

Our family was in mourning, as they were forced to send us off to America. All the day and night, people came into the house. Seamus listened to stories with father and the men, and they all acted brave and talked of the wonderful things to do and see in America. Seamus paid them little mind. But the women wailed and worried as if we were dead and gone and talked of how we would be missed. They all of them talked about us as if we were not there.

While I was scared to my bones, I held myself very tight together. I knew this was my chance to make good. I would not end up like my aunt Mary, who was a widow, left roaming the streets of Galway, or like Biddy Rafferty, whose husband beat her when he wasn't too far gone with the drink, and I never wanted a child of my own to die like my sister Kathleen, at age two from the cholera. And certainly, as much as I loved her, I did not want to end up like my dear mother, whose heart had been broken too many times, having watched two of her children die and now two of us leaving. She had my younger sister Mary by her side and the two boys, Sean and Peter.

As the potato blight had struck again, the English landlord of the estate where we lived and worked determined he must rid himself of tenants. Not enough he had taken our land—no Irish could own land—but when these terrible times struck, he sent us away so he wouldn't have to feed us. He gave Mother the money to send Seamus and myself away to America.

My mother blessed him as if he did it for our own good. In part of my heart I did also. But in another part of me, which is dark and deep and I hope God never knows of it, I cursed him terrible for the tearing apart of my family.

Another famine had come upon the country. My father said it was not as bad as the great one, the Black '47, but still people were starving in the ditches. And there was talk of a terrible plague starting up in Limerick, as if we Irish had not endured enough. Our landlord claimed he had little food to give us, so we gathered seaweed to eat and the few slimy potatoes that were left in the field. With two fewer mouths to feed, our family would be better off.

So many of our neighbors had fled to America that, as their stories came back to us, I felt I knew the country. I was often asked to read the letters home because I had some schooling. Mother took education very seriously. She herself had learned to read in English from her father. Not that she had much time with fieldwork and the children.

Father spoke Irish most of the time, but Mother insisted we children speak in English. She said it was the only way we'd get on in the world, for the English ruled our land.

The letters from America told of hard work—scullery maid, laundry worker, serving girl—but also of the money that followed. I kept remarking on the many opportunities for young girls. I knew that if those girls could do it, I—with my learning and not half bad looks—would prosper. Maybe I would do it by marrying a rich man, maybe I would find a way to start my own business and make enough money to bring over my whole family.

After all, my name was Brigid, named for the goddess of poetry, midwife to Mary, and the saint with the holy mantle. She was a protector of all that was wise and good.

My mother had always said that I was brighter than the moon in the sky.

In many ways, the day of my wake was when my life began. I had come into womanhood only months before. As she showed me how to care for myself during that time of the month, Mother talked to me of men. She said, "Watch out for the charming tongue. They will woo you and they will want you. But if you give in to them, they will leave you worse off. Before you do anything, pray to St. Brigid."

When we left the next day, my mother cried as if the heavens had broken and were pouring through her. I could hardly stand it. Even Seamus looked away. My father was still smelling of the wicked *potcheen* he brewed himself. But he tugged on my hair like he always did when I pleased him and called on God in Irish, *"Dia linn!"*

When I stood at the stern of the ship and watched the land slip away, falling into the stone-cold sea, I wondered if I would ever return. A mist covered my green Ireland and I watched until my eyes blurred over. I watched until only the spires of the cathedral poked at the sky. Then they too vanished. We were to sea.

I crossed myself, said a short prayer for my travels. I was going to this new country for a better life. I swore I would find it.

Even though Seamus acted as if I was a bother, I could tell he was glad to have me with him on the trip. He patted me on the head and said, "We will be back with bags of gold."

I laughed. I liked the idea. But I never believed in the gold.

Soon, I saw the air was clearing. Blue sky stretched out all around us. A good sign. I felt into the pocket of my cape and touched the small packet of dirt that mother had put there.

"Don't forget Ireland," she had said. "Don't forget us."

On that first day to sea, Seamus brought two boys to meet me. My brother made friends easily.

"This is my sister, Brigid. She's the smartest *cailin* in all the countryside round Galway." With those kind words, he waved in the direction of his two new friends. "Paddy and Billy."

"Dia dhuit!" they said in greeting to me.

"Good day," I answered. I would not speak Irish to them. We were on our way to America.

The two of them were from farther south, near Donegal where there had been much unrest of recent times, the people revolting against the English who owned all our land. Paddy spoke of the Molly Maguires, a secret society trying to take the land back for the Irish, telling stories of their daring.

The older, taller one's full name was Padraic Hennessy. He had black hair that hung over his face like a curtain and steel blue eyes. For all that he had a sweet smile. But his eyes did not smile. Closer to twenty, Padraic had worked cutting peat to save money for the passage. Of the two he was the quieter, but his mind seemed to be always working.

Billy was the younger and smaller, the same age as Seamus, with bright red hair and light blue eyes. When he smiled, his eyes sparkled like the sea. He smiled often. I'd have bet he was a good dancer at the *ceili*. He boasted that his uncle had lined up work for them with the railroad. He bragged of the money that he would make in this new land.

When Billy and Paddy left us, I turned back to Seamus. "Do they really have work?"

"Oh, they talk big, but they're just poor exiles like us. We none of us have anything for sure."

✳　✳　✳

In the cramped quarters of steerage, where all the poor travelers stayed, I had the upper bunk to a woman named Maureen Kelly. She had a sweet young daughter named Kate, who was after turning two. They slept together in the lower bunk. Kate had a face as wide and as dear as an angel. She could say, "mam" and, "da," and she learned to say, "Bigid." Maureen was going to join her husband in Brooklyn she said. She told me that was a town very near New York. She hadn't seen him in nearly two years.

"The babe's had no father," she crooned, rocking the sweet rosy thing in her arms.

Over the next few days, the baby grew sick. The little girl could keep down no food, crying all night long. The second day, I went to fetch the doctor. But the steerage captain, Mr. Vance, stopped me.

"There's a child very sick," I told him.

Mr. Vance looked like an ox. His shoulders were broad under his fine trimmed jacket and his face was wide, with a heavy beard covering his chin. His voice was low and deep. There had been complaints about him already among the Irish. I knew he would not plead our case.

"One of the passengers in first class is not well. You'll have to wait."

So I waited, leaning up against the railing of the ship and watched the water. A shark followed in the wake, his fin cutting through the sea like a knife. The sailors told me it was a bad sign to see one stick so close to the ship. I watched the sky turn dark and the ocean black, and still I waited.

Billy and Paddy came up and asked me why I was sitting there so long.

"There's a baby sick. I'm afraid for it," I said.

"Don't say that so loud. No one wants to hear that about any sickness. It could run through the boat." Billy shushed me.

"I'm waiting for the doctor."

"I'll go fetch him," said Billy.

But he too was turned back by Mr. Vance.

All through the night, I waited, from time to time running down to my bunk to check on the child and Maureen. Then I would go back to waiting on the stairs, sleeping what little I could sitting up.

Toward dawn, Mr. Vance came strolling up to me. "I would go to bed if I were you. In fact I'd take you to bed myself. You're a toothsome little wench."

His tone frightened me, but I ignored it as best I could. "You would let a baby die too, I see." I readied myself to slip down the steerage stairs if he made a move toward me.

He turned on his heels, then came back and said quietly. "I have no control over this. They have the money to pay for the doctor's attendance."

"Can't he just come for a moment? The poor thing is wasting away. It's all but collapsed."

"Tell me the symptoms."

When I told of the color of the child and her labored breathing, Mr. Vance seemed shaken.

"Don't go near to that baby. I'll try to hurry the doctor."

Late morning the doctor finally came. He checked on the child and told Maureen to keep her warm and force-feed her if need be, but he didn't sound hopeful. He ordered me to sleep away from them. I knew then that what little Kate had was contagious.

I said a prayer for the sick as my father had taught me. All my life my father had told me the prayers to say for everything we did: prayers for waking in the morning, prayers for lighting the fire, prayers for praise, and prayers for the dead. I hoped in my heart that I would not have to say the latter anytime soon.

After my long vigil, I slept hard that night on the floor. Even though the planks were hard and cold beneath me, I slept until I no longer knew where I was.

When I awoke, dear, sweet Katy had joined the angels she so resembled. The women wrapped her tiny body in a sheet. The captain said a few words and the keening went up from the women. Maureen shrieked and tried to follow her child as the bundle was dropped into the sea. The men held her back by the arms. I remembered my own sister's death and a sadness filled me like the sea.

On the estate so many Irish babies died before they could even walk. My mother's words came to me, "If a child makes it to the fifth year, then it might live to see its own children born."

The ocean opened and closed, and Katy was gone. But I prayed that her small white soul would fly to heaven like a dove to the sun.

Maureen stayed curled up in her bunk and cried. I brought her soup but she would not eat. She said she wished she were dead. I reminded her that her husband was waiting for her. Surely there was some good there.

"Perhaps he can give me another child," she said, and tasted her soup.

Was this enough? I wondered. I swore that I would have more than children as riches.

❊ ❊ ❊

Halfway across the ocean, the weather stayed fine and the steamship made good speed. The fever had not spread and we were all breathing more easily.

At night the sea glowed. The phosphorescence we moved through made the water shimmer, the sailors told me 'twas nothing but a tiny sea creature. I hung over the side of the ship, enthralled by the light that rose from such darkness.

An older man pulled out his fiddle one night and played at the end of the hallway. A few people started to dance. God knows, we needed the merriment. The children jumped to the music and people tapped the floor and swung their feet. When another song began, the fiddle quieted and a dark woman wrapped in a shawl stood and sang "The Wearing of the Green":

Then if the colour we must wear be England's cruel red,
Let it remind us of the blood that Ireland has shed.
You may take the shamrock from your hat and cast it on the sod,
But 'twill take root and flourish there, though under foot 'tis trod.

After her voice faded away, there was not a dry eye in the crowd.

The bottles of liquor came out and moved from hand to hand. Happier music and more liquor put that somber mood away. I saw that Seamus was in the drinking line. I hoped he would not follow in the path of our father.

I closed my eyes and imagined I was back in Ireland, going to a crossroads dance. Then I felt my hand grabbed and smiling Billy pulled me to the floor. Just as I had thought, he was a fine dancer.

Seamus's stance grew crooked with a bottle hanging from his hand. Paddy, standing off to the side, watched it all but showed little. I longed to know what it would take to make him smile.

✳   ✳   ✳

One night I hid in the shelter of a life boat until I could not keep my eyes open any longer. The night was stormy, but I couldn't stand the sickly dead-meat smell of steerage and the confines of the bunks.

Just as I was about to take myself to bed, Mr. Vance stepped out on deck. I huddled closer to the canvas, but he saw me move.

He came toward me slowly, like a dog approaching a bower of baby rabbits, straight on to snap their necks. But when he stopped before me, he was very civil.

"Not a good night for taking the air." He laughed, a heartless laugh, that of a bully used to getting his way.

Trying not to show my fear, I stood up. "Then I will take myself off."

He stepped right in front of me, which brought my face up next to his chest. He made three of me easily. His large hand reached out and cupped my chin. "Not so fast."

So quickly he grabbed me that I had no time to prepare myself. In a moment he had a hand on my mouth and one wrapped around my neck. He bent over and his heavy breath whispered in my ear. "It will be easier if you give in. I will show you what a man can do for a woman."

He pushed me into the hull of the boat and came in on top of me. I knew the Virgin Saints fought to their death, and while I have never been that holy, I figured I could learn something from them. I struggled away from him, but he grabbed my shoulders and pushed me back down. Lifting my skirts up, he ripped away my undergarments.

In desperation I turned my head and bit his hand. He slapped me across the face, then descended on me again.

His weight alone was crushing. The air was pushed out of me and with it some of my will to fight. Sure the force of him would tear me apart. I prayed to Mother Mary that I would not take his seed to child, as my mother had warned might happen.

The ship tilted as Mr. Vance made to push into me. A force struck him and he roared in my ear. Suddenly, he was ripped away. I was uncovered in the night and saw that Seamus and Padraic had him by the shoulders.

Seamus yelled, "Bastard!"

But Mr. Vance was so strong that he was not to be held back. He lifted his arms and shook off Seamus and Paddy. They were boys and half his size. He pulled away, but they latched on to his arms and grabbed his hair.

I pushed down my skirts and got ready to jump into the fight myself when lightning cracked and the sea rolled. In the flash of illumination I saw that Billy was on deck.

He jumped on Mr. Vance and grabbed him from behind, tearing at his face with his hands. The big man spun around, but Billy hung on. It was hard for me to see all what went on in the melee of arms and legs.

Even with Billy's arms around his neck, Mr. Vance hit Seamus in the face. My poor brother went down hard on the deck. I ran to Seamus and found blood gushing from his nose. With a sudden heave of his shoulders, Mr. Vance shook Billy loose and backed away.

Paddy dove at his legs, but Mr. Vance kicked him aside and turned toward me. I was caught with my brother in my arms. All I could do was put out a hand to protect the two of us.

At the same moment, Billy dashed forward and kicked Mr. Vance in the leg, then danced back toward the rail. Mr. Vance shook his head and charged at him. Billy, instead of ducking away, stepped into him and shouldered the big man up and over the railing of the ship.

The back of him was broad and dark as a stone as he sailed out of sight.

A man overboard is a deadly thing. Mr. Vance was murdered as soon as his feet left the deck.

The sky burst over us and rain washed the blood from the decks.

We ran to cover, huddling on the stairs.

"Not a word," Padraic said. "Not even amongst ourselves. Say nothing."

I could not stop shaking. Seamus had an arm around me, but I could feel the fear was in him too.

"Our lives depend on our silence," Padraic whispered. "If we do not wish to join him in the water."

Billy would look at none of us and his arms moved as if he was fighting the dark.

"We are all in this together," were the last words Padraic said before we went to our beds.

The next morning the word was put out that Mr. Vance was missing. The captain asked for any news of him. No one knew anything but we four, and we kept silent. After a day, the captain declared Vance's death an accident, as it was assumed he had gone over during the storm that had raged all night long.

The death lived silently between us. Seamus would not let me out of his sight and that was how I wanted it. Even Billy and Padraic stayed near. We were quiet, caught in our own thoughts, but drew strength from each other.

After wandering around after me all the next day, Seamus finally asked me if I was all right.

"Yes, considering."

Then he looked down at my belly.

I assured him, "He did little to me."

"Thanks to the Holy Mother," he said.

In the days following, Billy hummed dancing tunes, seeming far from it all. Paddy, who had always been quiet, kept even more to himself. He became a shadow man, leaning over the railing, watching the water take away whatever fell into it.

✳   ✳   ✳

Three days later, a hint of a dark green showed on the far western horizon. As we drew closer, it grew. Finally we saw buildings. Larger than can be believed. Like castles they were.

All classes of passengers lined the rails—from the fine ladies of first class to the dirty waifs of steerage. Children were hoisted on shoulders. A cheer went up. We could see the promised land.

Seamus smiled for the first time in days and threw an arm over my shoulder. Padraic came and stood near us. I looked down into the churning water and laughed, thinking we could swim from here if need be.

I reached into my cloak and pulled out the packet of dirt my mother had given me. We had arrived. I let the dirt fall into the water below us, the earth of Ireland no longer a weight upon me, but I knew I would always carry it in my heart. I brought my eyes up to see what was now my new home.

The Hunt Mansion

King of the bright sun
Who knows our every need,
Be with us every day,
Be with us every night,
Be with us every night and day,
Be with us every day and night.

—Irish prayer

St. Paul, Minnesota
November 22, 1878

I stood still for a moment, holding the tea tray, watching snow drift down out the front window. More than a year had passed since I had landed in New York. How lucky I was to find myself in the middle of the country, working for a wealthy family, getting their house ready for this holiday they called Thanksgiving. I knew my father would approve of this celebration, for wasn't he always saying we should be giving thanks every day of our lives.

I would have loved to have my family with me for the holidays. Even to see them for a day or two. Christmas at home had been simple fare, a rabbit if Father was lucky with the snare, stewed apples that Mother had put by. Homemade presents of knitted scarves and carved toys were all that were given, but joy in the making was what counted.

My family was never far from my thoughts. Missing them was a constant ache in my heart. I sent them a bit of money every time I was paid. Mother wrote when she could, assuring me that times were better, but I was hard pressed to believe her.

When Seamus and I had first arrived, we stayed with our uncle Jim in New York for a few weeks, but it was obvious the poor man could barely keep his own family together. Then Seamus left to work with Paddy and Billy on the railroad.

With an empty feeling, I had watched the train that took the three of them away until it was only a black smudge in the distance. I envied them, having each other, while I was left alone in the world, with no family at all.

How could I manage with only myself? But before leaving Seamus had promised we would be together again soon.

After days of walking New York's hard and endless streets, I managed to find work in a boardinghouse. There were ten residents and I was the only servant. Back-breaking work it was, and I was only fifteen. From six in the morning until nine at night there was no time to take a breath. I served food and cleared tables, then started all over again. I was forever exhausted.

Some of the men were handy, grabbing at a girl. But I learned to laugh at them and turn their words against them. Coming from a big family, I knew how to take teasing. Many of them were kind and would sometimes slip me a little extra money on the side. The woman I worked for, Mrs. Ester, was mean—and doubly mean with the money. I had little to send home to my parents.

Seamus wrote me soon after he left. He was in Pennsylvania, working on the railroad. As the rails went west so did he, with Paddy and Billy still by his side. Then I didn't hear from him for months.

In the meantime, one of the boarders mentioned that the girl he was marrying was leaving a position in a private home near Washington Square. With her as reference, I stepped into the job. My new mistress, Mrs. Lowdon, was cruel in her own unhappiness and her husband was a drunk, but at least I wasn't the only servant. They also had a cook and a manservant.

I slept in a cold attic, washed floors, emptied the slop, and did all the drudgery labor—but I also learned how to set a table and how to serve. I had moved up in the world. For all my raw fingers and aching back, I was learning the work of a house servant.

When I next heard from Seamus, he wrote from the Dakota Territory, a town called Deadwood. He, along with Paddy and Billy, had staked a gold claim. He bragged that they were on their way to making their fortune. I wondered what the three of them had gotten into.

He sent me a bit of money and told me I might try for a position with the Hunts, a wealthy family in Minnesota. He had become acquainted with the son as the family had some interest in his claim. I would rather have joined Seamus in Deadwood, but he wrote that I should not come. He described the new town as a raw and dirty world with men going deep into the earth and coming up with nuggets. "Bags of gold do line the streets."

As he had instructed, I wrote a neat letter to Mrs. Hunt about the position. She answered me with speed, asking me to come. I packed my bags and walked out on my job that day and bought my first ticket for a train.

I loved riding on the train all the three days of travel to St. Paul. In the early spring, the land turned green as I sat in coach and watched out the window. I lived on bread and bowls of soup, the cheapest food on the menu in the dining car, washing myself in the bathroom sink and catching what sleep I could in my seat.

As I stood in the enormous St. Paul train station I could see that over thirty trains a day came through from all parts of the country. I had been told that the population was nearly forty thousand in the city. Not as big as New York, and I was happy to be in a smaller town.

At my first meeting with Mrs. Hunt, I told her I was from Galway. She brightened, then bowed her head. "My father was born there. He's been gone now these past five years. May his soul rest in peace. We'll be glad to have you working for us, Brigid." Kindness lit up her eyes.

There were eight of us servants, and a stable boy and a groomsman attended to two teams of horses, a carriage, and buggy. There was Aggy the cook and her two kitchen helpers. Then there was Bigsby the butler, and Rose, Anna, and I, the housemaids. We were roomed down in the lower floor next to the boiler room. I didn't mind it. Sure there was not much light, but it was always warm. For the first time in my life, I slept in a heated room. Sheer luxury.

Mrs. Hunt was good to us all, making sure we were well cared for. She gave me—like all the other servants—two changes of uniforms, but she also handed down to me a good dress, an everyday dress, and even a coat that she claimed she no longer wore. More clothes than I would ever have imagined. I so wished my mother could see me. I wished she could sink into a tub full of warm water like I did once a week. I wanted my family to have all this too.

The hardest thing for me was learning the proper behavior of a servant in such a fancy house. Once I fell asleep in a chair in the parlour and Bigsby scolded me to high heavens, saying that I was never even to sit down on the job. He had to remind me often to walk slowly and quietly in the house, speak only when spoken to, and keep my own thoughts to myself.

With great effort, I learned not to talk when I was serving food. The first time I was allowed to serve the family, after I had set down all the plates, I bid them have a good supper, which I thought was just good manners. Bigsby had looked at me as if he wanted to turn me into a block of salt.

*　*　*

On that day before Thanksgiving, we were all awaiting the arrival of Prince Charlie. That was what the staff called Mr. and Mrs. Hunt's twenty-four-year-old son.

The house had never been in such a stir. We had polished and waxed and washed and dusted every inch of the house, cleaned all the fine silver, put new linens on all the beds, stacked oak logs in all the fireplaces. I never saw such goings-on.

Charles Hunt had been gone for nearly a year, tending to his father's new mining business in the Black Hills. Since I had worked at the Hunts' home only a short while I had never met him.

A letter had come that morning for Mrs. Hunt. She was reading it as I brought in her tea. In her early fifties, she held herself very upright. Threads of gray streaked her dark brown hair. Not really beautiful, more handsome I'd say, she had a wide face, deep blue eyes. I knew life had not always been this easy for her. At the start, she had worked alongside her husband and then had lost two children in her younger years. Now she had only Charles, her eldest, and Dorry, her baby as she called her, a sprite of a child at ten.

She turned to me and said, "Tomorrow, Brigid. According to his letter, he'll be coming sometime tomorrow. In time for the holidays. I can hardly wait to see him, my darling boy."

After Mrs. Hunt left the room with her letter, Bigsby came in and told me to sweep the snow off the front steps. Without wasting a moment, I put on my coat and grabbed the broom, anxious for an excuse to be outside in the crisp air.

Before stepping outside, I caught a glimpse of myself in the looking glass by the front door. A full face with a dusting of freckles looked back.

My eyes held the soft gray that is in a field mouse's fur. My curly hair was the blackness of shoe wax. No beauty, I thought, but I looked better since I had come to the Hunts' house.

As I pulled the front door open, a young man almost fell in on me. He had been about to knock. He was well-dressed and stood tall, with a smile that filled his face and lit up his eyes.

"Oh," I said and I must have sounded as if the wind was knocked out of me. Between the surprise of his appearance and his obvious good looks, I could hardly breathe.

"This is a good start," he said, looking down at me.

"May I announce you, sir?" I asked.

"Yes, please." He stepped in the door and pulled off his gloves. "Tell them Mr. Hunt, Mr. Charles Hunt is here."

He had his mother's handsomeness and his father's vitality. I ushered him into the entryway. "They're not expecting you 'til tomorrow," slipped out of my mouth.

He looked at me, then laughed. "You seem to know much that is going on in this house. For your information, I caught an earlier train."

"Your mother will be so happy."

"I am delighted to make her so."

I reined myself in. As Bigsby reminded me often, I had to remember my place. "Yes, sir. I'll go fetch them."

"No." He grabbed my arm. "Don't. Let me surprise her. Where is she—do you know?"

"Yes, she went to join your father in his office."

"Perfect," he said and went off to find them.

The Prince was here and now the holidays could begin. I retrieved my broom and finished sweeping down the steps. My thoughts went to Prince Charlie. My mother always said if you wanted to know the worth of a man, check his teeth. Mr. Charlie had good teeth.

I wanted desperately to ask him about Seamus, my brother. To think that Charlie Hunt had probably seen my brother in the last week made me miss him all the more. Had Seamus grown tall? Was he sporting a beard? I hoped I would get a chance to ask him or that he might think to mention Seamus to me.

The trees were laced with a cloth of white. Only a skiff of snow was on the sidewalk. Snow was a lovely thing when you had a warm house to sleep in. I finished sweeping the steps, then went back into the house to tell the others of the royal arrival.

"He's here," I announced to Aggy.

She was stirring something in a cast iron pot at the large black range that took up half the kitchen wall. The range often seemed like a beast to me, especially when I had to feed it wood. Aggy turned and yelled at me above the roar of the stove, "What are you saying, my girl?"

"I let him in the door. Prince Charlie, he's here. Just arrived. He went up to see his parents."

"Sweet Jesus, but I'll be glad to see that scalliwag." Aggy turned a little jig in the middle of the kitchen. She was a sight to see—this small, round woman moving her feet so fast that they almost disappeared.

"What are you stirring up for dinner tonight?" I asked. The range was roaring and whatever was bubbling away smelled good.

"Beef stew. That will make my Charlie happy."

"Does everyone like him so much?" I asked.

Surprisingly, her face fell. She pushed a few stray hair locks back up off her face. She sat down on her stool near the counter. "Not everyone. I guess that's too much to ask. Mr. Charlie is a healthy young lad with warm blood pushing through his veins. He's made a few girls upset and once more than that."

I went off to set the table and wondered about what Bonnie Prince Charlie might have done.

✻ ✻ ✻

That night at dinner, I helped serve. Bigsby had the night off. As it was just family tonight, they ate in the breakfast room—a warmer, more intimate space than the formal dining room. A wood fire blazed in the fireplace, and they sat close to each other around the dark oak table.

Mr. Charlie had much to tell of his time away. Often, I didn't want to leave the room to get the next course when he was in the midst of a good story. I would stand on the other side of the door to hear the end of it. "... then he slapped down his cards with one hand and picked a gun up in the other. But rather than shoot the man, he popped the light hanging over the table and glass rained down on them all."

Aggy had done herself proud with the meal: fresh potato rolls, a lovely beet salad, the beef stew, and for dessert, lemon cake. Mr. Charlie had seconds of the stew and, oh, Aggy beamed at that as I came flying back into the kitchen with his request.

"I suppose no one's been feeding that poor lad," she mumbled happily as she served up another bowl.

When I brought the stew back in and set it in front of Mr. Charlie, he smiled at me. I simply bobbed my head in answer.

Dorry was on her best behavior. She sat up straight and ate all her food without complaining. She watched her brother's every move. He teased her and called her Dorry Gumdrop. Sometimes, just Gumdrop. She looked as if she was afraid of him. All through dinner, she held in her lap the new doll that her brother had brought her. He told her the doll was from China. With straight black hair and a large white face, it looked like a Chinese baby and so was named Blossom by Dorry. She stared at her brother and kept one hand on her new baby doll, covering it with her napkin so no food would drop on it.

When I brought out the lemon cake, Mrs. Hunt stopped me for a moment and introduced me to Charlie. "This is Brigid Reardon, Charlie. Don't you know her brother out in the Hills?"

Mr. Charlie looked at me with new interest. He seemed to be weighing me. I nodded my hello. "Seamus's sister. There's little likeness," he commented, then remembered his manners and added, "How do you do?"

I curtsied. And that was all. He gave me no word of my brother while I served the cake.

After dinner, Mrs. Hunt sent Dorry off to bed in Rose's care, then went into the kitchen to consult with Aggy about Thanksgiving dinner. Mr. Charlie and his father went up to the study.

I was asked to bring up a new bottle of port for the men's after-dinner drinks. When I walked into the library, they were near to the fire and looked so obviously father and son, even sitting in chairs the same way, arms open, legs apart. The conversation stopped when I entered, so when I left I listened at the door, curious.

I heard Mr. Charlie say, "Father, I'm finally getting ready to make an offer on that claim of Seamus Reardon's. I think their claim is worth even more than they're asking and I'd hate to lose it."

At that moment, I heard footsteps at the bottom of the stairs. I moved quickly away from the door and wished Mrs. Hunt a good evening as she came up toward me.

She stopped and smiled at me. "Thank you, Brigid. Now that Charlie's home, we will have a true Thanksgiving tomorrow."

I descended the stairs, wondering if Seamus knew what he was getting himself into, doing business with Charlie Hunt.

3

Thanksgiving Day, 1878

In late November the sun set near to five. On this fine Thanksgiving day, the family would eat soon. I was sent in to light the candles on the table. We had only put in two of the ten leaves for the mahogany table. The dining room with its dark woodwork and tooled leather walls glowed with warmth. Roses tucked into pine boughs adorned the middle of the table. Mr. Hunt had twelve dozen roses shipped in for this holiday—a wild extravagance for so late in the year. They filled the room with their honey scent.

Mr. Hunt's sister's family had come to St. Paul for the holiday so there were ten sitting down to dinner. The gold-rimmed Limoges china glinted in the candlelight. Matching gold-rimmed wine glasses waited to be filled. We had taken the fine silver from the vault and polished it until you could see your face.

After I had lit all thirty candles, I stood back and looked at the room. The light from the candles made the gold leaf in the plaster ceiling shine all the brighter. Like a fairy castle it was. My mother would never believe such splendor existed. I would write and try to describe it in my next letter and explain how on the feast of Thanksgiving the Americans ate more food in a day than my family had eaten in a week.

Even old Bigsby looked smart. He wore a white carnation and had slicked his thin hair back into a shine. He had looked us all over. "Please, do yourselves proud today. The young master is back and we have company. Everything must be perfect."

As I was standing in the dining room watching the rosy light grow as all the candles caught and bloomed, I was spoken to.

"Quite a scene," Charlie Hunt said at my side.

I gave a yelp, which was quite unladylike. "Let a body know when you sneak up on them like that!" I said, speaking more familiarly than was proper.

"I'm sorry." He took my elbow and turned me toward him. "You looked like the little matchgirl, standing and looking in on the dinner."

I held up my long match. "But I don't plan on freezing now that my match has gone out."

"You've read the fairy tale?"

"I've read many books." I didn't tell him that most of them were from his father's library.

"My, my. I have underestimated you."

Mrs. Hunt walked into the dining room at that moment and saw us together. For a moment, there was an odd look on her face and then she smiled as she called to her guests. "Come everyone. Charlie's so hungry he's ready to sit down without us."

❃   ❃   ❃

After the family finished dinner and was settled in the library, playing charades, it was time for the servants' Thanksgiving meal in the kitchen.

Aggy laid out a fine spread for us: ham and turkey, potatoes and fresh rolls, beans and carrots, relishes and pickles. And then there were the pies: mince and pumpkin and apple. We ate as well as the family that day. Mr. Hunt even sent in several bottles of wine.

Rose and Anne got the giggles and went on about Mr. Charlie. "If he isn't as handsome as they come," one of them would whisper. They'd both laugh and then the other would say, "Those eyes, you could drown in them I'm sure. And a fine figure he has. Sure and he carries himself well." They turned to me and asked, "How do you find him, Brigid?"

"Oh, he looks healthy enough," I said.

This sent them off laughing again. Aggy frowned and Bigsby harrumphed, which did not quiet the girls one bit.

After our meal, I carried up warming stones to slip in between the sheets at the foot of the beds. I was kneeling down, lighting the fire in Mr. Charlie's room, when he walked in. I had heard his footsteps in the hall so he didn't surprise me this time. Quite the opposite. He hadn't seen me down by the fireplace.

Mr. Charlie flung himself on the bed, then lay with his eyes closed and a hand held to his forehead.

I stood up and gently cleared my throat.

He sprang up and said, "What the devil are you doing here?"

"I was only getting a fire going for you."

"That won't be necessary. I'm used to roughing it. This house is altogether too warm for me."

"All right, sir." I turned back to blow out the small fire I had started when I heard his voice again.

"Oh, leave it. I can suffer a little warmth, I guess."

I stood again and tried to gather the courage to ask him about Seamus.

"What is it?" he asked.

"Well, sir. May I ask you something?"

"Certainly. What is it?"

"You know that I am Seamus Reardon's sister. I would like to have word of him."

The light from the fire moved across his face. He did not answer immediately and I watched him weigh his words. This worried me.

"Is he not fine?" I asked.

"No, don't worry. There's nothing wrong with Seamus. He's healthy as a horse, God knows. When did you see your brother last?"

"It's going on a year this fall."

"And the rest of your family?"

"Still back in Ireland."

"How old are you?"

"I'll be seventeen soon enough, sir."

"A babe. How long have you been in America?"

"I was just after turning fifteen when I came." I was flattered by all his questions. "I need to get back to my work, sir."

"Yes. Take my word for it that Seamus is fine. I'd not say the same for those two he hangs around with—Paddy and Billy—they're troublemakers, I'm afraid."

I nodded.

"You're a pretty girl," Mr. Charlie said.

I was pleased to have such praise from him and could feel a flush warm my face, but I knew it would not do to let him know. "Oh, it'll be the wine and the firelight talking, I'm sure."

He laughed and said, "Yes, you're a fine Irish rose. I wonder if those thorns would prick if one got too close."

4

The day after Thanksgiving was glorious, the black trees standing out in the new white snow. Mrs. Hunt had asked a favor of me, something she did from time to time. Dorry's governess had gone home for the holidays, so Mrs. Hunt asked me to take her daughter sledding.

Watching Dorry was a wonderful reprieve from the housework. I know Bigsby wasn't happy when I told him that Mrs. Hunt had requested I chaperone Miss Hunt. Bigsby stared at me, then nodded his brittle head. I promised him I would be back at my post by four o'clock. "See that you are," he said.

I raced to my room, took off my uniform, and put on my maroon wool dress. I fastened up my high boots and put on my good coat with its fur trim at the collar. Gloves and a hat and I was ready.

Dorry was waiting at the door. She had long woolen pants that her mother had purchased especially for sledding and winter sports. Mrs. Hunt felt that getting outside was good for her child.

"Hello, Dorry. Are you all bundled up?"

"Yes, Miss Brigid. Thank you for taking me."

"It's my pleasure. I haven't been sledding before in all my life."

"Really?"

We walked out the front door and the cold hit us in the face. I looked longingly at Dorry's warm mittens, hoping my thin gloves would keep my fingers warm.

Dorry gave a little skip and ran down the steps. "We have a good hill. It's at the far end of the lawn. You just have to watch out for the tree at the bottom."

I had never seen Dorry so animated before. Her wan cheeks brightened with spots of red.

"We'll get the sled from the stable," she told me.

I followed her and she chattered away at me. "I can't wait for Christmas to come. Papa said we would have the biggest tree he could find. Won't it be grand to decorate the tree?"

"It will indeed." I held her hand as we came near the stable. I didn't want her to get run down by one of the horses. "Are you glad that your brother Charles is back?"

"Oh, I guess so."

"Not enthusiastic?"

Dorry laughed. "He's nice enough. But he teases me sometimes. I don't like to be teased."

"Tell him to stop."

"Oh, I couldn't do that. It wouldn't be ladylike."

"Never let being ladylike stand in the way of getting what you want." The words slid out of my mouth before I could stop them. What did I think I was doing, talking to a child like that, the daughter of my mistress? I had given her the advice I would have given my sister, but she was certainly not that.

She tipped her head at me like a wren and then pursed her lips and said, "I wish I could."

"It was but a thought."

The sled was lifted down from the loft by the stable boy. He set it in the snow for us and Dorry insisted on pulling it. As we walked toward the hill, Dorry continued to talk. "Charlie gets in trouble too. He was in trouble when he left the house. I think it was something to do with a girl. I was quite young then so I didn't pay much attention. But I recall Mama was quite upset and I remember it caused a scene."

"A scene?"

"Yes, a young woman came to the house and had words with him. He left the next day."

"What happened to the young woman?"

"I'm really not certain. I couldn't ask anyone because I wasn't supposed to know it even happened. I can hardly wait to be older and be allowed to talk about such matters."

We stopped at the top of a long hill. Down at the bottom, I saw the infamous tree, an oak with a few leaves still clinging to its branches.

"Should we go down together?" Dorry asked.

"Why don't you go first, and I'll watch and see how to do it."

"Good idea." She set herself on the sled, positioned her feet on each side of the front bar, and I gave her a push. The sled started slowly and then picked up speed. She maneuvered neatly around the tree, but a little shriek did escape her mouth at the end. I feared she would tip over, but she stopped without mishap.

"Well done." I clapped my hands as she pulled the sled back up the hill.

"Now it's your turn."

I sat on the sled and followed Dorry's example. With a foot on each end of the bar, I held the tow rope in my hands. She pushed and I started down the hill. I was cold, but I forgot that completely. The wind blew through my hair, my eyes watered, the world went rushing by. I tried to miss the tree and ended up overturning next to it. Snow in my coat and up my skirts. I lay in the snow and laughed. For that moment I was a child again.

Since I had set foot in America, I had not had time for play. I walked the crowded streets of New York until I found a job, and then I worked, hauling wood for fires, hefting a heavy iron on shirts and sheets, carting dishes and washing them until my fingers were chapped red. Even on my afternoons off, I barely had time to attend to my clothes, do a few errands, and maybe, if I was lucky, read for a while.

We sledded for another hour. Sometimes we went down together, often we traded off turns. My gloves were soaked through with damp and my fingers were freezing. My feet felt like two icicles in my boots. As we readied ourselves for the last ride, I saw that Mrs. Hunt and Mr. Charlie had walked up.

"Hello, Brigid." I heard an odd note in her voice and I wondered how I looked, for Dorry and I had tumbled into the snow a time or two.

"Let me push you," Mr. Charlie said and gave us a large shove that sent us careening down the hill. Dorry was steering, but she came too close to the tree and the end of the cross bar hit it. We both spilled out. This time I didn't laugh, although Dorry did. Mr. Charlie ran down the hill and helped us up. He walked up the hill with us and pulled the sled. I felt Mrs. Hunt watching me.

"I'll take the sled back to the stable," I told them and took the tow rope from Charlie.

"I'll escort you. Mama, you have Aggy make a big pot of hot chocolate. We'll be right in." He veered off with me in the direction of the stable.

"No need, Mr. Hunt. I'm sure I can manage," I told him.

"I'm sure you can. I'm just not ready to go back in the house yet. You looked like you were having a wonderful time." He smiled down at me.

"It was terribly exciting. I've never gone sledding before."

"No snow in Ireland?"

"Oh, we had it from time to time. Wet, heavy stuff it was, to be sure, but we had no sleds to play in it."

When we got to the stable, Charlie took the sled from me and put it back in the loft. Then he glanced down at my gloves. "Is that what you've been wearing on your hands? You must be freezing." Without asking my leave, he stripped the gloves from my fingers and began rubbing my hands between his. "This will warm them up. This is what we would do in the Black Hills to prevent frostbite. Also, it helps to stick your hands in your armpits—one of the warmest spots on your body."

I laughed and then suddenly he leaned into me and tipped my head back with one hand as if he were going to look at something in my face. He moved closer and kissed me. I felt it through my whole body, a jolt of warmth, and then I pulled away, catching my breath.

"Sir, you take advantage of me." The urge to slap him rose up in me, but I thought better of it. I turned and walked toward the house.

"Brigid, don't be so difficult." He caught up with me.

I stopped and turned to him. We were standing outside in plain view of the house and so I didn't think he would try anything again. "I am your servant. I work for your parents. Now I must be on my guard around you. You make me consider my circumstances here."

"I only did it because I thought you'd like it." He smiled at me and I saw a warmth in his face that had never been in the eyes of the men at the boardinghouse. "Besides, you have such a damnably kissable mouth."

The urge to tease him rose in me, but I could not do it. Such teasing might cost me my job.

I dipped my head and gently tried to explain my position. "My life is very different from yours. I have had to work hard to get to where I am, and I will not ruin my chances to get ahead by ill-conceived flirting. As your mother might be watching us through the window, I suggest we keep walking and part company at the door."

5

December 15, 1878

D alliances between housemaids and their masters were gossiped about among the servants. Rose told me the tale of a young girl at another Summit mansion who thought for sure the master's son would marry her and so had let him have his way. When the evidence of their trysting became too large for anyone to ignore, she was sent packing, ruined for sure. Who would hire a girl with an illegitimate child?

I avoided Mr. Charlie when I could. I took care to be with either Anna or Rose when I was around him. I never entered his room if I didn't know that he was out of the house. I took no chances.

Since my assault on the ship crossing over, I had grown wary of men. My caution had stood me in good stead when I worked at the boarding-house. I always tried to stay within sight of another servant, avoiding any chances of being caught alone by the boarders or, in my previous private home, the man of the house.

One night when all was quiet in the house, after I had finished up the kitchen with Aggy, we sat down to chat. She made some tea and we talked of many things—but much of Ireland. Aggy had come from Donegal. She talked of the heather and the gorse and the smell in the air this time of year with the peat fires going in every house. She leaned on her hand and closed her eyes. "Sometimes, you know, I miss that smell so it like to break my heart."

I could hardly bring myself to speak of Galway and the bright water in the bay but told her of my family. "My mother is the smartest woman I ever knew. She could tell what time it was by looking at the sky. She mixed up herbs for all the women around to help them through whatever ailed them. She always knew what was on my mind." I wondered if anyone would ever be able to read me like that again.

"Might they come here?" Aggy asked.

"My brother and I talked of it. We hope to bring some of them over if we can. But it's hard to save the money."

We both fell silent for a moment, tears sparkling in our eyes.

"Well, that's another life, isn't it?" Aggy wiped her eyes with her apron. "But it's done my soul good to have Charlie around."

"You know, Dorry mentioned some scene with a woman when Mr. Charlie left last year."

"Oh, Lord bless me, did that poor little sprite hear the goings-on? What a nasty scene we did have, right in the hallway at the bottom of the stairs. Bigsby would let the woman in no farther. The silly goose claimed that Mr. Charlie had seduced her and she flashed a cheap little ring as evidence that they were to marry."

"Why do you not believe her?"

"Our Mr. Charlie would do no such thing. Now, I'm not saying that he doesn't have a wild eye for the women. He does. But he's no fool. He takes care of himself, does Charlie. He would never have given her such a gaudy bauble. Not his style at all. And for one more thing, neither was she. She was a tarty blonde. He has always preferred dark-haired women. You have more the kind of looks he has a liking for. But he's a gentleman, our Mr. Charlie. Would never push himself on anyone. I've known him since he was in knickers."

I wondered what the truth was about our Mr. Charlie. While I couldn't help but feel somewhat pleased with his attention, I wondered if I had fooled myself by thinking I had seen warmth and kindness in his eyes.

❋   ❋   ❋

That night the Hunts had gone out to attend the Christmas concert at St. Paul's cathedral. They weren't expected back for a while.

I decided to let myself into the library and choose a new book to read. I often slipped one into my apron and read at night. I was always very careful and brought them back soon, so they were never missed.

The library was quite dark, but I had brought a candle with me. I enjoyed looking over the rows and rows of books. Such an enormous wealth to own them all. One afternoon I had gone into a bookstore in St. Paul and been astonished at all the volumes. An older woman with spectacles perched on her nose asked me if I was looking for anything special. I told her I was just browsing, but she gave me a skeptical look. I could only imagine the luxury of buying a book whenever one felt like it.

The library was where the family spent much of their time. Mrs. Hunt and Dorry would work a jigsaw puzzle while Mr. Hunt read the latest newspapers. A large couch filled the room, one end near the fireplace. I went to a shelf of books next to the fireplace and bent over.

When the clock struck ten, the chimes startled me. I pulled *Pride and Prejudice* from the shelf. I had read one other of Miss Austen's novels and had found it both enjoyable and refined. I opened the book to the beginning page and read the first line: "It is a truth universally acknowledged, that a single man in possession of a good fortune, must be in want of a wife." My thoughts ran to Charlie Hunt for a moment. He must find himself in such a position.

I clasped the book and turned to leave the room. Then I saw I was being watched. Mr. Charlie sat up on the couch.

"Hello, Brigid," he said quietly.

I was caught. He knew I shouldn't be there. "Mr. Charlie!" I didn't try to hide the book in my hand.

"What have you there?"

"Just a book. I was going to borrow it for the night. No one would miss it. I take such good care of them."

"I'm sure you do. Come here and let me see what you have chosen to read."

I walked toward him.

"I have heard that this Miss Austen writes a splendid romance. My mother has spoken well of her work," he said.

I said nothing.

"For a kiss, I will forget this ever happened."

I bowed my head, shaken that he would again take advantage of me. I must have been mistaken about him. I had brought this on myself. I should never have gone into the library alone, breaking my own rules for safeguarding myself. I dropped the book on the couch and left the room with nary a word to him or even a look.

✳   ✳   ✳

The next morning, as I fretted over Mr. Charlie's behavior, a letter arrived for me. I was glad when Bigsby handed me my mail, but when I saw the handwriting I feared something was wrong. The address was written in my father's hand. He could barely write. I was amazed the letter even arrived with the poor address he had scrawled on the envelope. I tucked it into my apron and at the first opportunity slipped away from my work and went to my room to read it:

> Dear Brigid. Sad news. Your mother has died. She turned very sick. Then she had no breath. The prist came. The wake was held. She is burid near the church. Plese pray for her. Tell your brother. Send monie if you can.
>
> Your father and the girls.

I slipped off the edge of the bed and curled up on the floor. She was in the ground already. My dear mother. I did not want to move. If only this letter wouldn't have come. If only I would have stayed in Ireland. If only my mother was still there. Tears spilled down my face. I cried as if something was being pulled out of me, wrenching hard.

I would never see her again. She was not in this world. Even though she had been so far from me, I had taken comfort in her walking on the same earth. I thought of her in heaven, but that gave me little pleasure. God did not need her the way I did.

I'm not sure how long I lay there. But finally I stirred. What was I to do with myself? Oh, what I wouldn't give to have my mother's arms around me again. All I wanted was someone to tell me what to do. I slipped off the bed and prayed to St. Brigid, prayed for words that would help me know my way:

Oh Brigid, maiden bright and fair,
help me come before God in his glory,
sit with me, stay with me, night or day,
may I be with you forever and ever.

After asking for her help, a calm entered me. Something turned inside me. I stood, knowing clearly what I must do. I went to my drawers and emptied the contents into my valise. I needed to be with my brother, my only family in this foreign country.

❋   ❋   ❋

I found Mr. Hunt in the library, sitting at his desk, reading a paper and smoking a cigar. His dark eyes were hooded as he bent over his reading. He had the look of a hawk. The room plumed with smoke.

"Mr. Hunt," I said from the doorway.

He looked up and waved me forward. "What can I do for you, Brigid?"

I had not spoken to Mr. Hunt very often, but he had always struck me as a fair and honorable man. Even though it would have been more usual to talk to the woman of the house, I felt I needed to discuss with him the terms of my leaving.

"Sir, I need to quit your employ. My mother has died and I must tell my brother."

"Can't you just send him a telegram?"

"I'd rather he heard it from me. I had been hoping to join him soon in Deadwood, so this will only speed up my departure."

He leaned back in his chair and studied me. "We'll be sorry to lose you, Brigid. Good help is hard to find these days. I know Mrs. Hunt has come to depend on you, as has Bigsby. Have you let her know?"

"Thank you, sir, for your kind words. I have yet to inform Mrs. Hunt."

He waited and then he asked, "Is there anything else?"

"Yes, Mr. Hunt. I was wondering if you could help me get a ticket on the train."

He looked surprised by my request. "This is a little unusual, Brigid. Usually when a servant leaves they don't ask for favors."

I could feel my face flushing, but I needed to take this chance. "I know, sir. But one of the reasons I feel I must leave your home is that your son has been paying improper attention to me." I hesitated and studied his face carefully before I spoke again. "I assume you know what I mean."

I saw in his eyes he did. He nodded. He lowered his head and said his son's name softly, "Charlie."

After folding up the paper, he tapped it on the desk with the sound of decision making. "I think a ticket can be arranged. You know the train will only take you so far and then you will need to transfer to a stagecoach. This will be a long and onerous trip. I speak from experience." He seemed lost in thought for a moment, remembering his last visit to Deadwood. "When would you like to leave?"

"As soon as possible." I feared if I waited I would change my mind.

He avoided looking at me. "That might be for the best."

I nodded.

He blew out a trail of smoke. "Yes, I'll see if there's anything leaving tomorrow."

I thanked him and turned to go.

"Brigid." He called me back.

"Yes, Mr. Hunt."

He regarded me with a sharp eye. "Deadwood is no place for a woman. Mind you take care of yourself."

Deadwood

God bless my steps
as they take me where I go.
Bless, also, the earth
beneath my feet.

—Irish prayer

6

Deadwood, Dakota Territory

December 24, 1878

The Black Hills rose before the stagecoach like dark clouds on the horizon. They were called *hills,* but surely they would have been mountains in Ireland. The horses worked hard to pull us up the steep roads. Sometimes the men passengers had to get out and push the stage-coach when the going got too rough and the road too muddy. I would get out and walk alongside of them. After the flat plains we had driven across, I felt as though we were climbing ever higher into a forested kingdom.

The coach took us through canyons so deep I had to tilt my head straight up to see the sky. At the top of one hill near Spring Canyon, the man next to me said we were more than 6,500 feet high. I could see the hills stretched out like a dark ocean of pine trees.

My body ached from the jostling of the vehicle. Although the Concord coaches claimed to be sumptuous because of their glass windows and leather curtains, they were not a very comfortable way to travel. The body of the coach swung high on leather straps tied into the frame, which was held high by the wheels. The rocking of the stagecoach had made me sicker than any waves had done at sea.

The driver told me at one of our last stops, in Whitewood, that the trip had gone as good as any he had driven. "Sometimes it can take up to five or six days to make our way, what with the Indians or bad weather or robbers. If you avoid all that, then something goes wrong with the rig. No, I think you've brought us all luck, Miss Brigid."

Well past nightfall, the snow that had been hovering over our heads the whole journey to Deadwood started to fall as we pulled into town. We descended into the bowl of the town, the tall trees standing sentinel on the hills. A few lights marked windows, but most of the houses and tents were dark, and the streets at this time of night were mainly deserted.

Twelve of us had made the three-day journey from Cheyenne in the Concord coach. I was the only woman. Early on the driver had asked his shotgun man, Sam, to watch over me. Sam handed me down from the stagecoach. He was returning with the driver. He tipped his hat at me and I blessed him. I felt immense relief to have made it to Deadwood.

Talking with my fellow passengers on our long journey, I had learned that Deadwood had only been founded two years prior, when the gold rush started. The town had grown to a population of more than five thousand in that time.

I had been set down on a small section of boardwalk in the heart of town. The main street was lined with many fine shops: Herrmann and Treber Wholesale liquor dealers, Wyoming Store, Stebbins Post & Co. Walking to the closest saloon—the only place open—I asked for the whereabouts of Seamus Reardon and company.

The heavily bearded saloonkeeper said, "What does a pretty girl want with them three Micks?"

"One is my brother, sir."

He looked chastened and told me I was quite close. "Two streets over and you'll see it."

The snow drifted over the streets, landing gently and starting to accumulate. There was little traffic on the mud-rutted roads; unpainted clapboard houses lined the streets. Smoke plumed out of the chimneys and mingled with the snow.

After walking two blocks, I saw the house he meant and noted with relief that it was all lit up. I hoped that meant people were still awake, and that there would be food. I was starving. All I had had on my journey was bread and bacon grease at the stagecoach way stations.

The thought of seeing Seamus filled my eyes with tears. I remembered when we were children. One Christmas he carved me a wren and built a little twig nest for it to sit in. I had given it to the younger children when I left home.

I could hear music as I approached the door. Someone was singing and many voices were talking. I knocked on the door.

A slightly weathered version of Billy answered. "Well, will you look at what the storm blew in. The prettiest lass I've seen since I left Chicago."

He threw an arm around me, and I wasn't sure he recognized me. I pulled back and looked around for my brother. My eyes lighted on him and the woman in his lap. Seamus's golden, curly hair told me who he was even if he had grown a beard since last I saw him. He was busy planting kisses on the woman's throat.

I was just about to say his name when a dark-haired man stepped forward. "Our own Brigid," he said and then I knew him. Padraic looked taller, and more somber, but his eyes held light. His nose was long, his eyes were slanted, and his shoulders broad. He was not handsome, but he looked intelligent and strong. He carried himself well.

"Paddy," I said.

He reached out a hand and rested it on my shoulder. "You've come."

At my name, Seamus swung the woman off his lap and stood. "The blessed sister has arrived. What a Christmas present she is." He pulled me from Paddy's arms and swung me around. "Did you fly? Jaysus, Brigid, it's too hard for any woman to do it—that long journey."

The lovely woman he had had on his lap laughed and said, "Not so hard as that."

Seamus put an arm around her. "Yes, but Lily, we have it for a fact that the men carried you on their shoulders."

She cuffed him on the arm as her face lit up.

"Darling Lily," he said and grabbed my hand. "May I present my sister, Brigid Reardon."

"I'm honored, I'm sure," she said. She turned her smile on me and I felt its warmth.

She was the most beautiful woman I'd ever seen. She wore her lovely blonde hair in loose curls piled high. A gorgeous dress of blue silk cut low in the front, revealing flawless white skin. She looked like a doll. But there was a slight blue shadow under her eyes.

"I too am delighted to meet you," I answered her. I addressed myself to Seamus, "You're having a party?"

"Sure and it's Christmas Eve. The weather's held and the gold is pouring in. We have much to celebrate." He held me by the shoulders. "What brings you here? Did you not like working for the Hunts? If they're all like Charlie, I can understand it being difficult."

I did not want to tell him the news of Mother with everyone. "No, they were a fine family. But I had not seen you for so long. I couldn't wait till spring."

My heart leapt to see Seamus. Mother would have been proud of him. He was handsome as the great Irish bards: thick curly hair, snapping blue eyes, and skin soft as a rose petal. He had also grown a smart, short beard. He too looked like he had been working with his body. His arms were muscled and his posture was straight.

"Well, it's time you were here. Our own family together now." He took my valise and coat from me. The rest of the party went back to their celebrating, only a few women in amongst the men.

Billy brought me a plate filled with a dark meat and biscuits swimming in gravy. I thanked him and sat down on a chair with the food perched on my lap. I took a bite of the meat. "Is it deer?" I asked.

"Venison to be sure," Billy answered and sat next to me, smiling. "I didn't recognize you. Little Brigid is no more. You're grown into a fair beauty."

Billy hadn't grown much. He was a small man with a great smile. Still covered with freckles, he looked more like a leprechaun than ever. He too wore a beard. I guessed it must be part of the miner's attire.

"Thank you, Billy. You're looking well yourself."

He blushed and pushed his hair back from his face. "Naw, I know that I look like the rough hand that I am. It don't worry me none. We can't all of us be such smooth customers as your brother."

Seamus came up carrying a glass in his hand and offered it to me. I could see by his behavior that he still liked the drink. Unfortunately, he took after our father that way. "Libations of the house, my dear sister. Have a drink with us."

"What is it, Seamus?"

"It's a distillate made in these very hills."

"*Potcheen*? You know I don't care for that."

"You always were the smart one," he said, both a bit of tease and warmth in his voice.

Paddy came up with another glass. "Try this. It's a light cider. You deserve as much after your hard trip."

Gratefully I tasted it. "Lovely."

Lily took the glass of *potcheen* that had been meant for me.

I wanted to get to know this lovely woman who had so captivated my brother. "Sit with me, Lily," I asked her.

She pulled up a chair and the men went off to argue about something. "A night off sure feels good." She took a big sip of her drink and made it look as if she were drinking water.

"What do you do?"

Her eyes opened wide and she blinked, then she said, "I'm an entertainer. I work at the Gem Theater."

"Oh, that makes sense. You have such lovely clothes."

"Thank you. It's part of the business." Her hands floated to her hair and arranged her curls.

"I can imagine."

"What do you plan to do with yourself here?" she asked me.

I had thought about it on my way in the stagecoach. They must need a woman to do some of the things I could do. "Well, I plan on working. I am a good servant. And I have some other ideas—maybe work in a store."

Lily laughed. "Only the ugly women work as servants. And even they don't have to if they don't want to."

"Oh." I wondered at the meaning of her words.

"There's a lot of men in this town." She smiled at me.

"Yes, I suppose, it being a mining town and all."

Lily laughed and it sounded like the tinkling of a spoon tapping on the finest crystal. "I'm sure you'll be well taken care of here."

At that moment, I heard music coming from outside the house. I recognized it as "Adeste Fideles." The others heard it too and Billy ran to the door and flung it open. The music poured in, sounding like a fine pipe organ in a grand church. After the first verse we all joined in and sang along with it. When the song was over, everyone raised their glasses and toasted. It was midnight. Christmas Day.

Lily had rejoined Seamus and they were singing another carol. Padraic came and sat next to me. "Where did that wonderful music come from?" I asked him. "It sounded like the angels had played on their harps from above."

"A set of triangles was made last year by a blacksmith here in town and played that very song at midnight. I guess it's become a tradition." He took my plate from me and refilled my glass of cider. "It will be so good to have you here, Brigid. I must warn you, we're gone most every day working in the mine, but we could sure use a woman's hand around here to cook and clean."

"That's just what I've come for. And maybe I'll find some other work."

"We can use your help around here, that's for sure and all."

"Well, I'd be delighted to help you three out. Are you trying to arrange a deal with Charlie Hunt for your claim?"

"What makes you ask that?"

"I overhead him and his father talking about it. He said that he was trying to buy you out, that they are putting together a number of mines. He mentioned some problems."

He looked at me, then said, "We have no problems. We're as clear as clear can be. They need to do some thinking and I'm sure they'll come around. We're to finish it all up when Mr. Hunt returns."

On Christmas Eve, we did not have to talk about such business. I was so glad to be among kith and kin, all that I had in this country. I smiled at him and said, "I'm sure, too."

After the food and drink, I could feel my body giving in to the warmth and the steadiness of the house. My eyes started to fall shut of their own accord.

"Listen, Brigid. This party might go on until all hours. You must be exhausted after your journey. Why don't you take my bed in the back room and I'll camp out here on the couch?"

Since it was either that or fall asleep where I sat, I thanked him and, after wishing everyone well and kissing Seamus goodnight, I followed Padraic back into a small room tucked next to the kitchen, where I saw a single bed and a box full of clothes.

He lit the small gas lamp next to the bed and turned to me. "You are the best sight I've seen since I left Ireland, Brigid."

"Thank you. Merry Christmas to you, Padraic."

"Merry Christmas." He patted my hair and then left me in the room.

❋ ❋ ❋

I piled my clothes next to me on the floor and stepped into my flannel nightgown. I was used to a warm room and felt the chill air wrap around my shoulders. I crawled under the covers and tried to warm them with my breath. After a few minutes, I heard a tap on the door.

"Who's there?" I called.

"Your own brother. I bring you some warmth." Seamus held in his hands a warmed ceramic hot water container. I lifted up the end of my covers and he slipped it in. Then he came and sat down on the floor next to me and took my hand.

"I can't believe I'm seeing you again. Life is treating us well here, Brigid. You'll see. Have you had a hard time of it all by yourself?"

To see him so close, to finally have a bit of my family at hand and him asking me this question, I was afraid of all that was piled up in me of these last years. "It's not been easy, Seamus," I admitted. "But I made my way."

"I knew you would. I have great faith in you, Brigid. You've always been twice as smart as even the priests." He squeezed my hand. "What brings you here? This can be no friendly visit in the middle of winter. You're lucky enough the weather held to let you come into Deadwood. Sometimes we're snowed in."

So he knew, or at least he suspected, something serious was up. "It's Mother," I said, sorry as I could be that I had to tell him this news on Christmas Day. "She's gone."

I watched Seamus's face and my heart broke to see it fall. "No," he whispered. "I wanted to do so much more for her. Bring her and the family over to America."

We sat in silence for a while. He did not cry. I did not expect that of him. That was not his way. But he shook from the sorrow of losing her. I took his hand and continued, "Father wrote to tell me. I've sent him some money. One can only hope it won't all be spent on drink."

"Curse it. Of all the good people to leave the earth, it would have to be our own mother." He bent his head and pounded a fist on the floor. "I hoped with all the gold I'm finding that I could bring the family over too. I just didn't do it soon enough."

"She might not have survived the trip."

"You might be right." Then he looked up. "You've come all the way to tell me this news?"

I thought of telling him my other reason for coming, but I was too tired and, thinking about Mother, too sad. "I did need to get out of the Hunt home. Bringing this news was a good excuse. And I wanted to come here soon anyways. We can talk more in the morning."

After tucking the covers up around my ears, he left the room. Sleep was slow coming to me. I had worked so hard to get to this town, I couldn't seem to relinquish this night.

The party died down after a while, and I heard the wind roaming around outside the house. I crossed myself and prayed for us all.

As I was drifting off to sleep, I heard a high-pitched wail that made me shiver. Surely it was the wind winding its way through a crack in the house, but making the sound of a banshee. It was told they would come and sing outside the window of a house when someone was about to die.

Christmas Day

Rarely did I remember my dreams when I awoke. I'd had too many mornings of being pulled from bed before I was ready in order to start the fires for breakfast, the dreams ripped from my head half-formed. But that first morning in Deadwood, I remembered my dream very clearly.

The dream came as several drawings strung together, images that I will never forget. I was standing in snow up to my ankles, but I was in my night-dress. A star fell from the sky and landed in my hands. The star glowed like an ember of coal in white ashes. I felt the ember burning my hands and I dropped the coal, then woke.

That first morning I felt as if I were coming out of a long illness. Many days of hard travel had left me exhausted. I realized that I was farther than ever from my homeland, from what remained of my family. On this holy day of Christmas I missed them all to the core of me. But at least I had Seamus.

In a very white and cold room, my body slowly came to itself. I watched a few flakes of snow drift down on the other side of the window. I could see my breath in the air and had little desire to leave my nest of a bed. I snuggled down deeper into the covers and listened, but no sound was to be heard from the adjoining rooms.

Though diminished, the party had gone on, as Padraic had predicted, until the early hours of the morning. Singing had woken me from time to time in the night. It was surprising to me to witness Christmas Eve cel-ebrated in such a fashion. But this was a town on the far frontier, and I sensed that the rules of ordinary civility did not reign in this place.

I had no idea of the time as I lolled in bed, but if the sun was up it meant it was past seven. I had not had the pleasure of lying in bed in the morning since before I left Ireland. Even when I had time off at the Hunts it was only in the afternoon. I had still been expected to do all my morning chores.

When I felt myself entirely awake, I dressed under the covers as I had as a child. No one was stirring in the main room.

Depending on what was in the larder, I supposed there was a Christmas feast to cook, not sure the men would think of it. I was starved to have some breakfast, even just a piece of bread.

The place reeked of cigar smoke from last night and peanut shells littered the floor. I walked carefully, trying not to crunch them underfoot.

Padraic was stretched out on the couch. Even in sleep he looked worried, his brow furrowed like a field in spring. I thought to run my hand across his forehead, but I did not wish to wake him. He looked like he had been working hard. Older than us all, he must feel somehow responsible, a heavy burden for one still so young. His blanket was slipping off his shoulder so I pulled it back up. He sighed in his sleep and turned from the light that came in the front window.

Lifting the lid on the woodstove cooker, I shoved the few pieces of wood I could find into the red pool of coals and blew on them. Within moments, the fire had caught. I warmed my hands and then walked toward the other stove, which was against the wall. That fire had gone out, and there was no more wood in the firebox.

There had to be a woodpile outside. I pulled on my coat and grabbed a pair of heavy gloves that were by the front door. Also I needed to use the outhouse. I was not looking forward to the cold, as I had been spoiled by indoor plumbing at the Hunts.

When I opened the door, I was dazzled by the white light. Everything was draped with snow, white caps on fence posts and big mounds near the street. Someone had shoveled a path last night, but even that had a bit of snow on it. I watched my step as I walked down the front stairs.

I looked up and saw the mountains encircling the town. Dark with pines, they were capped with snow. The town was crowded with wooden houses like the one my brother lived in. Tents dotted the outskirts. A small town, Deadwood was much more primitive than St. Paul.

There was no traffic on our side street. I walked around the side of the house and found the firewood neatly stacked up against the house, also covered with snow. As I walked toward it I saw another mound—was it a low-growing bush?

There looked to be a red flower blooming under the snow. I couldn't believe such a thing could manage to bloom in this cold weather. What could make this brilliant red?

I slowed my steps and stared. My mind did not want to understand what my eyes could see—the shape of a body under the new blanket of snow.

My hands flew to my mouth and I fell on my knees. Somehow—maybe a touch of the second sight—I knew even before I wiped the snow from her face that it was Lily, beautiful in her shroud of white.

In the center of the blood-flower was a dark stamen, a knife handle sticking out of her chest. Her legs were twisted under her. She must have been standing and then fallen straight down when she'd been stabbed.

My stomach turned inside of me and I bent my head into my hands and wept. For what? I didn't really know the woman. Maybe for women in this wilderness. Then I saw it was for myself. That I should be the one to find her, that I should be so far from home, that I had not a home any longer. What kind of place had I come to?

After my tears had been spent, I wiped my face and looked again at the sorry woman in front of me.

Her coat was open and she had been stabbed right above the rise of her breasts; her low-cut dress had left the spot bare. One of her hands reached toward the knife, as if to pull it out. In the other hand was her beaded purse, looking undisturbed.

I huddled in the snow and prayed to the Virgin Mary to take Lily's soul. This had indeed been a blighted Christmas season. I had been driven from my job, come to find my brother to tell him of our mother's death, and now I would be the bearer of yet more bad tidings.

I prayed the way my father had taught me. He would have said, "Trust in the One who sees over us, who is bigger than us, then put yourself in His hands. You cannot know what should happen. You can never know."

After that moment of silence, I lifted myself from the snow, shook out my skirts, and turned to find Padraic coming up behind me, perhaps to help me with the wood. I must have woken him when I left the house. He was standing with his boots untied and a blanket around his shoulders. His hair stuck up in back. He was smiling to see me and looked like he was happy, much happier than he had looked in his sleep. He walked toward me, flapping his blanket like a bird about to take flight.

"What have you found, Brigid?" he asked.

I thought to shield him from the sight, to keep him happy for a moment longer, then stepped aside.

"Oh, Padraic," I said. "Look there." I pointed down.

A look of pain and sorrow shot across Padraic's face. "Lord above, she's finally come to this," Padraic said and crossed himself.

"Who could have done this?" I asked.

Another emotion crossed Padraic's face, but this time I read fear. "I hate to think," he said. "We might all be blamed."

He walked up next to me and wrapped his blanket around the two of us. "This is bad, Brigid. Very bad."

Then he nudged her arm with his foot. "Lily of the Valley. Her real name was Faith, obviously not a name that worked in her profession. She was too beautiful to be anything but trouble, and trouble she's been since the day she arrived in this town."

"I guess you didn't care for her."

Looking down, he shook his head. "I really had no feelings about her. I barely spoke three sentences to her. She was so busy with all the moneyed men."

"But surely you have as much money as Seamus does."

"I have that, but not the looks. She fell over head and ears in love with your brother. Lately, he had even been talking of marrying her. She cast a spell on him, sure as the little people. Not that it stopped her from doing her job. Seamus was like to go crazy sometimes, wondering who she was with, what man was having his way with her."

"What are you talking about? What other men? How could she if she loved Seamus?"

Padraic looked at me as if I'd lost my mind. Then he said, "You don't know, do you? I wondered at you talking so friendly to her last night. What did she tell you she did?"

"Well, she told me she's an entertainer." By Padraic's face I knew I had missed something.

"Don't you know what that means out here, Brigid? The men only need one form of entertainment, and they'll pay top dollar for it."

I started to comprehend what he was trying to tell me. I had heard of such women but had never seen, much less spoken to one. How silly I was last night, too exhausted to understand what she had been telling me. I shook my head, still hoping it was not true.

In anger, Padraic spit out, "She was a streel. Nothing but a streel, but she had them all in the palm of her hand, all the men." Padraic shook his head. "Even that fine gentleman, Charlie Hunt."

Hearing Charlie's name tied to Lily's confirmed my worst feelings about him. He had only wanted one thing from me, that which he had gotten from this lovely woman. I promised myself I would think of him no more—I would put his fine stature and the warmth that I had seen in his eyes out of my mind.

Something white and solid hit Padraic in the side of the head. When we both turned, I too was hit with a snowball. Billy was standing in the snow in his long johns and boots with a fur cap on his head. He bent and scooped up another handful of snow. Before he had a chance to throw it, Padraic stopped him by holding up a hand.

"Merciful Jaysus, Billy. Can't you see we have a problem on our hands here? Stop your fooling around and tell us what you know."

Billy walked up and his face fell as he saw Lily lying in the snow. He shivered as he stood staring down at her. "Jaysus, Mary, and Joseph. What has been done?"

He fell on his knees in front of Lily and touched her as if she might move if only shaken slightly. "Oh, my God, Lily, who has done this to you?"

"Stop your blathering, Billy. I think you see it clear enough. She won't get up for no amount of wailing from you. What happened after I fell asleep last night, Billy? We might be in real trouble here."

Billy rubbed his face in his hands and stood again. "Not much. Seamus was half-seas over with the drink and insisted on walking Lily home.

He went out the door but wasn't gone long. He went upstairs and crawled into bed. I heard him although I was nearly asleep. That's all I know."

"Who was still at the party?"

"Not a soul. They had all gone."

"Why did Lily go home?"

"She said he was too drunk. And she was right. He's still snoring away. He can't have done this. I tell you he was too drunk to even hold a knife in his hands."

"I believe what you're telling me and I believe that Seamus is no killer no matter how much or how little drink he's had in him," said Padraic, "but I'm afraid, since he was the last person to be seen with her, it's going to look like he killed Lily."

We all three stared down at the red flower darkening in the snow.

8

We decided not to move her. I didn't like the idea of leaving her lying in the snow. But in fact and all, it was probably the best thing to do for her. In the snow and cold, she would keep.

Billy was for covering her up and leaving her until the spring thaw. Paddy seemed to consider it as a possibility. I was appalled. "Have you no sense of decency?"

Paddy turned dark and said, "You don't know this place yet, Brigid. There is not much decency to be found."

Before I could argue further, the choice was taken out of our hands. A tall, thin man passing by on the street looked over and saw what was spread out at our feet. His hand flew to his mouth and his feet carried him away.

"That stupid idiot. Calls himself the Professor. He has no more schooling under his belt than I," Paddy said disparagingly. "He's run off to tell the whole town. All we can do is prepare for it."

"Shouldn't we go and fetch the sheriff?" I asked.

"The sheriff is worse than the idiot. He's got a mean streak in him a mile wide and he hates your brother with a passion. He's lost his britches to him more than once at faro. Last time he swore he'd run Seamus out of town."

"Speaking of which, we have to wake Seamus," I said as we walked in the door.

We all trod silently up the stairs. I didn't know what the two other men were thinking, but for myself I felt sorely shaken, having just seen someone I knew who had died by the hands of another. The world seemed more dangerous, more impermanent. As it had that day on the ship.

However, what had happened on the ship was in the nature of an accident, certainly self-defense. Many were the nights I had lain in bed and prayed for our souls. I told myself there had been no other choice—it was him against us—but in my heart I couldn't help but wonder.

Padraic pushed open the door of the back bedroom and we stared at my brother. Seamus looked as if he had tried to swim across the ocean in his bed. His pillow was on the floor, his blankets were twisted willy-nilly around him, and his arms were flung over his head. From his open mouth came snorts and snuffles. But for all that, he looked like an innocent, free of any wrongdoing. I knew Seamus would not wake easily.

Padraic was his match, though. He stepped forward and lifted the edge of the mattress up high and dumped Seamus on the floor.

Seamus's eyes flew open and he looked as startled as a fish thrown out of water. "What do you want with me?"

Padraic stood over him. "I want you to wake up and talk. I want you to tell us what the hell happened with Lily last night?"

Seamus rubbed his eyes and held his head. Then he sat up and laughed. "I can't quite remember everything, but I can tell you this. She said yes!"

"Praise be to God, what did she say yes about, I'm afraid to ask?"

Seamus grabbed the side of the bed and pulled himself up. Even though he was pale, he was smiling. "I asked her to marry me and she said she would. She promised she would. She took the ring I had made for her. Remember that large nugget I found two weeks ago? The jeweler made it into a gold band for me. She slipped it on her finger and said yes she would be my wife."

Then Padraic collapsed down on the bed next to Seamus and held him around the shoulders. "I have bad news. About Lily."

Seamus's face got hard. "Lily, my own?"

Padraic continued, "I'm sorry to be telling you this, but she's dead. Someone has stabbed your fiancée and left her for dead in our yard."

"No." The word came out of him like a snake out of a deep, dark hole. "Not my Lily."

"You need to think who could have done this, my good lad, because the sheriff will be wanting to pin the deed on you. You and he have never seen eye to eye. I'm afraid for you."

Seamus stood up and pulled his pants up as he did. "I'll kill whoever did this. Lily was my own. My love." He moved toward the door, but Paddy stood in his way.

"Hold yourself, Seamus. There's no good rushing to see her. First we must talk. The sheriff will be here soon enough. What happened last night? Tell us now."

At Paddy's words, Seamus sank to the floor, the air let out of him. He crumpled into himself and rubbed his face with his hands.

"Come on now, Seamus. You need to tell us."

Seamus turned his face up and it was wet. "And surely it is my fault. Why didn't I see her safely home? All I remember is slipping the ring on her finger. I walked her home. I think I did. Billy, what did I do?"

"You left with her, but you weren't gone long. I would say you were back within five minutes. Not nearly long enough to have walked her all the way back to the Gem. Surely she wasn't working last night at all, was she?"

"No, and if I had my way she'd never work again." Seamus's shoulders shook again. "But then what does it matter. She'll never do anything again. My poor, dear Lily."

"You weren't mad at her, were you, Seamus?" I asked.

"Never at all. She had just said she would be my wife. Why would I be mad at her?" He looked me straight in the eyes. "Why would I want to kill her? I loved her and that's all I know."

I didn't remember seeing a ring when I had looked at Lily's hands. "I saw no ring."

Padraic stepped in. "Forget about the ring." He turned to Seamus. "First and foremost, you need to clear out of here for a while. I do not trust the sheriff to see that justice is done. Let's not give him a chance. I want you to pack up and ride out of here. Get dressed. Billy, run and get him a horse."

❋ ❋ ❋

I packed up some food for Seamus: cold venison, part of a loaf of bread. My hands shook as I worked. *My brother running off to avoid being charged with murder.*

I heard Seamus clomp down the stairs and then out the front door. From the side window where I was working, I could see him in the snow. He stood tall and looked down at Lily and then fell to his knees and took her in his arms. His head bent into her neck as if he could hide there. After a few moments, he stood and came back into the house.

I touched his face and made him look at me. "Seamus, I'm forever sorry for you."

His face broke and tears swam in his eyes. "Nothing works out, Brigid, no matter how hard we try. Leaving our family, coming here. In the end, what we love is taken from us."

I did not try to tell him differently. I was all too aware that I was losing my own brother again, after only a few hours together.

Instead I looked him over to be sure he was ready for his trip. He was dressed for the trail: high leather boots with his wool pants tucked into them, a layering of shirts, a vest, a buckskin jacket, and a scarf at his throat. A felt hat was pulled down to his ears and he carried leather mittens in his hands.

Right before he left he told me, "You'll be fine, Brigid. These two will look after you. I'd trust them with my life."

"Yes. You won't be gone long?" I was shamed to hear my voice break. Tears pushed behind my eyes but I blinked them back.

"When this matter is settled, I'll be back. Padraic knows how to send word."

"Well, that's fine then."

He took a bag from his pocket and handed it to me. "Some gold for your needs. Buy yourself some things with it. We will be getting much more when we settle the claim with the Hunts."

"When will that be?" I asked.

"Charlie was supposed to be back any day." Then he reached into his jacket and pulled out a piece of paper. "And I am giving you my share of the claim. I think it can be worked a while longer yet to good avail. Billy's against, but I'd argue that there's gold to be had yet. I trust you to guard my interest."

I looked down at the table.

"You help Padraic. You've got a good head, Brigid." Seamus rubbed the back of my neck.

✻ ✻ ✻

Banging sounded at the front door. Billy ran in from the back and Padraic told Seamus and Billy to leave. He spit out, "The sheriff's here with Professor Pete and Al Swearingen, the owner of the theater where Lily worked. They've got guns."

Padraic turned to me. "Brigid, you need to go and stall them. Tell them Seamus has gone off to the claim. That will keep them busy for a while."

As I heard Seamus go out the back, I walked slowly, taking my time. I knew they could see me through the window in the door so they would stay put. I looked in the mirror by the door and tidied my hair. Then I pulled open the door and stepped out on the front steps.

"Oh, Sheriff," I said, grabbing his arm with the rifle in it. "I'm so thankful you're here. Look what I've just found." I pointed off to the side yard. I could see more footprints in the snow. They had already walked out that way. I wasn't telling them anything they didn't know. "Lily, and she's been murdered."

The three men grunted and tried to push past me, but I held my place. "I don't believe we've met. I am Brigid Reardon. I just arrived in town last night. I'm Seamus Reardon's sister."

The tall man with a badge swept off his hat and said, "Howdy, ma'am. I'm Sheriff John Manning." I looked him up and down. He stood tall in his boots, a thick dark beard covered much of his face, and his hair was pulled back in a ponytail. Not an ugly man, but very coarse. He looked like he had earned the right to be sheriff the hard way, by fighting for it.

Al Swearingen said, "We have it on good authority that Seamus was the last person seen with her. Nellie said she left Lily at the house, and Seamus said he'd bring her back to the theater. And now he's gone and murdered her in cold blood."

"Who saw her with Seamus?"

"A man that works for Charlie Hunt. He was on his way home when he saw the two of them. He said they were wrestling, but he thought it was all in fun until he heard about the killing."

"Where's Seamus?" the sheriff asked and looked past me into the house.

I had to do something to give Seamus more time to get away. Putting a hand to my forehead, I swooned. Sheriff Manning wrapped a tight arm around my waist.

Professor Pete looked like he wanted to shake me. He bent close to me and shouted, "Miss Reardon, this is serious business. You need to tell us where your brother is."

"Seamus has been gone since early morning. He went off to check the claim. He doesn't even know about Lily. I found her body after he left, when I went out to get wood for the fire."

As they turned to go, I stalled them a little longer. I grabbed the sheriff's arm and pleaded, "Let me go with you and tell him. Lily's death will break his heart. They were to be married."

Professor Pete gave a harsh laugh. "He was in a long line. She had more men dangling than any other fancy lady I know."

A buckboard pulled up to the side of the road. A short man with a dark overcoat on and a thatch of white hair stepped down from it and lifted his hat to us, then walked toward the body.

"That's Doc Hammer. I sent someone for him," Professor Pete told me. "I reckon he's come to take the body."

People were gathering at the edge of the yard to see what the commotion was all about. Ill news flies fast enough. The doctor walked up to Lily and bent to see her better, going down slowly as if his joints ached. He ran a finger across her cheek and then lifted one of her hands and looked at her fingernails. He let the hand drop and patted her on the shoulder as if consoling her.

When he stood, two men walked forward with a blanket. They set it down on the snow and brushed her off and then, gently, lifted her onto it. Other men from the crowd rushed forward and they carried her in a sling to a wagon.

The sheriff shot his rifle off into the air. The sound of it thumped on my chest. Padraic came out of the house and put a hand on my shoulder. The crowd looked up at the sheriff as the men on the buckboard reined in their horses. He had everyone's attention.

The sheriff raised his voice. "We are looking for Seamus Reardon in connection with this killing. Anyone who has any information should come to my office this afternoon. Or bring him in. I want to talk to that damned Irishman."

Padraic squeezed my shoulder and whispered in my ear. "Don't worry. He's off. I told him to head to Cheyenne. The sheriff has no jurisdiction there."

My brother gone so soon. I shivered as I wondered when I would see him again.

9

It was Christmas, after all, and I tried my best, but the chicken came out half-burnt, half-raw; the woodstove cooked that uneven. I boiled potatoes and Billy helped mash them. We had turnips and onions for side dishes. I found a jar of peaches in the cupboard and divvied them up into three bowls. There were no matching plates but at least there were three of them. I found some mugs we could use for the cider Padraic set on the table. He pulled a lump of butter off of the windowsill, where it had been placed to stay cool.

I couldn't help but think of where I might have been—in the warmth, security, and grandeur of the Hunt mansion. Instead I was serving a dinner to Irish men in a place that seemed at the edge of the world. How I wished I was setting one more plate.

The three of us sat down together. We all missed Seamus. With him we would have had such a festive meal. Without him the dinner was empty of joy.

"Haven't had a feast like this in ages," Billy said and piled food onto his plate.

Padraic put out a hand to him and stopped him. "I think we need to say grace before we dig in."

A banging at the door caused us all to stand up. Padraic pushed his chair back and went to answer it. Before he could get the door, it was flung open and the sheriff came in. "He's not at the claim. And no one's been there today. I need to search the house."

Padraic said to the sheriff, "That would be fine. Let me go with you." He told Billy to stay with me.

I covered the bird to keep it warm. Billy and I sat down at the table again and listened to them go into each room upstairs and tear things around. Billy swore under his breath, then begged my pardon. I told him I was cussing in my mind. The messing they did would just give me more cleaning to do tomorrow. Then they all were clattering down the stairs and looked into the back room.

"Where is he?" Manning asked, standing close to my chair.

I decided I might as well speak. "Maybe he heard about Lily, coming back from the claim. He might be hiding out someplace. As it is, you're not giving him a chance to clear himself."

"Well, this sets it up just fine. He kills a girl and runs off. I'd call that a pretty clear case of guilt."

"Or he knows the sheriff he's up against," I said.

I got him to think twice on that one, not sure if it was a compliment or not.

"I'm sorry to interrupt your dinner, ma'am." He took off his hat and dipped his head. "If Seamus shows up here, we want to know."

"You can be sure you will, sir," I promised, knowing full well we'd not see my brother again until his name was cleared.

Then they left. Padraic slumped down in his chair. Billy kicked at the table. I uncovered the chicken and cut it up.

"How do you come to have such a confidence with men about you?" Padraic asked me.

"You know what they say—a woman sleeping equals three men waking." I didn't feel like telling more.

"I want to know," Padraic said, "what have you done with yourself since last we saw you?"

"For a year I fed a dozen men three times a day in a boardinghouse. I learned how to handle much of their talk and antics."

Padraic looked at me with admiration. "I've no doubt of that. Now I still think we need that prayer."

"Fine idea," Billy said. Then they both looked at me. We rested our hands on the table together and bowed our heads. I thought of the home I had known in Ireland, my family gathered around the table, my mother

pinching someone's ear to make them behave, patting another on the back
of the neck, father smoking his pipe. I said the prayer that we would say
before many meals:

> Remember the plentitude of five loaves of bread
> And two fish shared with five thousand.
> Let us ask for abundance from this bountiful King,
> May He give us our fair portion.

I dished out the food and they ate with a semblance of manners. We
had a quiet meal, eating all that was in front of us in our hunger. When we
finished, we sat and looked at each other.

"Who could have killed Lily?" I asked.

Padraic leaned back and folded his arms over his chest. "That is the
question, right enough."

Billy laughed. "Any one of her many men could have been waiting for
her at the Gem. All he'd have to do is threaten her, walk her back to this
house, and stab her. Everyone knew about Seamus and Lily. No secrets in
this town."

"That's the job of the sheriff," Padraic said.

"He's so determined that it's Seamus, he'll look no further," I reminded
them.

Padraic nodded. "Not to worry. It'll blow over like a bad storm. Seamus will find his way to Cheyenne. The sheriff won't be bothered to leave
Deadwood. We can sell the claim as soon as Hunt gets back and join him
there."

"You don't plan on doing anything?" I asked him.

"There's plenty of work to be done."

"So we'll do nothing to clear Seamus's name?"

Padraic put out a hand to calm me. "Seamus is safe enough right now
wherever he is. Things will sort themselves out."

In my heart, I doubted his words and thought of what I might do to
help my brother. For he needed my help.

❀   ❀   ❀

A few hours later a knock came at the door, a gentler rapping than before. We were all gathered around the fire in the front room, and Billy got up to answer the door.

The woman who walked in looked familiar. I was sure I had seen her on Christmas Eve. She turned and let Billy slip her coat off her shoulders, which were broad indeed. She was what was called a strapping lass. A lovely green satin dress clung to her ample figure. Her hair was swept up into a chignon. Black beads decorated her ears and her throat. She was not really pretty, but she had a generous air about her.

She turned to say something, but all that came out was, "Lily." Then she burst into tears. Billy patted her on the back.

When she quieted down, Billy introduced us. "Nellie, this is Seamus's sister, Brigid. I don't think you two met last night."

"Hello," I said. "I'm so sorry about Lily. She was your friend?"

Nellie collapsed into a chair that Billy held out for her. "Like a sister to me she was. Through thick and thin, and I'm telling you, sometimes it got pretty thin. What will I do without her? Damnation, why would someone want to go and kill her?" Another gale of tears approached, and Billy headed them off by asking if she would care for a glass of cider.

"I think I need that, I really do." She sniffed. She looked around the room. "Where's Seamus?"

"He's gone away to do some business. He's very broken up about Lily," Padraic explained, then asked her: "You don't think Seamus did it, do you, Nellie?"

"Lord above, that boy was as smitten as could be. Which doesn't mean that they couldn't have had a lovers' quarrel, but no, Seamus was not one to kill a girl. I'm telling you, though, I do want to find the son of a bitch who killed her."

I decided to jump right in. "Professor Pete said she saw many men." I grew embarrassed when I realized how silly that sounded. That was, after all, her line of work.

"Oh, Lily was very popular indeed."

"Nellie, we need your help. You knew Lily so well. Could you tell us what other men she was seeing? Were there any who might have a jealous streak, who might not want her to marry my brother?"

"I can list the men who saw her if you have all day." Having said this she burst into laughter, then wiped at her tears again.

"I do."

"Oh, you're a smart one. Lord knows we need a few bright women around here."

"You're not working then tonight, Nellie?" Billy asked as he cozied up next to her.

"I told Al that there simply wasn't nothing going to make me work tonight. I put my foot down. I'd guess he understood. We're not as busy as you might think. The weather is turning bad."

I thought of Seamus out on the trail and sent out a prayer for his well-being.

Padraic said, "We'll need to get out to the claim tomorrow, Billy. Make sure no one's touched anything. I wouldn't put it past the sheriff and his posse to have put some holes in our equipment just to teach us a lesson."

Billy stirred the fire, then struck a pose. "And now a prayer for our dear departed Lily, who's gone down the flume before us. Brigid, you're the one who knows them all. Give us a prayer for Lily."

I thought a short one would do as well as any. "Hour of grace, our hour of death, this hour is good, by God's will and by Mary's."

I heard a howl come out of Nellie and saw hard tears again running down her face. She threw her arms around Billy. He wrapped an arm around her shoulder and the two of them slowly went up the stairs, wishing us a good night. I couldn't help wonder what had become of me that I was staying in a house where an unmarried man and woman slept together.

❋ ❋ ❋

"What will happen to us, to Seamus?" I asked Padraic as we sat together by the fire. The question burst out of me with an anger and sadness that surprised me.

Even saying my brother's name caused me sorrow. I missed my brother so much I wanted to kick something. After such a long time of seeing none of my family, I only had a day with him. Not even that. How could he leave me? I felt myself becoming furious at Seamus for getting involved with a woman like Lily, getting too drunk to know what he was doing, and then leaving me in the mess he had created.

Padraic only shook his head, not looking at me.

"What is he up to, this brother of mine? Does he have no sense?" I asked.

Padraic lifted his head and looked at me. "Sometimes more than the rest of us, but, when it comes to the ladies, not much."

"And now see what it has brought on us all."

We sat for a moment, then I asked him what had been on my mind for a while. "What would the sheriff do if he caught up with Seamus?"

"Well, that depends on all sorts of things. But Manning isn't so awfully unfair. He'd probably bring him in. However, justice can be pretty rough here. A man was hanged last year for hiring a horse from a livery stable and not bringing it back. A 'suspended sentence' can be administered on the spot."

"I had no idea," I murmured. I put my head in my hands. All the weariness from the last days of travel came back upon me. I did not cry. I simply closed my eyes and breathed deeply.

"Brigid," Padraic said.

"I'm fine. Tired," I assured him. "What can we do for him?"

Padraic shrugged. "I don't want any more trouble."

"But trouble has landed on our doorstep. We need to clear Seamus's name."

"The man who killed Lily won't want to be found, you know. Looking for him would be dangerous."

"It was dangerous for me to come here, dangerous for all of us to come to America. We faced danger, together, on the ship."

At the mention of that horrible night, Padraic tensed. "You're right there. I'll do what I can, Brigid."

"Thank you, Padraic." I stood to go to my room.

"Stay a moment. I have not forgotten the day." He slipped his hand into his pocket and brought out a small brown package. "Merry Christmas."

I held the package in my hand and did not know what to say. I hadn't had a present since Seamus gave me the little wooden bird. "Oh, Padraic," I said, words for once failing me.

"Are you just going to stare at it? Open it, you silly girl."

I unfolded the coarse brown paper and found a piece of tissue paper inside. Unwrapping that, I held up a simple chain with a golden locket. I had never had anything so elegant before in my life. I opened the little clasp and found two places for pictures. "Oh, Padraic, isn't it grand? How did you ever manage to get such a lovely thing?"

"'Tis nothing much. I bought it today when I went for supplies. I thought the day called for a present."

"Would you help me put it on?" I knelt down by him and turned my back so he could work the clasp. He seemed awkward with it, but finally he patted my back and said, "There you go."

The locket hung down onto my dark dress and made such a nice glow. "Such a fine thing." I settled back into my seat.

Padraic stretched his feet out in front of the fire. "I haven't had a day off like this in many a week. We've been hard at work at the claim."

"I'd like to go see it and help if I can."

"Oh, it's awful work, Brigid. But you sure can come to see it. In fact, you'd better." He smiled at me. "Just before he left Seamus told me he had signed his part of the claim over to you. Congratulations. You're part-owner of a gold mine."

10

When I walked out the front door the next morning, I heard a swishing noise coming from next door. A young woman with a large red scarf was sweeping off her front steps with a broom. I had heard nothing about our neighbors and wondered who she was. She looked close to my age.

I stood still in the sun for a moment and let it warm my face. Then I called over, "Good morning."

She lifted her head with a jerk. When she saw me, she smiled and waved me over. "Good morning."

She pushed her scarf off her head and her hair shone brown with shots of gold in it.

"I'm Elizabeth Wellington," she told me. "I saw you yesterday but didn't get a chance to introduce myself." She had the flat nasal sound of someone from out East, born in the States.

"I'm Brigid Reardon. Seamus is my brother."

"Seamus has been so very nice. All those three. They help me now that my husband is gone." She sighed. "It was horrible to spend Christmas alone. My husband, William Wellington, that is, wanted me to stay behind in Yankton, but I didn't know anyone there. I wanted to be with him. We were only married six months ago. I'm originally from Philadelphia. Have you ever been there? It's a lovely city."

"No, I lived in New York for a while, but I've never been to Philadelphia." I walked up closer to her and stood at the bottom of the steps, looking up.

"I think it is the nicest city back in the States." She looked down and her lip quivered. "I can't believe I am out here in the wilderness. William warned me. He told me I wouldn't like it, but I didn't believe him. He was

69

right. And now he won't listen to me when I am so lonely. He says I asked
for it. But how could I have known?"

"'Tis a hard life out here."

"Yes, that's it. A hard life." She smiled and looked pretty. She took a
step back and motioned me up the steps. "Would you like to come in for a
cup of coffee? I could put some on to brew."

"May I come another time? I'm off to do some errands."

"Yes. That would be nice. Something to look forward to. I'm nearly
almost always here. Come and knock on my door. I would love to have
another woman to talk to."

"I look forward to it. Goodbye, Elizabeth." I backed up.

"I'll make some cake."

"Fine." I turned away and then heard her say something again. She
seemed to not want me to go. I wondered what her life must be like—
alone in this shanty town where she had no family, waiting for her husband to return. I had no desire to marry just for the sake of it, for even the
sacred institution offered little security.

"Awful about that woman getting killed, wasn't it?" she hollered at me.

"Did you hear anything that night?"

"No, just some singing. I fell asleep before midnight."

✳   ✳   ✳

The church deepened into darkness as I walked into it. I had hoped I might
find a mass in progress at St. Ambrose, but the nave was empty. I could
smell the incense hanging in the air like burned wool. I crossed myself,
genuflected, and slid into the second pew from the altar. The quiet did me
good, falling on my shoulders like a wanted rain. With my brother gone, I
could hardly remember why I had come to Deadwood and wondered if I
should remain. For a moment, I wished I had never left St. Paul.

Here I was. Nearly a grown-up woman, on my own, part-owner in a
mining claim, with a golden locket hanging around my neck and my best
dress on for the third day in a row. I wasn't sure I wanted to go back to
being a chambermaid, plus I knew I couldn't have stayed at the Hunts' too
much longer.

In the darkness I stayed quiet a long while, letting my thoughts wander, saying a prayer, thinking of my mother. It was a wonder to me that I did not have to work, that I could sit here for an hour or two and no one would question if my chores had been done. A sense of freedom shot through me as loudly as the rifle crack from yesterday. I could do whatever I wanted.

I stood and walked to the altar of the Virgin Mary. I had seen Mary looking better. Her head was tipped to one side, her eyes gazing in two slightly different directions, and one hand was missing. I lit a candle and prayed for my mother's soul. I wished her a safe journey and hoped she wouldn't have to waste too much time in purgatory but could get right on into heaven. I knew my mother would be happy to see my little sister Kathleen. I liked thinking of them together, my mother holding her up in her arms and spinning her around and around and Kathleen laughing with the song of a wren.

Then my thoughts darkened. Would Lily be there too? Ah, she would have to spend a lot longer in purgatory to make up for her sins, but then I didn't even know if she had been Catholic. If my mother did meet her, she would be kind to Lily. There had been a woman who lived down the road from us who made some money from visiting men. My mother would still say good morning to her on the way to town, unlike some of our neighbors. She said, "We all need to get by. Her husband left her, and how is she to feed the children? It would be a far greater sin to let them starve."

How might I pass judgment on Lily when I had watched a man be killed and said nothing of it? I said a quick prayer to God for forgiveness for all I had done.

I turned to go when I saw someone move at the front of the church. A priest had been on his knees in front of the altar. I hadn't seen him before because he was so still. He walked down to greet me. "May I help you, my child?"

"Father, I just needed to say a prayer for my departed mother. When do you have masses?"

"Every morning at eight and twice on Sunday. Confession is heard Saturday in the afternoon. Where have you come from?"

"From St. Paul. My brother and his friends have a claim here, and I've come to help them out."

"St. Paul? That's a handsome town. Right on the Mississippi. But where are you from originally, my child?"

"My name is Brigid Reardon. I'm from near Galway, in Ireland."

"I am Father Lonegran. You are a long way from home," he said solemnly as he walked with me toward the door of the chapel. "Please feel free to come into the sanctuary and pray and think. That is what the house of the Lord should be used for."

He blessed me and I walked out into the light of day in Deadwood. I would have asked him the way to the Gem Theater, but I wasn't sure he would have approved of my visiting there.

❋   ❋   ❋

Padraic and Billy had left early that morning for the claim. They said they'd be back for dinner at noon and then would take me out on the town, but I had wanted to see some of it myself. I also had a strong feeling that Nellie might talk to me differently if I were to show up with the two men.

The snow of yesterday had melted into a slush that mixed with the mud of the streets and created an unholy mess. My light boots would not hold up to it. I might need to buy myself a few more pieces of clothing. I even considered buying a pair of dungarees for riding horseback. Padraic had told me that the only way to get out to the claim was by horse.

The main street in Deadwood ran near the creek and had two- and three-story false fronts on each side of the street. Wagons rolled down the streets. Horses were left tied to railings.

All around were the hills, some bare from the fire or from cutting for building and firewood, but on other hills pointed trees perched up near the sky like so many fingers pointing heavenward.

After a couple of blocks I saw the Gem Theater. I entered and found it crowded, smoky, and noisy. Not a pleasant atmosphere. Women walked around wearing scanty outfits and hanging on men's arms. My entrance caused a small stir—men stepped back and watched me pass. I walked quickly so as not to elicit any more attention.

Groups of men surrounded what I assumed were the faro card games, gambling with bags of gold dust as the dealers threw out the cards. Most of the dealers were men, but I even saw a woman dealing toward the back of the room.

I walked up to the bar and asked for Nellie. The bartender pointed toward the back. The stage was empty so I went up the side stairs and found Nellie in one of the back rooms.

"Hello, Nellie."

At first Nellie didn't seem to know who I was. Finally I seemed to come into focus for her. "Holy Jesus, girl, what do you think you're doing here?"

"I wanted to see if there was anything I could do for Lily."

"Does Billy know you're here?" Her words sounded oddly slurred as if I had woken her from a deep sleep.

I shook my head no.

Sitting in front of a mirror, Nellie was wearing a brassiere and corset with a filmy skirt around her waist. I felt hot and stuffy in my coat and wool dress. I could not imagine sitting around in public with so little on, but she seemed very comfortable, almost sleepy. She gave me a vague smile. Seeing her up so close, she looked older and coarser than she had last night. Her eyes were rimmed with red and her teeth looked dirty.

Another woman was sitting with her, applying makeup to her eyes. She looked Chinese and had beautiful hair, like a blue-black wave falling over her shoulders and down her back. I wanted to put my hand out to stroke it. The face under it was rather homely with a long chin and small eyes. She didn't smile, only looked at me as if I were an oddity. She was wearing a silk robe opened to the waist with a dark corset on underneath.

Nellie was smoking a cigarette, something I had not often seen a woman do. She pointed to another room and said, "You wanted to see about Lily. We've got her all laid out in back. The doctor brought her over this morning, and we all worked on her. Go take a look at her. I think she looks lovely. Like an angel. That's what she was, an angel."

Tall maroon curtains were drawn with only a sliver of sun coming through them to light up the room. Lily looked so pale. They had dressed her all in white, down to her pigskin gloves. Her hands were crossed on her stomach and her chest was covered with an eyelet white dress. Without the wound showing she looked as if she was resting.

I crossed myself and said a prayer for her and told her Seamus was fine. I would tell him I had seen her and she was properly taken care of. He would be glad of that. Or I hoped he would. How well did I really know my brother after these years apart?

When I walked back into the dressing room, Nellie introduced me to the other woman. Her name was Ching Su. "Her name doesn't mean anything, she says. She says it's just like Nellie, only a name that girls get when they're born. Her stage name is Sugar Sue. I like that. It suits her."

Sugar Sue gave me a little bow with her hands together, then went back to putting on her makeup. Her face was covered with white powder. She looked like a doll, with a faraway look on her face. I wondered what her voice would sound like. I had never heard a Chinese person talk.

Nellie shook her head. "We've got a show to do in just a few minutes. Why don't you go out front and watch and then come back when we're done."

I hadn't wanted to stay so long. I needed to get back and get dinner ready for the men. "If it's too long, I'll have to leave. I'll come back later."

Sugar Sue lifted her face to me. She had finished putting on her makeup and was busy dressing her hair. Her hands wrapped it around and around in a thick, dark coil. "Are you looking for work?" she asked me. Her voice was soft like a slight breeze with only a hint of an accent.

"No, I have a houseful of men to take care of," I told her.

She nodded knowingly.

"Oh, I mean, I cook and clean for them." I felt I should explain. "That's all. One of them is my brother."

She covered her mouth and laughed. Then she pulled out a small pipe from a drawer in her dresser. "Would you like some?" she asked, offering it to me.

Nellie knocked her hand down. "No, she doesn't do that. She's book smart. She has learning and everything."

Sugar Sue put the pipe away.

"Chop-chop, darling," Nellie tapped Sugar Sue on the head. "We need to get onstage."

As Sugar Sue stood up, I noticed something else about her. Her feet were like two small balls on the ends of her legs, smaller than any feet I had seen. She was standing with them in red slippers that looked like they would fit my big toe. I could not help myself and gasped at the sight of them.

Nellie gave out a laugh. "Don't you know about the celestials?"

"What are celestials?"

"The Chinese. The women still bind their feet. Supposed to make them more valuable. I'm not sure for what. Means Sugar Doll can't do any dancing. Right, sweetie?" She nudged Sugar Sue, who almost fell down from Nellie's weight.

"Celestials? What a lovely name—but why are they called that?"

"Because many call China 'the celestial empire.' But sometimes I think they call them celestials to make fun of them."

I left them to their final preparations and went out front. I felt uncomfortable with all the men around, so I slipped into a seat and hunched down. Professor Pete was at the piano playing some popular song. I wished I had not come by myself. I was afraid that one of the men would accost me. In New York, I had been careful in the streets, crossing over if a group of men were coming my way, but I had never before experienced the leers that surrounded me in this theater.

Sugar Sue hobbled out onstage first. She was still wearing the robe and it was fastened up to her neck. She looked almost demure. Sitting down on a chair, she nodded her head to the music with a Chinese sound to it. Then I recognized it as a Gilbert and Sullivan tune. I had seen the play from standing room only on my afternoon off. The song was sung by Yum-Yum:

I mean to rule the earth,
as he the sky—
We really know our worth,
the sun and I!

Nellie came strutting out in the same outfit she had on backstage, and I felt sick for her, having to parade around in front of this group of men like that. She had a big smile plastered on her face, but her eyes still looked far away.

Around me men were erupting, hooting, and hollering, yelling, "Whoa, dollie!" and "Will you take a look at that!"

With all their stamping and whistling, it was hard to hear the song, but I realized that I was probably the only person trying to listen. The men stood at the foot of the stage and threw money at the two women. Partway through the song, Sugar Sue let her robe slip off her shoulders and reveal the corset she was wearing underneath. The men went wild around me.

After the show, Nellie came walking out and pulled me to a table. She leaned in close to me, her eyes wide in the dark room, and said, "I think it's the men that Lily met here that brought her to her death."

"You don't think Seamus did it, do you?"

"Not on your life. But there's a few others who've been seeing her that might have. Wouldn't put it past that Charlie Hunt. Always thinking he should have anything he wants."

"But is Charlie here?"

"Not sure. I heard he was coming back soon."

I certainly knew that about him from the way he had treated me. It was one thing for my brother to fall in love with a working girl, but quite another for Charlie Hunt, who could have any woman he wanted, to take up with her and then not want anyone else to have her.

"Two others come to mind: Moses Walker, a poor miner who's made a right pest of himself, and Ching Lee. He's Sugar Sue's brother. He runs the laundry in Chinatown. Very rich. He gave Lily the most beautiful silk fabric to make her dresses."

"Anyone see Lily after she left Seamus that night?"

Nellie shook her head. "I'll keep asking around, but so far no luck."

"Thanks."

"The funeral's tomorrow. Will you come?"

"Yes, of course."

"All us girls pitched in and bought her a casket and a plot up on the hill. She'll be buried close to Wild Bill Hickok. She would have liked that. She always thought he was a gentleman."

Just then a man came up and leered down at Nellie. "I've got gold dust, sweetie. Plenty of it. Let's go to your room."

I watched Nellie stand and follow the man, glad I was not in her place.

I had heard about such places where women went to work and sold their bodies, but I never thought I would enter one. Yet if my uncle hadn't given me a place to stay in New York and if I hadn't found a job quickly in the boardinghouse, who knows what might have become of me? More than ever before I resolved to take care of myself and find, in this wild country, a means to security.

Then and there, I promised my dear departed mother that Nellie's path would never be mine. As soon as this mess with Seamus and the sale of the mine were settled, I'd find a proper job.

11

Cooking smells assailed me as I walked in the door of what I was quickly coming to consider my home. Padraic had the potatoes on to boil and Billy was after skinning a fresh rabbit. It did my heart good to see two men doing the cooking.

I threw off my coat and entered the fray. "Sorry I'm late."

"Don't worry about it. You are your own person, Brigid. You don't need to answer to us." Billy grinned, tossed the rabbit pelt on the wood box, and sliced the flayed carcass into quarters.

After finding a sack of flour under the counter, I began to stir up some biscuits. I had made them so many times at the boardinghouse that I didn't need a recipe.

"There's much to see in this enterprising town," I told them.

"And what did you see in our fair city?" Padraic asked me with a smile on his face that looked a little false.

I realized they both wanted to know where I'd been but didn't feel like they could ask me. Without Seamus around, they did not exactly know how to treat me. But I determined I would not lie to them or even avoid the truth. "I went to see the church."

"To church? And what did you find there? God?" Padraic teased.

I ignored him for a moment as I spooned out the biscuits onto a cooking sheet. "Only his humble servant, Father Lonegran, but then I'm sure you two know him well."

Padraic shrugged his shoulders. "Only in passing. After losing half my family to famine and most of the rest to sickness, I'm not sure I want to meet the God responsible for all that."

"Who is left in your family, Paddy?" I asked, sitting opposite him at the long wooden plank that served as a table.

"I have a brother who made it to Dublin, I hear. And an aunt who still lives in Donegal. She writes me from time to time. That's all that's left. I once had three sisters and two brothers and my mother and father. I was the oldest. They had all died by the time I left Ireland. There was nothing to keep me there. My aunt had taken my brother in, so I didn't have to worry about him."

"I don't know if Seamus told you, but our mother died this last month." I smoothed down my dress.

"No, I had not heard. Seamus spoke so well of her. You must be very heart sad." Truly I felt that Padraic looked more moved by my mother's death than his own family losses. Maybe it is easier to feel someone else's pain than to squarely face your own. Especially for men.

"I am at that." I felt tears pushing behind my eyes and changed the subject. "Also, I went for a short visit to the Gem. I wanted to see what it was like. Nellie was performing while I was there."

Billy dropped the rabbit in hot grease and then jumped back from the splattering. "You never did, Brigid. Jaysus, a lone woman like you."

Padraic's eyes turned black and he banged his fist on the table. "What were you thinking?"

I could tell he was on the verge of saying words that we would both have trouble ignoring, so I spoke before he had a chance. "Now, Padraic, as Billy said to me when I came in, we all have a right to our own lives. I want to be able to do what I need to do to clear my brother's name. You must see that."

He closed his eyes for a moment as if to clear them of their storminess. When he opened them, he appeared calmer and nodded as he spoke. "Yes, I think I would have to agree with that, especially as it was laid out for me so clearly and directly."

"I'm sure there are some people who would think I shouldn't even be staying with the two of you."

"Of course, Brigid, you must stay with us. We need a woman's hand around this godforsaken place."

I could tell that Padraic was feeling badly. So I reached out my hand to his and rested it there. "I will help around the house and assist as much as

I can with the claim. And I will try to find out who killed Lily. Surely you can understand that. I appreciate your concern for me. But now I'm all on my own, and I want to be able to make my own decisions."

He took my hand in his and looked at it as if it were a precious metal. "You're a well- spoken woman, Brigid Reardon. We're lucky to have you."

"Would you go to the Gem with me later?"

He didn't answer immediately. He seemed to be trying to pull himself together. "It would give me great pleasure."

We all laughed at his slip of the tongue.

*   *   *

That night at home Padraic and Billy sat down with me and went over the business. A year ago, they had bought their claim for three hundred dollars from money they had saved from railroad work. It had been Billy's idea. He was sure they would make a fortune. They had taken over the claim from a miner who was too sick to continue to work. Since then they had pulled nearly three thousand dollars' worth of gold out of it; however, much of the money had gone back into the workings of the claim.

While they felt there was much more gold to be had, they didn't feel they had the equipment or the money that was needed to do so. They were hoping the Hunts would offer to buy their claim for ten thousand dollars.

I was stunned. Ten thousand dollars was a huge amount of money. It could set you up for life. Even with a three-way split—nearly thirty-five hundred a piece. That was what a chambermaid would make if she worked her fingers to the bone for ten years and never spent a penny.

"When are you expected to let them know if you will accept?" I asked.

"When Hunt left he said he'd only be gone a month or so. Just over the holidays. He might be back any day now," Paddy explained. "But it's not all as easy as that. They are bringing in their own man to do a test on an ore sample. That will happen as soon as Charlie is back."

I thought of seeing Charlie Hunt in Deadwood. Wouldn't he be surprised to learn that he would have to be dealing with me to buy the claim?

I remembered the conversation I had overheard at the Hunt house between Charlie and his father. "From something I heard at the Hunts' we might be able to ask for more. I think their interest runs high."

Billy smacked his hand on the table. "I have a good feeling about this."

Paddy stayed calm. "At present, we're both going to keep working the mine. If we stay at it for eight to ten hours a day, we should take out about twenty to thirty dollars a day. At that rate we can't afford to hire another miner. We could really use Seamus right now. An extra hand would be good."

"Is there anything I can do?" I asked.

"We'll take you up there. I don't think you would want to go down into the mine, but you might help us check the sieves. Keeping the house in order here and figuring out the banking would be a big help."

"What if I find a gold nugget? Do I get to keep it?" I asked, wondering what that would be like, to find money on the ground.

"You might need it for some new clothes," Billy said.

"I'm fine in what I've got."

"This might not be the time to talk about this, but you're going to need to buy yourself a pretty dress, Brigid." Billy said to me, pushing back his chair. "There's a dance come New Year's Eve. You might want to get something new to wear for that."

"A dance," I said in wonder, then felt bad thinking of such fun. "I don't know if I would feel like going. But I've never been to a real dance before."

Billy winked at me. "I'll teach you the new steps so you can keep up with everyone. As I remember, you're light on your feet."

"As I remember, you throw your weight around."

We both grinned at each other across the table. Standing up, Billy started humming a waltz. I stood and curtseyed. He took me in his arms and, without running into many pieces of furniture, we danced around the room.

The next thing I knew Billy was roaring out the words to an Irish ballad in my ear and we were all laughing and trying to keep up with him. Padraic tapped out the rhythm of the music with a knife on the table, and I felt a bubble of happiness push up inside of me.

Billy's voice was true and clear as if it poured from a holy spring. The words came out and I felt my heart yearn for Ireland again, for the music of my people, even for the sound of the Irish language. What were we all doing in this strange land?

I wondered how my dear brother was faring on this cold night, if he had found safe refuge in Cheyenne or wherever he might be. I hoped beyond hope to clear our family name and to gain enough money from the sale of the mine to set us up well, with no worries ever again.

And that I might actually go to a dance.

12

The next morning as we were preparing to go to the mine, Padraic handed me a leather pouch.

"This is what the fine gold dust looks like," Padraic said.

I took the pouch in my hand and opened it. Gold dust. Particles of burnished gold, dirty looking, but worth twenty dollars an ounce, he told me. I dipped my finger in and stared at the bits of gold that clung to it. The streets of America were not lined with it, as promised, but here I was holding a bag of the precious metal in my hand.

"How ever do you gather it when it's so fine?" I asked.

"You will see."

Billy joined us on the front steps and laughed when he saw what I was holding. "So he's letting you hold his balls?"

I was shocked at his language, but Billy hooted again and even Padraic cracked a smile. He pointed at the bag I was holding. "It's made from a bull's jewel sack," he told me.

I carefully tapped the gold off my finger back into the bag and looked at the fine leather with new respect. A grand pouch it was. "May it only increase in size," I said as I handed it back to Padraic. They both got a laugh out of that.

Billy ran off to fetch the horses and Padraic looked me over. I was outfitted in a pair of Billy's dungarees. They were a bit big around the waist so I had tied them over a shirt with a kerchief. There was not an item on my body that belonged to me but my socks and even they had been covered with a heavier wool pair of Paddy's.

A chinook had blown in—a warm southern wind that had melted most of the snow during the night and turned the street into a sea of mud. The sun was out, and I could feel its warmth on my face and through my jacket.

Paddy went inside and came back out with a brown felt hat that he placed on my head. I pulled it on tighter for a better fit. Then he surveyed me.

"You look like a boy," he crowed.

I felt stung by his comment. "Well, what do you expect with all this gear on?"

"A fine looking lad you are, to be sure," he said to make me feel better.

We were riding up to the claim. I wanted to see for myself what they were doing and understand the mining process. Now that a share of the claim was mine, I intended to make sure that we did what was best with it.

I wished again that Seamus was with us. Last night, lying in bed, I had questioned what I was doing staying in Deadwood without him. I thought of traveling to Cheyenne to join him, although we still had not had word from him. But I felt I needed to stay on and safeguard our share of the money from the sale of the mine. With it, we could bring the family over from Ireland—I was determined to not let another one of them die there.

I tried to think what I might do with a bit of money—start a business, set up my own household—it all seemed so grand. And with some money of my own, I was sure I could make a better marriage. Who would want me as I was? Without a pot to pee in, as my father would say.

❋   ❋   ❋

Billy rode up on a bay and held the reins of two other horses. The smaller one, a pinto, was for me. I walked to her head first and patted her on the nose. She stared back at me with reassuring dark brown eyes. Paddy helped me put my foot in the one stirrup and hoisted me up onto the saddle. I felt very high up off the ground and hoped that my horse had a gentle disposition.

Padraic patted me on the leg and said, "Gertie is as sweet a horse as there is. Give Gertie her head and she'll take you the right way. She knows this path well."

Paddy grabbed the reins of his horse, a black gelding, from Billy and swung up into the saddle as if he were climbing over a fence. He clucked and pulled the reins in the direction he wanted to go, and the horse gave a little jump and sashayed up the street. My horse followed with a nice rhythm to her gait. Billy fell in behind me.

I hadn't ridden since I had come to America. In Ireland, Seamus and I would steal out in the dark and hop on the backs of the landlord's horses, wrap our hands into their manes, and ride over the fields until we fell off. Somehow, riding without a saddle I stuck on the horse better. Now I felt as if I might slide off the worn saddle at any moment, only my feet in the stirrups keeping me propped upright.

We rode for half an hour. The claim wasn't far according to Padraic—up over a steep hill and then following a trail alongside Whitewood Creek for a half a mile. Patches of snow huddled into nooks on the hillside. The sun shone and the soft wind blew moist against my cheeks. A very pleasant day for a ride. I was enjoying the slow easy walk of my horse as we picked our way along the path.

Padraic pulled up and pointed down through the trees to an area right around the creek that was stripped away. Trees had been cut on either side and a sort of wooden chute built right over the creek. We turned our horses toward the claim and they gingerly picked their way down a gentle slope to the creek bed.

A sign posted on a tree claimed the land for my brother and his two friends. Padraic jumped down and tethered his horse to a tree. I waited until he grabbed the bridle of my horse to swing down off the saddle. Even that short distance in a saddle and I felt an ache in my legs.

He waved his arm and said, "This is the Green Isle claim."

A long wooden chute was built along the creek bed. The creek had been torn up and water ran right through the chutes. Piles of rock lay on the banks and shovels were close at hand. The scene looked like they worked until they were too tired and left things where they dropped them. So typical of men.

Padraic explained how the whole system worked.

"We panned at first, but that's just too blamed hard. Then we set up this rocker." He showed me the box with small holes in it, which he called a riddle, set on a trough. The gravel was placed in the top of the box and water poured over it. This washed the sand, gravel, and silt through the riddle. After removing the big rocks and pieces of gravel, the slurry of gold

and sand was washed down into the trough where it passes over other rif-
fles where the gold and garnets are caught and held. At the very end of the
trough they had put a sheepskin to catch the last bits of gold.

"Don't you know we call it the golden fleece." Padraic rubbed his hand
over it and then looked to see if anything was stuck on it.

"We can't work this right now as the waters froze. But we've been digging to find the good gravel. We've got a pit going over here." He walked
me over to a hole that I thought I could barely fit in. "I think we've located
a lode. We've found some decent ore down there."

"How do you determine that?"

"Well, sometimes we just figure it out by running it through the rocker.
We can see what we have pretty quickly. But the Hunts want to take a sample to determine the worth of the claim."

"How do you decide where to take a sample?" I asked.

Padraic pointed out where the pit had been dug. "It's part the smarts
and part just guessing, the same way it is with most things. You can see the
way the land runs. You learn where the bedrock lies in your land. The gold,
because it's very heavy, settles down on the bedrock. The pit is dug on one
of the lowest areas on our claim, in the crease of it, so to speak. We dug
to bedrock and brought up the gravel that we found right above it. We're
going to dig a mine shaft right there. Billy's working on it already."

"Why are the Hunts so interested in your land?"

"Besides the fact that we've got a good solid claim here, I think they
want our piece as part of a bigger scheme. They mean to buy up the whole
valley if they can."

I looked around at the diggings, which were all dirtier and danker
than I had expected. The two men went to work, Billy climbing down into
the pit and Padraic clearing away a channel.

I started examining the slurry that was brought up out of the pit and
was astounded when I would find the smallest chip of gold. The gold
looked darker than I thought it would. But so sweet to find it. Once I
found one piece I could spot others. I quickly picked out more pieces of
gold. Imagine picking money up off the ground. I held the pile of small
chips in my hand and thought what I could buy with them: a suit, a muff,
some decent shoes, books if they were to be found in this uncultured

place. Then I thought of grander things: real china, a fur coat, a home with servants, my own carriage. From working at the Hunts, I knew what real money could bring. I pictured my father and the children getting off the boat in America. I kept digging to find more of it.

✳ ✳ ✳

After working about two hours, they called for some dinner and I took out the basket I had packed. I spread out a tablecloth and we all set to eating. Simple fare. Leftover biscuits and rabbit thighs. But out in the clean, cool air it tasted wonderful.

I showed them the small chips I had found.

"She's become a miner herself!" Padraic laughed at me. "We'll have to be giving her her own set of balls to keep her gold in."

As we ate, Padraic told stories of the mines in the hills, of the Indians who hunted around us, of the cavalry that came through. I was surprised to hear what a storyteller he had become. They went back to work for a while longer, but the sun was almost touching the tops of the mountains, and we didn't want a cold dark ride down out of the mountains.

Billy was chipping away at a piece of stone he had brought out of the pit. Suddenly, he was up and dancing around.

"It's a nugget," he cried. "The biggest I've ever found. This is surely a good sign for our claim. I know we will be rich." He ran over and showed us. A dirty yellow stone the size of my thumbnail. He gave it to me to hold and I ran my fingers over it.

As I held the nugget in my hands, I thought of how I had felt finding my own gold. Lily's death, might it have something to do with the gold thirst? This gold lust seemed to be the impulse behind most everything in this small, new town.

13

The next morning the two men of the house went off early to work on the claim. I was left, as my mother would say, to my own devices. I had a good morning of cleaning and putting everything to rights in the small house. At first I was content humming to myself, and then it was not enough. I needed to hear another's voice; I needed the company of a woman. I tidied myself up and decided to present myself next door.

When I knocked on Elizabeth's door, it took her a while to answer. When she came to the door, she looked unwell, her face puffy and her eyes streaked red. Nonetheless, she grabbed my arm and pulled me into her house.

"I'm so glad to see you," she said and ushered me to a chair in the main room near the fire.

"I thought I'd stop by."

"Yes." Elizabeth nodded her head. "Yes. I'm so glad. I baked a cake. I'll make some coffee. Get warm here by the fire. My husband piled up a whole lot of firewood for me before he went. So I've not been cold."

"It's very cozy in here." I looked around the room.

The house looked very much like the one I was in although a woman's touch was evident. What looked like gingham fabric had been pasted to the walls like wallpaper. Elizabeth had chosen to use a bright gingham with red and white squares. Two painted portraits were hung up high on the wall, a stern looking man and a mousey woman who bore a great resemblance to Elizabeth. I assumed they were her parents. There was a bookshelf filled with books, and I made a note to myself to ask to look at what she had, for books were a great treasure out in Deadwood.

Elizabeth sunk into a chair herself. Her face looked slightly green and she was sweating. "I'm not myself these days."

"Yes," I said. "You seem a bit under the weather."

She tucked her head down and whispered, "I think I might be with child."

"Oh." I felt part relief that she was not going to pass the influenza on to me, but also a certain alarm, not sure how to view her predicament with her husband gone and all. I tried to put on a happy face. "You're to have a baby. Isn't that lovely?"

"A baby would be company." She smiled and I saw what a pretty girl she must have been back in Philadelphia, before she followed her husband out to the wilderness. "And at least it won't come till spring. That's a blessing. The warm weather will make everything easier."

I couldn't imagine having a child in this wilderness, and yet I knew women did it all the time. "Does your husband know?"

"I said nothing before he left. I wasn't sure. But with each passing morning I am surer of my condition."

"Would you like me to get you something to eat?"

She stood and insisted on serving me. "No, let me get you a piece of cake. I'll just sit and watch you eat it."

She brought me a piece of pudding cake and told me how she had made it. I wondered if her leavening was off as it seemed not to have risen much. I took a few bites and set it to the side.

We sat and chatted about how it was to live out East, finding out we had lived very different lives, no surprise to me. She had been the pampered only child of a wealthy family. I did not go on about my hardships in New York, not to mention my life in Ireland, but I saw clearly that they had better equipped me for the life we were leading out in Deadwood.

"I just don't know what to do with myself. Every task here seems impossible. Even keeping the fire going is hard. I never knew how much wood one must haul to stay warm." She wrapped her shawl around her thin shoulders.

"Before I go, I'll bring in a load for you." I decided I'd mention it to Padraic and Billy to bring in wood for her in the morning. An easy enough task to do, but one she seemed not made for.

Finally, I got around to the question I had come to ask. "Elizabeth, I wanted to ask you about Christmas Eve."

"When that woman was killed?" She stirred with interest.

"Yes. I know you said you went to sleep early, but did you hear anything unusual that night?"

"I think I told you, the party did keep me awake for a while, but then I drifted off to sleep. Then later that night, toward morning even, I heard your brother singing. Lovely voice he has. Some Irish tune. You're Irish, aren't you? I can hear it in your voice. I don't remember the song, but it was a happy one."

I could picture Seamus singing. The woman he loved had just said she would marry him. His sister had arrived for a visit. Early Christmas Day and he had poured enough drink in himself to float a ship. This new piece of information went far in convincing me once again that he was not a murderer. What killer sings as they stab their lover?

*   *   *

I dressed in my second-best clothes, my gray serge dress, but I couldn't stand the thought of trying to slosh through the mud in my lace-up boots, so I put back on Billy's pair, Kensington's they were called. They didn't show much beneath the hem of my dress.

Paddy and Billy had said they'd be back in for supper. I told them I would be out for part of the afternoon. I intended to order a new dress from one of the dressmakers in town. But ever since Nellie told me of the other men in Lily's life, I was determined to have a word with each of them.

Billy told me that Moses Walker lived above the dentist's office. As I walked I kept my skirts in my hand because the mud was more than ankle deep in some places. I bet the laundry in this town did a booming business.

A sign hung down with a pair of teeth painted below the name of the doctor. I supposed that was to help draw in the men who couldn't read. Alongside the building was a stairway that led to a door on the second floor.

I took the stairs up and paused outside the door, composing myself. All I could do was simply ask the man how he had spent Christmas Eve, then watch him carefully.

However, when I knocked, a woman answered the door. Mrs. Moses Walker, she tartly informed me. She had a very small child in her arms and a slightly larger one attached to her skirt. Both of them with snotty noses and crying besides. A heavy-set woman, she had one eye that turned away from her face. Wall-eyed. She looked me up and down and then bellowed, "What do you want?"

"Is your husband in?" I asked, keeping my composure. I caught a glimpse inside the room and was amazed at the walls. They were covered with colorful pictures from newspapers and magazines.

"Not for the likes of you. He's off to his claim. Can't you leave a decent man alone? We have children to feed, and it don't help none, his bringing his money down to the theater to spend on such trash."

"Ma'am, I'm not—" I got no further.

"Don't bother to tell me such lies. Woman as pretty as you. What else are you good for? You've got the look. I can tell. I've seen too many like you. Preying off the men, that's what you do. And what other woman would come bothering us to see my husband? I suppose you'll be trying to tell me you have business with him."

"Of a sort."

"And just what kind of a sort would that be?" The children had quieted, listening to their mother caterwauling at me. The baby had stuck a finger in his mouth and was sucking on it, the limpet child's mouth was hanging open as he stared at me.

I decided to be truthful. There seemed nothing to gain either by trying to deny that I was a lady of the night or making up a bogus story to tell her.

"There was an accident that happened on Christmas Eve late, and I'm trying to find anyone who might have witnessed it. Someone said that your husband had been out for a walk and I wanted to ask him some questions." Close enough to the truth.

"That's a blamed lie. Take it from me—that someone is wrong." She yelled at me as if I were standing clear across the room. "My dear husband stayed with myself and the children all of that blessed night. He drank himself into a stew and slept by the fire." She stepped toward me and I backed up, feeling the railing of the stairway cut into my back. "Now, leave him be. He's a good man if he keeps away from the drink. He wouldn't look at your sort if he was sober, not my Moses."

"I don't doubt that."

"I heard one of your kind was kilt t'other night."

"Yes," I said and stopped at the top of the stairs.

"My husband has not a mean bone in his body. He wouldn't do such a thing. And he was here with me."

"Thank you." I believed not a word the woman had told me, except that her husband was a drunk.

*　*　*

Wolf and McDonald's haberdashery had a lovely woman's suit on a mannequin up at the front of the store. I stood and stared at it, then reached out to finger the fabric, a wool tweed with a handsome edging of satin and velvet. Wouldn't I just love to wear such a suit one day. But first I needed a dress that I could wear for the New Year's Eve ball. I didn't know if it would be possible for them to outfit me so quickly. I hoped they had some nice dresses readymade.

The store was as big as any I had seen in St. Paul, with bolts of fabric all along one wall. Men's clothes in shelves along the other side. Overalls, big brimmed hats, and wool socks overflowed bins.

I marched over to where the men's boots were lined up and found a pair that would fit me. I also found a pair of dungarees that would come close, especially if I cinched them with a belt. Thus outfitted, I could ride out to the claim in comfort if not style.

Piling my clothes on the long wooden counter, I addressed my request to the man standing behind it. He looked me up and down, and I guessed he was trying to understand how I fit into this town. After a small exhalation through his nose, he sent me on to the back, where he assured me a Mrs. Bisbee would help me out.

Mrs. Bisbee was formidable, dressed in enough fabric to make five dresses, and she was not a big woman. Her gray hair was tied up tight in a bun on the back of her head, and around her wrist she wore a kind of corsage made from a pin cushion. I was impressed to see a woman managing a part of a store. It occurred to me that I might try for such work, but my handwork left much to be desired. Still, she was a working woman, not a sporting girl—which was what I wanted for myself.

I told her what I was looking for.

She shook her head as if I had misbehaved in some way. "I don't see how that can be arranged. However, we might be able to sell you something off the rack."

Then, looking skeptical, she showed me several dresses, but they were not what I had been thinking of. Very dowdy, not really dresses one wore to a dance.

"I was hoping for something a bit more elegant. A dress for the ball."

Suddenly, she snapped her fingers. "I had a dress that I had started but . . . Let's see if that might fit you."

She walked behind some curtains and brought out an elegant dark blue dress, with some flounces, but not so many that you looked like you might fly away. I tried it on and Mrs. Bisbee went to work with her pins, her hands pinching my sides, plucking at my arms.

"The shoulders must be let out. The waist is just right. The hem let down an inch or two. I think it will do." She talked to herself as her hands flew around the dress.

When she was done fitting me, she stepped back and turned me toward the mirror.

I let out a gasp. Never had I seen this creature who stared back at me. The blue brought out her eyes, and the sheen added glossiness to her hair. She looked like she could walk into any party on the continent of Europe and fit in. This dark-haired young woman looked like a princess. Running my hands down the skirt, I stared and stared and still couldn't believe that the woman in the mirror was me.

"Oh, yes," I said. "This will do nicely."

The price was very reasonable. I guessed it was probably already partially paid for. This Mrs. Bisbee was a businesswoman. For all I knew, she was getting paid twice for the dress. I did not care. I would not have been able to leave that dress behind.

Because the gown was so reasonable, I decided I could also buy a pair of shoes. I chose a pair of pumps that were soft as suede, almost like little slippers. I slipped them on my feet. They fit like they were made for me.

"I'm so pleased that the dress fit you," Mrs. Bisbee said as she ushered me to the door. "We'll have it ready by the day after tomorrow." Then she added, "Poor Lily will not be needing it where she's gone."

14

Billy said he wouldn't go to Lily's funeral. He made no pretense about it. He stated it was a woman's affair and that he hated all that wailing and weeping. Said he had better things to do than watch them put a body in the ground. I think all the sorrow frightened him.

Padraic had said he would go, but in the end he changed his mind. "I'm not much into church affairs," he explained.

I was dressed and ready to go, standing by the front door when he said this. He looked at me to see what I would do. I pulled on my gloves. "I feel like my family should be represented. After all, she was my brother's fiancée."

"I think you're taking this engagement more seriously than either Seamus or Lily would have taken it."

"Really?" I asked.

"In this place, people promise much, but it doesn't often happen." Padraic shrugged his shoulders.

"Well, I gave my word to Nellie that I would go to this funeral and I am going." I straightened my hat.

"As you like," he said and told me how to get to the cemetery.

The weather had turned bitter again. I had to walk up a very steep hill to get to the cemetery, which overlooked town. From this vantage point, I could see the slate-gray clouds moving in. The clouds looked as stuffed full of snow as pillows are of feathers. As I rose higher above the town, the wind grew in force and buffeted my skirts about me.

When I made it to the top, I saw the funeral cortege and moved to the back of the gathering. There were about ten women and a handful of men. I saw Ching Su next to Nellie, dressed all in white. How odd, I thought. But her hair stood out against her coat like the trees against the snow. Nellie had on a purple coat that made her look a bit like an eggplant. She was crying into a handkerchief, a harsh sound that was raw with grief.

Behind the two women stood a Chinese man. He had eyes that cut across his face and a small silk hat that tucked tight to his head. I guessed that he was Ching Su's brother. Although a small man, he looked very forceful. Except for Sugar Sue, I had never met a Chinese person before, or a "celestial," as they were called in Deadwood.

Lily must have been of some Protestant sect, for the service was not familiar to me. I bent my head and listened to the words that droned on. Then suddenly everyone looked up as charging up the hill came a carriage, which pulled in behind the funeral carriage. Out stepped Charlie Hunt.

To see him here unnerved me. My hands turned cold, then hot, and my face flushed. I bent my head to be unobserved. Charlie appeared larger than I remembered. Maybe it was his high top hat and a dark and handsome waistcoat that fit him to perfection. His shoulders pushed through his jacket and his face looked so healthy and clean, in such contrast to the men I saw on the street in Deadwood. Clearly he was no miner. He was a businessman with hands soft and smooth as his mother's.

Charlie had with him a man who had been at the Christmas Eve party. I particularly remembered this man because he had such a large mole on the end of his nose. He was all over a knobby man, about forty years of age. Unfortunately, I did not need to wonder why Charlie Hunt was at this funeral: he was paying last respects to one of his mistresses. It made me angry to think he had kissed me too.

I lifted my head to get a glimpse of him and found him staring at me. Now that I was not a servant girl in his house, I did not need to watch myself around him. I stared right back, then turned back to the proceedings.

The pastor said something and people responded. I needed to attend. I managed to hear his next few lines and answered, "Amen," with everyone. Nellie threw a dark red rose down onto the casket and then the men tossed in spadefuls of dirt. I said a silent prayer for her soul.

And then, out of nowhere, I was hit with deepest sorrow. The body entering the ground. I knew my mother had been buried in the earth, but I had been unable to be there. I would never see her again. Tears threatened to spill out of me. I forced myself away from thoughts of my mother. No one here needed to see me cry. They would not understand and might find it strange that I would grieve so openly about Lily's death when I had only met the woman once.

After I pulled myself together, I walked up to Nellie to give her my sympathy. Her face was blotchy red with crying and her handkerchief wet. As I came closer to her, I recognized the reek of whiskey on her breath.

"Nellie, I'm so sorry. But it was a lovely funeral."

"It was, wasn't it? There aren't many sporting girls like us can claim as much, but I promised Lily she'd have a nice one."

"Did she fear she would die?"

"Oh, it's just one of the things the girls talk about. You never know what's going to happen with a customer." Then her red eyes filled with tears that gushed down her cheeks. "But I'll never have a friend like her again. We told each other everything. Like a sister she was to me. A dear, dear sister."

"You were lucky to have her," I murmured, thinking of my own dear sisters at home, wishing they were with me.

When I turned to go, I felt a hand on my arm.

I lifted my face and found Charlie Hunt very close, leaning over to converse with me. I pulled back slightly and he stood up straighter.

"I am so pleased to see you, Miss Reardon."

"It's good that one of us can say that."

"I see you've honed the tongue."

"I see you've polished your boots. They won't last long in this town."

"I know. May I give you a ride down to town?"

I meant to say no. I meant to say it immediately. But my feet were cold and flakes of snow were descending like needles from the sky. I would need to do business with this man. Refusing a lift seemed melodramatic. I had no time for that effect.

"That would be kind of you."

I let him lead me to his carriage and lift me up. The mole-nosed man climbed up on front with the driver. A horsehair blanket awaited my lap. Charlie secured it around me and sat down across from me. He leaned back into the seat and looked me over. "Yes," he said. "You are as handsome as ever."

"Handsome is for men."

"Yes, and a few women who are uncommonly good looking. Who have a bold look."

"Now that's the second time I've been called a *streel* in two days' time."

"A streel?"

"It's Irish for a good-time lady."

"You have not that look, and I would never deem to call you that."

"And yet you treated me like one."

He looked down at his gloved hands and said quietly, "I'm sorry if you think I took advantage of you at my parents' house."

"I have missed the luxury of your parents' house. And the books," I said boldly, remembering the last one I almost read.

"Yes, I imagine."

"What brings you back to Deadwood so soon?" I asked. I already knew much of the answer but wanted to hear what he would tell me.

"Business and pleasure. I hear that I might actually be able to mix them by dealing with you."

"How so?"

"I've been told that you've taken on your brother's share of the claim."

I was astounded. This man couldn't have been in town more than a day and he had already found out more than I liked him to know about my business. "How do you know this?"

"I have my ways."

I turned to look out the carriage window. Charlie cleared his throat and then asked, "How fares your brother?"

"Your network has failed you. I assumed that you could tell me much about him that I do not know."

"Nellie told me you had taken on Seamus's share."

"Oh, so you've moved from Lily to Nellie. Well, I suppose a man must find his comfort wherever he can."

"I can explain . . . ," he started.

"You do not need to explain anything to me. Because I am young, you might assume I am unknowledgeable about such matters. I have certainly acquired a wealth of information from the places I have worked. Even your parents' establishment."

He looked at me dumbstruck and I hoped that I had set him properly in his place. Instead, a most explosive laughter burst from him and I experienced an overwhelming desire to strike him. He quickly sobered up and assured me, "I have always assumed you to know much about everything."

"Well, I look forward to doing business with you."

"Might I be so forward as to ask if you would join me for dinner in two nights' time? We could try Delmonico's. I've heard their food is quite good."

"I will have to see. I am keeping house for Padraic and Billy, and they might require me to be there."

"As I was dealing mainly with your brother in negotiating the deal for their claim, I thought I might continue my dealings with you. However, if Padraic is going to take over, please let me know."

"I will certainly."

We rode in silence. The snow kept falling and it quieted even the clopping of the horse's hooves. I felt tucked into myself. Charlie too seemed to have sunk into himself, staring out the window.

I longed to ask him many questions about the household I had left: what Dorry had received for Christmas, what Aggy had prepared for the meals, how his mother was, but I resisted asking anything of him. His presence reminded me of all I had left behind in St. Paul, back in the States. While I was glad to no longer be a servant, I had grown fond of his family.

As we neared the main street, he asked me where I wished to be dropped, and I told him right by the bank. As the carriage slowed, he stepped out first and then reached up to hand me down. I came down next to him, and he continued to hold my hand, looking down into my face.

"Brigid, I know I must give condolences to your family also. I had heard that Seamus and Lily were engaged."

I nodded and turned away quickly, thinking Lily might have been a sister to me.

✻   ✻   ✻

I had only gone a block or two when I realized I had turned in the wrong direction. Charlie had so unnerved me that I had become disoriented.

Most unlike myself. Thank goodness, Deadwood was not a large town. I looked up and could easily make out from the hills around me where I was and headed back in the right direction.

I saw a new milliner's shop that had opened, Madame Laclaire's, and wondered if I should stop in and see if they had a new waist that I could purchase and wear with my velvet skirt. The skirt had been a hand-me-down from Mrs. Hunt, and one of the other maids had fitted it to me. She had always been very generous to us.

As I was daydreaming, looking in the window at the lovely hats and gloves, I saw my reflection and adjusted my hat. Then the window exploded. A gunshot cracked loud close by. I ducked into the doorway and heard the zing of another bullet as it hit the sign hanging above my head.

A final bullet sung through the air, but I didn't know what it had struck. I pushed open the door and fell into the shop. A dark-haired woman stared at the window and then at me. She stepped out from behind the counter where she had been sorting linen handkerchiefs.

"Shooting. They're shooting," I gasped out.

She pointed at two drunk men down an alley firing off their guns into the air. "They are crazy. *Fou, complètement fou.* They shoot for the fun of it."

I closed the door behind me. "Even in town?"

"They have ruined my lovely *chapeaux*," she said, in what I could only guess was a French accent. She was staring at the hats in the window, which were covered with shards of glass.

Then she looked at the hat I was wearing. "They have also ruined the hat you have upon your head. Very unlucky," she declared.

I unpinned it and looked at the slash a piece of glass had given it. How had I been spared?

"I might need to buy a new one," I agreed.

15

"What has brought you to Deadwood?" she asked in her high, sweet voice as she wrapped up my several purchases. "I'm staying with my brother and his friends."

She smiled. "Oh, your family is here. How nice." The milliner's name was Clarice Laclaire. I put her age at near fifty, but she was a lovely woman with small red lips like a little bow. When she talked, I noticed, she kept her mouth quite small, never opening it much. She seemed to me to be the quintessence of femininity, and I felt large and awkward next to her. Another woman with a career and a foreigner like myself. So such a thing was possible.

I handed her my bag of gold, not quite understanding the etiquette of who did what when the gold was weighed out. She took it from me and with a very careful hand and a small spoon put a small pile of gold dust on the scale. My purchases, a beautiful black velvet hat, a lovely lace waist, and one handkerchief, came to just under three dollars. It seemed so odd to watch this dainty woman weighing out what looked like a thimbleful of yellow dirt. But it was the way things were done in Deadwood.

"Is your husband here with you?" I asked, assuming they had opened the shop together.

She ducked her head and said, "He was killed during the Civil War."

The war had happened before my coming to America, but people still talked about the tragedy of it. "I'm so sorry."

"Yes, so am I. He was a good man. But he left me with some money, and I've always liked adventure, so here I am. My own shop. For, you see, I make hats. That is what I am good at."

"Yes, you are."

"If you would like, you could leave the other hat with me and I would fix it for you so that it would look like a new hat. Very much *à la mode*."

"Do you miss your country, France?"

"Many things I miss, the food, the culture, but I do not miss the small world that women must live in. That I do not miss. Here I can own myself a shop. So you see!"

I laughed. I loved her spirit. "Yes, I do!"

She waved her hands around at her shop. Then her eyes lit upon the front window and she sighed, "*Ah, le pauvre vitrine.*"

I could guess what she was saying even though I knew no French. "I'm sorry about your window."

"The men in this town are animals. Shooting, shooting, always shooting. It is not your fault. You were very lucky you weren't hurt."

❄   ❄   ❄

In a shop window on Shine Street, I was surprised to see a wanted poster as I was walking home from the funeral. No photograph, just his name in big type: SEAMUS REARDON. The reward was five hundred dollars. I needed to renew my efforts to find out who had killed Lily. The stories that Billy and Paddy told about how justice was meted out in the frontier scared me. I didn't want my brother hunted down like a common criminal and shot in the back.

When I got home, I found that Padraic had gone back out to the claim and Billy was sleeping on the sofa. I was slightly offended to find his body carelessly draped over the only decent piece of furniture in the living room. The sofa was placed right in front of the fire and looked awfully cozy. I cleaned up around him, sweeping the floor, shaking out the rugs, rearranging the wooden chairs, but none of my activity made him stir.

I pulled up a chair near the fire to warm myself and stared at him. What an odd little man, I thought. Much like the leprechauns that are said to inhabit Ireland, though they are talked of more here in America than back home. His face was darkened with the shadow of a beard, and his hands were rough and torn from the mining work. I wondered how long

Billy would last. He seemed to go at life awfully hard, and he might simply, in the end, be worn down by it all.

"What you staring at?" Billy opened one eye at me.

"The mess that someone has left lying on the couch."

He gave a snort and came to life with all limbs flying. He sat up and shook his head, then asked, "How was the funeral?"

"Simple. I think it served its purpose. Nellie seemed pleased." I looked over at Billy to see how he would react to her name. I was uncertain of their relationship.

He nodded. "Good. Nellie's a fine woman. But you know what they say about the three worst smiles . . ."

"I don't know that one."

"The smile of the wave, the smile of a sporting woman, and the grin of a dog about to leap at you."

I laughed at his triad. I hadn't heard a good one in a long enough time. Billy always brought me back to Ireland and I loved him for it, as scruffy a little leprechaun as he was.

"Oh, and I forgot to tell you: Mr. Charlie Hunt attended."

That got his attention. "He did, did he? Well, it's nice to know he's back in town. Now he can take the claim off our hands and we can clear out of here. I'm tired of this godforsaken place." He put his head down into his hands and rolled it back and forth.

"Where will you go next, Billy?"

He lifted his head up and said loudly and clearly, "Where there's money to be made. Maybe California. I've heard great stories. They say the sun shines there every day and the trees are taller than the tallest building in New York City. Will you not come along?"

"I'd like to see California, but I'll need to see what Seamus wants to do. I'd also like to bring our family over."

He rubbed at his eyes. "You need to forget about your family."

"How can you say that?"

"They brought me into this world and I've already done my time for that. My father's a drunk and my mother had too many children. Lord help them, because I can't."

I realized he was describing my own family as well, but unlike him I missed them terribly: my mother's hands, my father's laugh. "But they sent me here."

"To be rid of you. Once I left Ireland, I decided to never look back. Not that my belly doesn't wrench at the thought of the lovely land I left behind. Maybe someday I'll return, but until then I'm setting my sights on the treasures right here."

I didn't want to argue with him, but just the mention of them made me long for my family.

We sat a moment in silence, watching the red flames lick at the dark logs. Dreams, immigrant dreams, to return home wealthy. But few of us would ever return and fewer would become wealthy. I hoped I would be different. Once the mine was sold, I'd have money and the opportunity to make even more. I had to keep my head about me.

"Billy, do you know Moses Walker?"

"By sight. He has a claim near enough to us. Why?"

"I need to talk to him."

"You might well find him out there today."

❋   ❋   ❋

The livery stable saddled up the small horse, Gertie, for me and I rode out. When I got through town and to the beginning of the trail, I reined in the horse. I wanted to take a minute and breathe. I pulled off a glove and reached my hand down into the horse's hair. Her coat was long for the winter, like prickly down it felt. This horse was a solid little mare. The snow had let up, but the air felt crisp. The mud had frozen, which made it easier to ride through town and up the trail. I didn't like going out by myself, but I had to do it.

I reached into the pocket of my coat and felt the cold metal of the derringer that Billy had given me. He said he had picked it up in a card game and had no use for it. When I told him about the shooting incident in town, he told me I should be armed. Now I needed to learn to use it. In this country, a woman needed to know everything a man knew. While I might never become an Annie Oakley, I thought I could become a decent shot.

As I climbed up and out of the valley that Deadwood settled in, I could see the lay of the land and how beautiful it was. I noticed more this time than when I had ridden out with Billy and Padraic. I think being alone allowed me time to study the land, and I felt more at ease on the horse.

Like a dark line drawn on white paper, the trail was easy enough to follow through the snow-covered woods. The pine trees towered over me and the snow cupped into the hollows on the hills.

Halfway to the claim, I ran into three miners going to town. They looked like they had packed in from a way out, their animals loaded down with gear. Two were on horses and the last rider was on a mule.

The first man tipped his hat and said, "Good day to you, miss."

"A good day to you, sir."

"Sir. Did you hear that, fellas?" He moved his horse off the trail for me.

I realized that to pass them I would have to move into the midst of them. They would surround me. I questioned the wisdom of being out on the trail by myself. But then I straightened my shoulders and clucked at my horse and rode with confidence I barely felt. The other two stepped their animals off the trail.

"Are any of you Moses Walker?" I asked.

They all shook their heads. "He's close by here, I think. Our claim is farther up the creek, nearly to Blacktail."

As they moved off, I wondered that they had frightened me. They looked a sorry lot, hungry and tired from the damp, cold work they were doing. Padraic had told me that many did little on their claims in the winter. Only the desperate did much work in this weather. He'd laughed and said, "The desperate and the crazy like us."

I rode on easy and found the path leading down to the Reardon claim. My horse took the turn with little encouragement. I patted her on the side of the neck.

Padraic was shoring up some of the timber on their claim. When he heard me, he shot up and turned toward me, his hand reaching back for his gun. His face cleared when he saw me, then he shouted, "What brings you out here, Brigid? Is it news of Seamus?"

I shook my head and reined in my horse next to his. I slid down off the saddle and tied Gertie up. "It is not Seamus, for good or for bad. I needed a ride, and I wanted to question Moses Walker. Also, could you show me how to use this?" I brought out the derringer.

"You've taken to carrying your own firearms, is that it?" He walked toward me, shaking his head.

"A few bullets went flying by my head today and so Billy gave it to me. I thought it might come in handy. And if I'm to carry it, I should know how to use it. Don't you agree?"

"I agree with everything you say."

"How good of you."

"Let's see this pretty little thing."

I handed over the derringer and the pistol seemed to shrink in his hand. He flipped it around, examining it from several angles, and then handed it back to me. He showed me how to hold it in my hand. After telling me to point it down at the ground, he walked over to a stump and set an old bottle on it. Then he walked back and stood behind me and had me raise up my arm.

"You sight down the barrel. Try that a few times before shooting at anything. Just practice lifting the pistol and sighting at the bottle."

I worked on this maneuver until he was satisfied.

In his quiet, thorough way, he showed me how to hold it in a good grip and how to pull the trigger. Then he stepped back to the side of me and said, "Let her rip. Do it all at once."

I lifted the pistol, let my eye slide down the barrel, caught the bottle in my gaze, and pulled the trigger. The gun snapped in my hand, twisting off to the side, and a chunk of wood flew off the stump.

"Fairly close," Padraic said.

"Horridly far away, I'd say."

"Load her up and try again."

This time I kept my eye on the bottle as I pulled the trigger. The bullet grazed the top of the stump quite close to the bottle.

"Try again."

I was determined. I sighted carefully and held steady. I felt like I moved into the bottle as I pulled the trigger. Immediately, the bottle blew into bits.

* * *

"I would like to stop and ask Mr. Moses Walker some questions on our way home if we have time."

Dirt was smeared across Padraic's cheek. His eyes shone brighter than I had seen them before. Work agreed with him. He had been digging and messing around for an hour since I had arrived. I had tended the fire and watched him. The sun had dropped behind the hills, but that still gave us another hour of dusk before the light fell away from the sky entirely. I liked being out in the woods with Padraic. He was a very easy man to be with. We talked and he showed me stones and bits of rock. He asked me many questions about my life working as a maid in the fine houses. I liked talking about my life. So few people were interested in it.

I thought to myself this would all be perfect if Seamus were waiting for us when we returned home. But I knew there was only one way to get him back. As we climbed on the horses, I explained to Padraic what I wanted to ask Moses Walker.

"If you don't mind, let me do the asking. I think he will answer more easily to a woman."

"Who could keep the truth from you?" He gave me a hand up into the saddle.

Padraic was surprising me. I had seen a new side of him today: a lighter, more joyful side. He had joked with me, nearly flirting.

We rode up to the main trail, then down another side path to a similar claim site. Two men were sitting by a fire, drinking a bottle of whiskey. One of them was big as a bear. A huge beard covered his face like a forest, a red cap sat atop his head. The other was a small whip of a man with pegs for teeth and not much hair left on his head at all.

"Just what we were saying we needed—a fine lady," said the bigger one, standing up as we approached.

I was glad to be up on my horse and next to Padraic. "Is one of you Moses Walker?"

"That's my name," the big man answered.

"Christmas Eve. Do you remember what you did?"

"Who wants to know?"

"A pouch of gold dust was found near our house and someone said you were there close to midnight. Is that true?"

At the news of a pouch of gold, the big man's eyes lit up, but then he shook his head. "Blamed luck. No, I was with the missus at home playing Christmas with the children all night long."

I wanted to laugh. The man wasn't even smart enough to lie. How had he lasted so long in this place? "Thank you, sir."

"Why would you bother to try to find the owner? I'd pocket it myself if it were my finding."

"We might have to do that."

As we rode up the hill back to the main trail, Padraic said, "Crafty girl. Remind me to stay on the good side of you."

I smiled back at him and said, "Partners we are, Paddy. Come what may."

"And it will come, I assure you of that."

16

The Chinatown in Deadwood was called the Badlands. The next day, I gathered up some laundry and my courage and struck out on my own to go to Ching Lee's laundry. I had been warned by Billy and Padraic not to go down into the Badlands alone. They explained that there were opium dens and unsavory characters, both of which I looked forward to seeing firsthand. Plus, Ching Lee was one of Lily's regular men.

The day was gentle. A weak sun shone through the pine trees. I walked down the hill and turned onto the wooden sidewalks that lined lower Main Street. Wooden two-story buildings stood on either side of the very wide street. Carts with loads of firewood rumbled down the muddy road. Signs in front of the shops showed the flavor of the place: tin shop, Oyster Bay restaurant and lunch counter, and then Hong Kee Washing Ironing. There were many laundries, and it took me a while to see the sign for Ching Lee's establishment.

Down a side street a door opened and I stopped dead in my tracks, staring at the interior of the place: small cots with people stretched out in various attitudes of repose as if someone had thrown them down. The man who walked out was a miner, and he had an air of detachment about him that made me notice him. Not exactly sleepy, but dreamy in a way. I wondered about this drug that could make one dream while still awake; this must have been what Nellie took to be able to work at the Gem. When he looked up at me, I hurried on.

After my sighting of what I believed was an opium den, when I walked into the laundry and smelled an unusual smell, I wondered if they smoked opium right out in the open. When my eyes adjusted slowly to the darkness of the interior of the shop, I could see where the scent was coming from.

In a small alcove behind the counter sat a fat round man carved out of green stone. In his small green hands he held a burning stick. The smell from this stick circled the room and made it both rich and pleasant. I stood at the counter with my arms full of dirty shirts and sniffed. The man on the other side of the counter did not say anything. He waited for me to speak. I stared at him for a few moments because I had never seen anyone like him up close. I had seen him at the funeral, but then he had been hidden in shadows.

Ching Lee looked like the full moon. His face was golden and smooth and wide. He wore his hair shaved up high on his head and then pulled back into a braid that hung to the small of his back. Billy told me they were called queues. A small smile sat on his face and his eyes were half-closed as he watched me.

Finally he said, "May I help you?"

Again, I was surprised. The voice that came out of him was an American voice with only the slightest sound of an accent. More American than my own Irish brogue.

"What is that wonderful scent?" I asked.

"That is a joss stick. It is to purify the air and to keep evil spirits away."

"It reminds me of the incense in the Catholic church."

He nodded. "Yes, it is similar."

I hoisted the shirts up onto the counter and said, "You may help me. I'd like to get these shirts cleaned."

He sorted through them and told me how much it would be: one dollar for eight shirts and another dollar for my undergarments. Most of the laundry was Billy and Padraic's shirts. I had grabbed a few of Seamus's too. Also some of my own petticoats and crinolines.

"Would it be possible to have two of them done by tomorrow for New Year's Eve?" I asked.

"They will all be ready by tomorrow. But you must pay me now for them." He bowed his head and brought it up slowly as if to say, that is the way we work here.

"Wonderful," I said and smiled.

He returned my smile in full.

"I saw you at Lily's funeral," I told him as I paid him for the shirts. I had taken some of the gold from the pouch Seamus had given me, and I watched carefully as Ching Lee weighed it out on his scale.

He tipped his head to the side and continued to look at me. Then his eyes widened and he touched the side of his nose with a finger. "Ah, yes," he said. "You left in the carriage with Mr. Hunt."

"I did," I said, surprised that he should remember me. Although once I thought about it, maybe a young woman climbing into a carriage with Charlie Hunt would cause comment. Little did I care what people thought of me in Deadwood.

"You are the sister of Seamus Reardon," he stated. "So you too are from the country of Ireland."

"I am."

"Why are you here?" he asked.

"The shirts." I pointed to them.

"No, I mean, why are you in Deadwood?"

I was surprised that he wanted to know. Most people assumed you were in Deadwood to make money. He was in Deadwood for that reason alone, I was sure. I knew why I had come and I knew why I was staying, but it was still a good question and one I should ponder more.

"I'm visiting my brother."

"But we have heard that your brother has left."

"I'm staying to attend to his business."

"Yes, that is good."

It amused me that I had come to his laundry to ask him questions about his relationship with Lily, and before I could he was quizzing me.

"I was about to sit down to have some tea. Would you join me?" he asked. He held his hands together in front of his chest in a form of supplication.

I must have looked surprised. All I managed to say was, "Tea?"

"You are here to talk to me, are you not?" He bent his head.

"I would like to ask you some questions."

"It is as I have heard. Please take some tea with me." He waved his hand toward the back room. A dark silk curtain hung down in the doorway. He parted it for me and we moved into the back.

I noticed his clothes as I walked behind him. He was wearing loose

black silk trousers, blue socks with slippers that had an upturned toe and
wooden soles, and over it all a loose black tunic held close with lovely red
silk frogs. His dark hair had the sheen of raw silk, reminding me of a lovely
dress Mrs. Hunt had had made from a bolt of silk fabric she had bought
from China.

He motioned me into a small room with a desk and two chairs and a
small round lacquered table. Papers covered the desk so completely it was
hard to see its hardwood surface. The small table was in contrast all cleared
off, and it shone brightly. Ching Lee pulled the two chairs up to it and we
sat. I took my shawl off as it was quite warm in the laundry, the steam from
all the clothes making the room feel almost tropical.

He had left the door open, which made me more comfortable, and
I could see down the hall to the laundry. Several men were working and
they looked much as Ching Lee did, their dark hair pulled back in a braid,
though their dark blue tunics looked more like uniforms. Two of them
were ironing, but I did not see them spitting water out of their mouths as
Aggy had told me they did to steam the clothes.

We had only been seated a moment when a woman shuffled up with
a pot of tea. I tried not to stare at her feet. I couldn't believe any grown
woman could fit her feet into the small shoes that encased them. Little
brocade slippers peeked out from under her skirt, the size of an average
potato. My feet had been that size when I was seven.

She set down a white and blue teapot and two small cups with no
handles. Her hair was pulled back into a tight bun at the nape of her neck.
The woman was dressed very similarly to Ching Lee: instead of trousers
she wore a long black skirt, but she too wore a tunic with exquisite em-
broidery on it. Her eyes were downcast as she served us, so I was unable
to give her a smile. She carefully poured out the tea, then backed up and
out of the room.

"Who was that?" I asked, wondering that he hadn't introduced us.

"My wife," he said, stirring his tea.

"Might I be introduced to her?"

"Why?"

"Is it not the polite thing to do?"

"Maybe in your culture. In ours, the wife remains in the background."

"She will not join us?"

"No," he waved his hand toward the back of the store. "She has the children to watch and the laundry to attend."

My first sip of the tea was so hot I could barely taste it. Unlike the dark tea we drank at the Hunts' there was a flowery taste to it. As I sipped it again, I could smell a sweet scent.

"This is wonderful tea. What is it?" I asked.

"Jasmine."

"Very lovely and delicate. I must get some. A nice drink for the afternoon, isn't it?" I asked.

He nodded his agreement and sipped his tea, waiting for me to start my questioning.

Suddenly, I felt that I was showing such bad manners to come and ask a man like him, a well-respected businessman, to tell me his whereabouts on a certain night. Especially after he showed me such hospitality. I determined to make pleasant conversation a while longer, so I commented, "Your English is excellent."

"I have lived in the United States all my life."

"So your parents came from China?"

"My father left China after the Opium War in 1845. He lived near Canton and was able to get to the coast and board a ship. He came to this country, as we called it *Gam Saan,* the Gold Mountain."

"And your mother?"

"She was sold into slavery and my father rescued her in San Francisco. I was born there in 1852. My father went back to China when I was twenty. I accompanied him and stayed for a year. Then I came back to run our import business in San Francisco. Recently I tried my hand at this laundry. So you see my English comes naturally." He paused, then added, "Yours is also quite good, for a foreigner."

I took another sip and then set down my cup. With that slight insult, I felt more comfortable asking my questions. I had a sense of us sparring with each other. But first I would tell him a bit of my history. "I am a recent immigrant. I came over from Ireland not long ago."

"Will you go back?"

"I hope to someday. Not to live but to see my family."

He sipped his tea and nodded his head in understanding.

Enough pleasantries, I decided. "I would like to ask you some questions about Lily. May I proceed?"

"As you wish."

I could read little on his face. But then he smiled and I felt more comfortable.

"Let me explain," I began. "I am trying to find out all I can about Lily's life in the hopes that I might discover who killed her. I'm sure you've heard that my brother has been accused and that the sheriff is determined to attribute this murder to Seamus. But I am sure of his innocence."

Ching Lee nodded.

"Your sister Ching Su told me that you had a close relationship with Lily."

He nodded again and then he spoke, "She was a woman I saw from time to time."

I was surprised how easily he spoke about his relationship with her. "Had you heard that my brother intended to marry her?"

At this he burst out laughing. "Your brother was a fool. No one should have married Lily. She had gone into the business of pleasing men. Why not leave it at that? Why should he think she would be happy with only him?"

"Were you jealous of my brother?"

"Not at all. I thought your brother a good man. He was fair in business, always paid his debts. These things are important in a small town like Deadwood. Many people drift in and out. To be able to count on a man is of great importance."

"What if he wouldn't let you see Lily after they married?"

"First, I did not think they would marry. Second, I have two wives. Number-one wife you saw here and number-two wife is in California, still running our business there. For me Lily was like her name, a flower you pick, admire the scent, then toss it away. You cannot hold her, she will fade."

His attitudes scandalized me. I had never heard of anything like the life he portrayed: two wives, mistresses, California, trips to China. "Why are you telling me all this?"

"Because you asked."

"How do you know everything that is happening in Deadwood?"

"This is a small village. My people work everywhere. I am an important person among the Chinese, a leader of my family guild. It is my business to know what goes on and to prepare accordingly."

"Did Lily have any enemies?"

He thought about my question, his eyes half-shut. Then he leaned forward and said in a low voice, "I would not say enemies. But there are not enough women here, and she was one of the most beautiful. She was desired by many. This leads to problems. Lily was not a cautious woman."

I wondered what problems. I knew her so little, but I thought her feelings for my brother seemed true. "I guess we will never know if she and Seamus could have been happy together."

"We will not know," he agreed.

"Thank you for the wonderful cup of tea and for answering my questions. I hope I have not offended you." I stood up to leave.

He rose with me and said, "A beautiful woman like you with hair that waves like the ocean would have to work hard to offend."

I wrapped my shawl around me and repinned my hat. As we stood next to each other, I realized we were about the same height. "Thank you again." I gave him my hand and he bowed over it.

"I am pleased you liked the tea. I will have a pound sent over to you for your enjoyment."

I turned to go but then thought of the one question I had not asked him, the one question that I should have asked before all others. "Do you know who might have killed Lily?"

He narrowed his eyes. His hands came together in front of his chest. "We have a saying: Look for the coin in your own hand before you search the floor."

His saying took me by surprise as I felt a certain truth in it—even as I worried that he was pointing at my brother.

17

Charles Hunt sent a note inviting me to have dinner with him at Delmonico's. I had talked it over with Padraic and Billy. Billy insisted I should go, but Padraic thought I should not go alone.

"He must like our Brigid. Alone she might find out more from him. That can only be to the good for our deal," Billy pointed out.

"Tell him nothing, pour him wine, and listen hard," was the advice Padraic gave me. I meant to use it. I had been planning on going anyway, but I listened to them as if considering their arguments and then smiled and said I would indeed go to dinner with Mr. Charlie Hunt.

My new waist was ready from the dress shop and my velvet skirt was in good repair. I dressed myself and walked over to Elizabeth's as she had promised to do my hair for me. She knew all the latest fashions.

Before I sat in the chair she had proffered me, I took a book off her shelf. It was one I had longed to read, *Little Women*.

"Take it. I found it rather romantic," she laughed. Her color was better and she seemed in high spirits.

"Is your husband due back soon?" I asked.

"I'm not sure. He said he would not be gone long. He was to be back in time for the ball. But I don't really care if he is."

This was such a change from the way she talked about him before that it surprised me. "Don't you miss him?"

"There are a lot of men in this town, and some of them know how to be quite kind to a married woman in need."

She brushed my hair back from my face. I thought of twisting around to see her face, but I didn't want to ruin her concentration. "The absolutely latest style is fringe, you know. Let me cut you a few curls. Your hair waves naturally on its own. I wouldn't even need to use the curler."

"Are you sure?"

Elizabeth took up a pair of scissors and snipped several times. She handed me four long tendrils of my hair, dark as coal. She rolled and twisted my hair and pinned it and fussed with it. "They are wearing the hair higher on the head, even putting in switches and something called 'lunatic curls' this year. I've read about the new styles in *Lady Godfrey's*." She arranged the top and asked me if I would like to borrow a pair of her earrings to wear.

"Do you mean it?" I asked.

"I have a pair of ruby drops that would go well with what you're wearing." She ran to get them and came back with a small pot of lip rouge.

"Oh, I couldn't, Elizabeth. Not makeup."

"Yes, you could. All sorts of nice women wear a bit of it. Not so much that you'd notice, but a little to enhance what they already have. I'll put it on quite sparingly. Then I'll show you the glass."

When I looked in the mirror she held out for me, I gasped at the change. I looked like a young actress who had done herself up to have her calling card or *carte de visite* picture taken. The curls around my face softened it and made me look sweeter somehow. The faint color of lip rouge matched the rubies hanging from my ears.

"Elizabeth, you're a genius."

She smiled. "Well, I know you're off to have dinner with this man you like."

"Speaking of men, did I see a young man leaving your house after dinner last night?" I asked.

"Yes." She sat opposite me, her skirt sighing as she sunk down into the couch. "I met him a while ago. He is a military man and helped me carry some packages home from the store one day. I gave him some tea and we had the nicest talk. He is from Pittsburgh. He had heard of my father." She pulled out a handkerchief. "He had been gone for a while with his regiment. He might be leaving again soon. Truth be told, I will miss him more than I miss my husband."

Many of the rules of etiquette I had learned in society did not seem to apply in this town in the Black Hills. Since I had come here, I had found myself thinking about what kind of man I might marry. I could not imagine marrying without love, but I wondered how it could thrive without the security of money.

✽   ✽   ✽

I stood inside the door and waited until I saw the light of the carriage out front, then I pulled my shawl over my head and ran through the snow that was falling from the skies. A dusting, the flakes sparkled in the air and hovered around the carriage lamps like a swarm of bees.

The driver was waiting with the door open and a big horsehair blanket at the ready for me on the seat. He tucked me in and said that Mr. Hunt was awaiting me at the restaurant. I sat tall in the carriage, feeling the warmth of the blanket on my legs, and watched the snow fly. Somehow I had moved from being a young girl, a mere housemaid, to being a woman of the world, having dinner in fancy restaurants with rich men. I wrapped my arms around myself and squeezed, wondering if this might become my life.

When I walked into Delmonico's, I was dazzled at the glamour of it. A rich burgundy carpet was laid on the wooden floors in the vestibule. A young woman took my wrap and showed me the way to the ladies' room to check my coiffure. In the large, handsomely framed mirror that hung on the wall, I was able to see nearly my whole self. I flicked away the flecks of snow that had landed in my hair. My cheeks were as rosy as if I had indeed applied a whole pot of rouge. No pinching would be necessary. The earrings glowed in the lamplight. I was ready to meet Mr. Hunt.

As I walked into the dining room, the size and splendor of it overcame me. The ceilings appeared a good fourteen feet high and were decorated with fine plaster work, and the walls were adorned with the most lovely gold and pink flowered wallpaper. Gas lamps lined the walls and on each table was a tall set of tapers. Several other couples sat at tables along the walls and a large group of people gathered around a long table by the windows.

And then I saw Charlie Hunt. He stood up as soon as I came into view.

He looked completely at home in this place. His hair was freshly cut, his dark jacket fit him as his clothes always did—perfectly. No paper collar for him: starched cotton encircled his neck with a diamond stick pin at his throat.

He pulled back a chair for me and pushed it in as I seated myself, then leaned over me and whispered, "You are certainly the most beautiful woman here."

I looked up at him and replied, "And you certainly have the sweetest tongue."

He sat down next to me. "Dear Brigid, do you never believe a word I say?"

"I feel you flatter me."

"I try to."

"Why?"

"Because I like you."

I looked down at the place setting. I had set many a table like this but never eaten at one that had so many pieces of silver. Thank goodness I knew what to do with all of them, from serving the fine dinners at the Hunts'. I was uncomfortable about how our conversation started out and felt it was upon me to change it. "How are your dear mother and sister?"

"Very well indeed, but sad to have lost you. I think your absence grieves my mother. She had come to count upon you for many things."

"I was sorry to have left her also." I remembered many kindnesses Mrs. Hunt had done me: giving me her clothes, always having a quick smile and gentle talk, trusting me with her child. "Was the Christmas holiday a fine one?"

"I left shortly before it so I'm afraid I cannot tell you."

A shiver ran through me. "I thought for sure you intended to stay on through the holidays."

"Business forced me to return. Mr. Hearst, our business partner, was concerned that we finish up some of these negotiations. He has plans for starting construction on the biggest mining business this area will ever see—the Homestake Mine."

"This is what I hope talk to you about," I started.

Before I could ask him more about that, the waiter came and took our order. After consulting with me about my tastes in food, Charlie ordered for the two of us something called "Beef à la Mode aux Champignons," asparagus in cream sauce, and a bottle of fine wine.

The wine came immediately, and the waiter and Charlie went through the ritual of his smelling the cork, then swirling a bit of the dark red liquid around in a glass and tasting it. He proclaimed it fine and poured me a glass of it. He lifted his glass up and I raised mine to his, and the rims of the glasses touched together with a delightful clink. Then I took a full sip.

The wine tasted as good as I had ever sampled at the Hunts' and yet I have to admit that there was something much sweeter about it having been ordered for me, served so well, and drunk in a warm and elegant room. I felt the warmth of the fire on my face and gave in to the delightfulness of being served fine food in elegant surroundings with a cultured man sitting opposite me. To think that a week ago I had been eating bacon grease on bread and shivering in the corner of a stagecoach.

"This is wonderful," I said.

"I'm glad you like it."

"Let's talk about the claim before the food arrives."

Charlie nodded. "We are bringing in an expert who will take the ore sample within the week."

"Oh," I said, glad to hear the deal would be settled so quickly.

Charlie smiled at my enjoyment and asked, "So we need say no more about that."

I was taken aback by his sureness and wondered what we would find to talk about the rest of the evening.

He reached out and lightly touched my hand, a seemingly casual gesture. "I would rather talk about you."

I pulled my hand away, surprised at the turn the conversation had taken. "There's not much to tell. My main concern right now, aside from the business with the mine, is my brother's innocence."

"Brigid, this should not be your worry. You need to think about yourself, beautiful young woman that you are."

"I hope you might be right, but I'm not so sure."

"This country is a grand place. Just look at my parents. Father had come from Boston with no money, and my mother was working as a waitress at a soda shop in St. Paul. Despite the fact that between them they had nothing, they married a year later. They worked hard. They succeeded mightily, as you know: the second-largest house on the finest street in St. Paul, a stable of horses and carriages, and, of course, servants to do their bidding. But this is America. All those rules of supremacy, aristocracy, what will you, don't matter here. And now you are your own woman." He looked through lidded eyes at me. "I think you will do very well in this new country. I'd like to help you do well if you will consider that."

One of my hands was wrapped around the stem of my wine glass, the other was clutching my napkin in my lap. I had heard all that Charlie had to say but couldn't bring my eyes to look at him; rather, they remained fixed on the fire. I was thinking of the story of his parents and wondering what he meant by telling it to me. For once in my life, I found no words at the ready.

Charlie reached out and took my hand from the wine glass. "Brigid?"

I pulled my eyes away from the fire and looked at him, really looked at him. *He had a wide and open face like the prairies surrounding us, his eyes were the blue of a perfect sky, his dark brown hair cut crisp and brushed back from his face.* For all his taking advantage of me, I found I had not forgotten the look of him. I was surprised to discover that some yearning for his charm stirred in me. If we could meet as equals, if I did not have to worry about how his attention might harm me, what might come of getting to know him better?

"I don't know what to say."

"Lord above," he laughed. "I've caught you out."

The rest of the meal went by in a dream. The food was fine, the beef a bit tough but I loved the sauce. Charlie made sure that my glass always had wine in it. By the end of the meal, I could feel my cheeks were warm with it. He told me stories of when he was a child and what it had been like for him to go out East to school. The glamour of his life dazzled me: private schools, staying in the finest hotels, always being waited on, and never knowing want.

"I think at heart I'm more of a Westerner myself," he said.

The waiter came and asked if we would like some dessert.

"They have the best ice cream," Charlie said.

"I'd love that."

He brought us each two scoops of chocolate ice cream in cut-glass bowls with a lovely wafer cookie.

"It's like eating snow," I laughed with delight.

Charlie looked out the window and said, "It's coming down pretty hard. Maybe the chef stepped out the back door and scooped it up."

"No, he just held out the bowls and sprinkled some chocolate on it."

Charlie laughed and tapped his spoon on the edge of his bowl. After a few moments, he frowned and said, "Brigid, let us take a moment to talk about your brother."

"Of course." I had raised up my hand to bring one more spoonful of the delicious ice cream to my mouth, but at his words it hung in the air. Then as he spoke, I swallowed, but the ice cream had lost its taste.

"Yes, I know you believe he's innocent, but I have to tell you I spoke with the sheriff yesterday."

"Why?" I put my spoon down.

"On your behalf."

His presumption inflamed me. "How did you dare to do that?"

"I was only looking out for you and your brother."

"And what gave you the authority to do that?" I found my voice rising.

"Calm down. I know the man. I thought I could find out how he was thinking on the matter, for you."

I knew I needed to hear him out. Maybe he had good news for me. Charlie Hunt, after all, was a powerful man in this town. "Go on."

"He has asked around, and no one saw anyone with Lily except your brother that night. A number of witnesses saw them leave the party together." He shook his head. "I have to say, it doesn't look good for Seamus."

I sat stunned. This was not the news I wanted to hear. I needed to make Charlie believe me. "He did not do it."

"Brigid."

"Don't use that tone of voice with me as if you are trying to get me to be reasonable."

He said nothing.

I thought how to convince him of my brother's innocence. "Let me ask you this. If someone came bursting in here right now and said that your mother killed your sister, would you believe them?"

"Of course not. There's no comparison."

"Yes, there is. Seamus does not have a violent nature, and I would know better than anyone else, for I have lived with him most of my life.

That's my first point. My second is this: he was in love with Lily. He had asked her to marry him and she had said yes. Those were the first words out of his mouth that next morning. Now, does that sound like a man who had killed someone?"

"Brigid, he was drunk. The drink can cause people to act in ways they would not otherwise."

I decided it was time to pull out my final point. "Yes, he was drunk. He walked the woman he loved home. Then he came home alone himself, singing as he went. Our neighbor heard him. He was singing. Now, I ask you again, does that sound like a killing man?"

Charlie looked me in the eyes and said what I wanted to hear, "No, Brigid, it does not."

"Then why are you tormenting me this way?"

"Because you might be able to convince *me* of your brother's innocence, but I doubt you could do the same with the sheriff, and he's the one who matters. This is a rough town, and laws don't hold the same here as they did back in the States."

I looked down at my plate. Disappointment flooded me. Charlie did not want to believe me. Maybe having Seamus out of the way, he thought, would work to his advantage. The last bit of my ice cream had melted into a puddle. "I want to go home now."

"You won't stay a while longer?"

I couldn't believe I had been considering Charlie Hunt as an ally, maybe even a friend. If he did not understand that my brother's safety meant everything to me, he did not know me very well. "No, I think our business is finished. I thank you for the fine meal."

I stood.

He stayed seated. "Have I offended you by speaking so bluntly?"

"Your family is safe and well in St. Paul. I do not think you understand what my brother's well-being means to me." I turned and made for the door with a heavy heart.

Charlie followed me, grabbing my arm. "I'll take you home. My carriage is waiting out front."

"Are you sure you want to be seen with the sister of a murderer?"

"Brigid, don't act like that."

A young woman brought my wrap and Charlie helped me into it. The carriage was called and he handed me up and then climbed in next to me. He covered our knees with the blanket and took my gloved hand in his. While I did not pull my hand away, I refused to say anything to him until we were close to my house. My feelings were in an uproar: what did Charlie want of me? Why would he not help my brother? Is he trying to hide something? When exactly had he come back to Deadwood?

When I pulled my hand away, he said, "Don't be angry with me, Brigid. Not when we have just come to an understanding."

I stopped long enough to say, "I'm not sure what you're talking about. Any understanding will have to wait until my brother's name is cleared."

18

December 29, 1878

The next morning, I heard stirring out in the big room and lay abed for a while, thinking of last night. Charlie Hunt wanted to have an understanding with me. Last night I had actually felt like he saw me as a real woman, not just a servant to be teased. In the carriage on the way home, he had not tried to take advantage of me. Maybe he was telling me the truth about my brother's situation and I was just not willing to listen to him. After all, he never said that he thought my brother had killed Lily, just that it looked bad for Seamus.

This could have been a happy day for me, but I felt the weight of my brother's troubles more heavily than ever. I also felt my head throbbing and my eyes would not focus as they should. The wine that I had drunk last night was still swimming in me. I could hardly think of a good reason to get out of bed.

I couldn't help but wonder why I was so resistant to Mr. Charlie Hunt. He had wit and charm, that was sure. He had more money than I could comprehend. He was handsome and well spoken. And yet . . .

In the middle of our meal last night, he had asked me to attend the New Year's Eve ball with him, but I told him I must go with my brother's friends. In a part of my heart I wanted to give Charlie a chance, but I was not at all sure I trusted him. In the past month or so, I had come to trust no one. Even my own brother was, in certain moments, a subject of uncertainty.

I so wished Seamus were here with me, telling me what I should do. I missed him more than when I had not seen him for years. Our short time together had only left me wanting more. He was my family.

I prayed to St. Brigid as my dear mother would have advised.

✳   ✳   ✳

When I walked out into the kitchen, Nellie was sitting at the table dressed in a flannel shirt of Billy's. While I wasn't surprised to see her there, I still felt uncomfortable with the impropriety of the situation. I had put on an old dark work dress of mine, as I intended to get some chores done around the house today. The room was warm and I was glad for that. Nellie had the cookstove going.

I greeted Nellie. "Top of the morning to you."

"What makes it the top, I'd like to know. I made some buns. They'll be out of the oven in a minute. Wouldn't you just like something nice and warm inside of you." She cackled.

I ignored her joke and asked, "What has become of Billy and Paddy?"

"The two of them hightailed it out of here at dawn's first light. Had to get to the claim. Ain't you three up to sell that piece of land or something? Sounds like a good idea to me. Backbreaking work that mining is, and there's much better ways of striking gold here in old Deadwood."

"Yes," I agreed as I slid into a chair opposite her. Nellie was in full bloom this morning, her hair wild around her face. Everything about her was a little bigger than it should be, an umbrella opened to its fullest.

"I heard you went out on the town last night." She poured me a cup of coffee and slid it across the table to me.

"I did."

"Did you have a good time?"

"In a manner of speaking."

"And what manner is that?"

I did not want to talk to Nellie about my relationship with Charlie Hunt. "I had a fine meal. We talked business."

"Righto. Indeedy. What kind of business?" Cackling again, she watched me carefully.

I should have known better than to think she would take any subtle hint from me. She might back off if I gave her some information. "You know I worked for Mr. Hunt's family. Well, he had news to tell me of them. And then of course there is the claim. We discussed that a bit. All in all, it went well, I think." I took a sip of my coffee and it seemed to rush straight to my brain. I needed my wits about me, so I was glad for the sensation.

"Oh, that Charlie. He is a sweet talker. You're a lucky lady."

"Nellie, what can you mean?"

"Listen, I know the man myself. He likes a pretty woman, and you are one of the better specimens here in Deadwood. Ask yourself why he got back to town right on your heels."

"When exactly did he get back to Deadwood? Do you know, Nellie?"

That shut her up for a moment. Her eyes looked around the kitchen while she thought. "I've a mind that it was a day or two after Lily was killed."

"After?" I asked, to be sure.

"I can't speak for sure when he got here, but he paid his respects shortly after his arrival."

Nellie whooped up out of her chair and opened the oven with the flannel shirt tucked around her hand so she wouldn't burn it. "Look at those buns. Nice and golden. Won't we just feast now?" She pulled them out of the oven and set the pan on the table between us. Butter and knives were already there, and a big jar of golden syrup.

"What is that?" I asked.

"Oh, that's the best honey you'll ever find. Comes from the bees of the prairies. Try it on your bun."

I slathered a bun with butter and honey and took a big bite. "Delicious," I told Nellie.

"I aim to please," she said between bites.

"Nellie, what was Charlie's relationship with Lily?"

Nellie laughed. "Easy, you might say. He liked her fine, he did. Treated her right. Gave her presents and good money, too. But he had his use for her and that was that."

I ate more of my bun. "What was Lily's story?" I asked.

"Oh, now that's a good one. Let me pour us both another cuppa." She filled up our coffee cups and settled in.

"This is like I heard it from herself. Lily grew up in Chicago. Came from a decent family. Her mother was a seamstress and her father was a teacher. I don't think they had much money, but she was well loved and looked after. Lily got a job early in a dress shop that her mother did sewing for. She was probably only sixteen, but already a looker."

Nellie pulled out a package of tobacco and a thin sheet of paper from a pocket in the shirt and proceeded to roll herself a cigarette as she kept talking. I had never seen a woman do this before and was nearly as fascinated with the care she took in the rolling, the tamping, the twisting as I was by the story she was telling me. "One day a fine gentleman walked in and wanted to buy something for his mother. Lily helped him out. He continued to come in from time to time and finally asked her out for a walk. He was only a bit older than her and came from a very well-to-do family, you know the kind. After they had been stepping out together for a few months, he up and proposes to her. Well, Lily can't hardly believe her good fortune. The boy, his name was Lucas, takes her home to his family. His mother is none too happy about all this. She's an old battle-ax with a broom up her butt, don't mind my language." Nellie stopped to take a puff on her cigarette and then blew out a cloud of smoke.

"However, the father takes quite a shine to Lily. So much so, that a few days later, he stops by the shop to see Lily. He tells her that he is quite happy about his son's decision to marry her, but that he would like to get to know her a little better himself. She thinks that is fine. A few days later, he asks her to dine with him at a restaurant in a fancy hotel. His son has gone away for a few days and Lily is delighted to meet with the father. She can't believe her good fortune that she is to marry into this family. But then the old bastard gets the poor gal drunk and takes her up to a room afterwards." Nellie's voice roughened as she came to the hard part of the story. She took a final puff on her cigarette and stubbed it out on the underside of the table.

"Lily doesn't remember quite all that happens, but she finds herself naked in the bed in the morning when she wakes. Once the old fellow has had a taste of her, he won't give it up, and he threatens to tell his son if she doesn't go along with him. Lily doesn't know what to do, but she gives in to him. Then one night she meets the old man at the hotel. They skip dinner this time and go right to the room. When she's in the blankets with the old man, the door pops open. The son walks in. He has a gun. He shoots his father. He slaps Lily and walks out. She dresses and sneaks out herself. The next day, the son finds her and gives her some money and tells her to leave the city. If she stays, he says, he will go to the police and tell them that she killed his father. They already think that's what happened anyway."

Nellie ate the last morsel of her bun and licked each of her fingers. "It did something to Lily. Made her a little *loco*. To have come that close to a huge pile of cash and then to have lost it all. She left Chicago and went out to Denver. She had no trouble making money. Then when she heard about Deadwood, she decided to try her hand here. I met her my first day in Deadwood about a year ago, and we were best friends ever since."

There were tears in Nellie's eyes, but she ignored them. "There weren't nothing bad about Lily. She just stirred things up by being who she was."

I had heard of such things happening to girls. Such tales made the rounds among the servants I worked with, but it was still awful to hear one told of someone my brother had loved. I was sad that I hadn't known her better.

"Do you think that she and Seamus would have been happy?"

Nellie laughed and threw up her hands. "Now, that's a stupid question if I ever heard one. No one can predict happiness. We all of us are just trying to get by in this here life. I think they had an understanding of each other. Both of them had suffered hardships. You know Seamus's better than anyone. There was love there. There was more than that. Lily had given a part of herself to Seamus that she didn't to most men, if you get what I'm trying to say."

I nodded.

Nellie smiled at me. "It's like me and Billy here. Don't get me wrong, we're not going to up and marry. That's for neither of us right now. But Billy sees me as who I am, and he's the man I want to spend my time with when I'm not working. Sometimes, we just sleep together, nice and quiet like. It's enough."

In part of myself I was shocked. I could not believe I was talking like this with a sporting woman and prayed my mother was not watching from on high. And yet Nellie said it all so matter-of-fact that it was hard to take offense. What would I come to, here in the Black Hills? "I know so little of these things."

"That's one of the good things about you, Brigid. You're fresh and young. Don't waste it. You make that Charlie Hunt marry you before you give him a taste."

19

New Year's Eve, 1878

The start of the ball was only an hour away, and my beautiful dress was finished and laid across my bed in the back room. I smoothed the silk fabric with my hand and reveled in the luxury of it. I felt like Cinderella about to go to her first ball. After all, I certainly had swept out my share of fireplaces, cinders and all. Never had I worn such a dress or even imagined wearing one in my whole life.

But I couldn't stop thinking about my brother and wishing he was here with us to celebrate. I swore to myself that I would continue my quest to find out what happened to Lily as soon as the new year began. Maybe even at the dance. With that thought easing my mind, I picked up the dress to put it on.

Earlier that day, I had managed a bath in the tub in the kitchen while Padraic and Billy had been at the claim. Elizabeth had fixed up my hair again and I had tried to help her arrange her own, although I was not as skilled as she. She showed me the dress that she was to wear and it was lovely, even if she did apologize for its oldness, saying it had been the latest style a year ago in Philadelphia. To me it looked like the height of fashion. I was glad to have a woman friend to help me with my toilet. There had been little time for friendship when I had been working.

I had to call Billy down to help me with my corset. I hardly ever wore one and needed a strong hand to pull it tight. At the Hunts' I would have asked one of the other maids to help me.

I told Billy to look the other way and put the ends of the ties into his hands. As he pulled, I attempted to fasten it shut, breathing in and holding my breath until another hook was clasped. The top of the corset squeezed my ribs until they felt as if they might snap like kindling.

"So that's the way those things work," he said at the door as he turned and got a good look at me.

I sailed a shoe at him and he left laughing.

A ball, I thought—a real ball, even if it is in the farthest reaches of civilization.

I stepped into my dress and pulled the confection up around me. Made of a heavy dark blue silk suited for winter weather, the garment was fairly low-cut. There was little bustle in the back and the train had four layers of flounces. What I was really happy about was how the dress fit my waist like a glove.

The shoes I slipped into were lovely soft things. Even though my feet were on the dainty side, they were large compared to the Chinese women's bound feet. What an odd custom that was to tie your feet so tightly that they couldn't grow and you'd be hobbled by them the rest of your life. Although I admitted to myself that I wouldn't have been able to run far in these delicate shoes.

I fastened the locket that Padraic had given me around my throat. Hopefully I would have a photo of Seamus to fill it soon. I would wear my black wrap and my muffler at my neck. The weather had stayed rather mild with the night temperature just dipping below freezing, a perfect night for the ball.

Padraic and Billy had their backs to me as I came out of the room.

"I think I'm ready," I announced.

They both turned and in their eyes I received all the compliments I needed that night.

"Blessed Virgin," profaned Billy.

"Lord above," agreed Padraic.

"Do you like it?" I asked, twirling about to show them the dress from all angles.

"An angel in our midst," Billy said.

"A piece of heaven, to be sure," Padraic breathed out.

The look in their eyes told me that what they said they meant. I thrilled to the novelty of such praise.

"You two look quite handsome, like gentlemen indeed." I walked closer and checked them over. Clean white shirts, dark wool pants and overcoats, all very presentable. And the finishing touches: silk neckties tied correctly at their throats, sleeve buttons in their shirts, and gloves at the ready.

Padraic gave me his arm. "We can walk the short distance to the hall, but I must insist that you slip on your boots and carry your shoes. Or else I will be forced to hoist you up in my arms."

*　*　*

We walked the two blocks to the hall and crowded in with everyone at the entrance. There was a flurry at the door of women slipping out of wraps and gentlemen helping them. The sound of a small orchestra tuning up could be heard over the hubbub of the people.

When we stepped into the hall, I stood still and took the room in. The floor shone from its new coat of wax, wooden chandeliers carved from shipping crates were filled with tallow candles, bright oil lamps lit the corners of the rooms. Handsome pictures of George Washington and the recently deceased General Custer held the place of honor at the head of the room. They had been decorated with green paper laurels. At each end of the room great fireplaces were lit, throwing out a cheerful light.

I clapped my hands and turned to Padraic. "This all promises good for the New Year," I said.

He nodded his head and looked around him. "I think you are going to be very busy tonight, dancing with all the men."

I followed his glance and noticed that for every four or five men there was maybe one woman. And some of the women were older and not so well dressed as they might like to be, but all of them were smiling and talking to the men crowded around them.

Then I saw Elizabeth enter on the far side of the room and wondered if the man she walked with was the young soldier she had talked about, or if perhaps her husband had showed up on her doorstep.

Padraic turned toward me and asked in all seriousness, "Before you promise yourself to everyone here, I'd like the honor of the first waltz with you."

"Of course, Padraic. I didn't know that you could dance."

"Billy taught me, and a rough job it was."

Billy laughed and asked for the first set dance with me.

A few men started walking our way, and then a line of them assembled in front of me, asking me for the pleasure of a dance. I hated to give all my turns away. I had hoped to have at least one dance with Charlie no matter where things stood between us.

Then the band struck up the first song of the night. I was not surprised a wit that it was "Garryowen," as everyone knew it to be the favorite song of General Custer. His defeat at the Battle of Bull Run was still much talked about.

After that the dignitaries were invited to form a group at one end of the room to do a set dance. As they whirled around to the calls, swinging their partners and following the patterned steps, Padraic pointed them out to me. "The sheriff and his wife, the mayor and his wife, the richest banker in town and his daughter. I'm not sure who the rest of them might be."

I was thrilled to be in this company, out in the world. I had danced many times before, but it was with the servants down in the basement of some house to the sounds of a piano and a fiddle, if we were lucky. I had never attended such a grand affair before in my life. I had heard that there had been balls at the Hunts', but none had taken place while I was in their service.

They called the next set, and Billy and I went forth to dance with many other couples. The caller had a clear loud voice and he proved a bit of a comic, calling off in new ways that made us laugh and lose our steps. Billy swung me and twirled me, he allemanded me left and right. I followed as best I could, not knowing the steps as well as he.

When we finished the set, I was claimed by another man and after that another. I could smile at these men, cleaned up in their best clothes, and let them swing me around, but it was difficult at best to talk to them over the swell of the music.

In between the dances I confess I watched for Charlie but saw no sign of him. I feared he would not come, and that took some of the charm out of the evening for me. My own vanity surprised me, but there it was. I wanted him to see me in this lovely dress, to see me as I could be, not just a servant girl who worked for his family but a woman with real possibilities. For the first time I felt I looked as lovely as I often felt.

When I heard the first notes of a waltz struck up, I looked around for Padraic. He was sitting in a far corner, watching the dances. He seemed to be amused, as I could see a smile upon his lips, but he always appeared quite removed from the affair. I ran over to him for our dance.

"You've come to fetch me?" he asked as he stood.

"Not very ladylike, I imagine," I said.

"No, but very full of enthusiasm. So like you, Brigid." He moved in close to me, and the next thing I knew I was in his arms. Waltzing differed so greatly from square dancing. Dancing in sets was almost an athletic venture, following the turns and swings of the whole group, but waltzing— waltzing was intimate.

Padraic's hand was very properly placed under my shoulder blade and his other held my hand. His grip was firm and he waltzed as he moved through the world, silently, competently, but with a slight remove. I relaxed in his arms and followed his sure lead around the room. I had never had such a night as this, and the waltzing made me feel like I had drunk champagne, which I had only sampled once after a party at the Hunts'.

"You're enjoying yourself then?" he asked.

"Oh, I feel as glamorous as Jenny Lind."

"Whoever that might be, I'm sure she's not half the beauty that you are, my lovely Brigid, *mo shearc.*"

The words of Irish brought tears to my eyes. That he had called me his love seemed simply part of the evening's magic. As we moved, the room twirled around us and the colors spun in my head. I laughed in Padraic's ear from the joy of it all. At this sound, he held me closer, and suddenly he was moving with more grace and form. He was dancing with some of the passion he brought to his mining work. I felt a pull to him I had never felt before. I had come to regard him as a brother, but in his arms, dancing so close, I was reminded that he was nothing of the sort to me.

When the dance ended, I stayed in his arms for a moment, sad to relinquish him, but then I felt my hand pulled away. As I stepped back, I saw that it was Charlie Hunt who was separating me from Padraic.

"I had to see the belle of the ball," he said, spinning me out and looking me over. "Very nice indeed," he said, viewing with a pleased look. "Brigid has always used her wit to charm us, and now she has pulled out her whole arsenal and brings to bear the full power of her beauty. Can anything stop her?"

Padraic ignored Charlie's courting and bowed over my hand, which he still had in his grasp. "Thank you for the dance. If you have any left, I'll try to claim another later in the evening." And he left us.

Charlie Hunt was resplendent. I had read that word so many times in his mother's novels that it jumped into my head quite easily when I saw him standing before me in all his fine glory. He wore a dark maroon necktie with a diamond stud. His vest fitted him like a glove. His hair curled back from his face and his eyes shone with delight. I could not help but smile up at him. "I'm sorry I'm late." He bowed his head down close to me to talk above the music.

"I'm sure it's nothing to me."

"I suppose not. You look like you've been quite busy. And, as you are the most beautiful woman in this room, there can be no question that every man has been clamoring to dance with you."

My face grew warm, but I said nothing.

"May I have this next waltz?" he asked.

"I'm afraid that it is promised."

"I will take care of that," he said and watched the man approach to claim his turn. Charlie stepped aside with him, said something in his ear, and the man slunk away.

"What did you tell him?" I asked as Charlie took my hand.

"I merely said that you were my wife and that we had not seen each other for weeks. He appeared to understand."

"You are very bold," I laughed.

"Only when I have to be." With those words he took me in his arms. He was a big man, Charlie Hunt, and yet quite nimble on his feet. He danced with authority and gusto, seemingly the way he did everything in his life. While he was a good leader, I felt that any woman could be in his arms and he would dance the same. I had felt a little more special with Paddy. Then I pulled myself up, gave him what I hoped was a brilliant smile, and finished off the waltz.

He bowed low over my hand. "I know you think me a lout, but I'm enough of a gentleman to know that I cannot monopolize you all evening. It is an hour to midnight. Pray save me a dance, for I would like to see the New Year in with you. Until then, Brigid of the Hills."

After that I danced many more dances. My new shoes pinched my feet a bit, but I ignored them. Men made various propositions to me and I laughed at the silliness of it all. They claimed I was the most beautiful woman they had ever seen, and I knew full well that they would say the same to the next woman they danced with. But still and all, I drank it in: the swirling of so many full skirts, the sprightly music, the warmth in the room, the high spirits of all. For a few moments, I forgot that my brother was missing from my life, and in dire straits to boot.

One of the men I danced with was Moses Walker. He seemed in high spirits, and I doubted whether he even remembered who I was. He kicked my ankle once in his exuberant dancing but did it with good humor.

I inquired how his wife was and he said, "The missus is busy as could be dancing with all the young men. She'll be in fine fettle tonight when I take her home, which will be good by me. She's often cross with having to watch the young 'uns."

One older gentleman told me of his claim and all the gold he was taking out of it. Then he asked if I might not want to join him in sharing all his wealth.

"What I mean, ma'am, is a proper proposal. Nothing untoward about it. I could use a wife."

I took care not to laugh—he seemed a nice old man—and told him that it was a very decent proposal, but not one I could consider at the moment. He took it well. I had never had such a night in all my life and did not know if I ever would again.

Close to the midnight hour, a group of women at the door surprised everyone. The dancers stopped, and I looked and saw that it was Nellie and some of the other sporting women who worked the theaters. They were all dressed up in low-necked gauzy gowns with lots of bangles on their wrists and flowers in their hair.

As a couple of men barred their way into the room, I heard one of the women yell out in a voice loud and clear, "We're good enough to visit at the Gem but not to dance with in public, eh? Well, we're here to have a little fun." Then she waved at a few of the men and called them by name. There was laughter at her boldness.

A number of men, including Billy, stepped forward and claimed their hands for the dance. I watched the sheriff walk over to the side of the room with the mayor and wondered what they were plotting. Several women had stepped off the dance floor, embarrassed to be seen in the same room as these working girls. I was sure I could not care. I waved at Nellie and Billy as I danced by. Charlie was nowhere to be seen.

However, I did notice, lined up against the side wall were a number of the celestials. Only the men of course. They were dressed in lovely dark outfits with their queues all nicely braided. How odd it must feel not to be asked to join in. But then, from what I understood, their wives rarely left the house.

I picked out Ching Lee, standing at the front of the line. As I looked at him, he glanced up and caught my eye. He nodded and I knew I had been seen by him. Feeling full of the spirit of the evening, I dropped him a full curtsy. He had been kind enough to send me some jasmine tea; I could at least show him equal courtesy.

Needing a break from the dance, I took myself off to the ladies' room to make sure my coiffure was still in place.

In the ladies' room, I walked up to the long mirror and surveyed myself. My color was high and my eyes bright. Arranging my hair, I turned my head to the side and readjusted some of the pins. I looked forward to dancing the last dance before midnight with Charlie. I had heard that a light supper would be served of ham sandwiches, potato salad, and cake. I realized with surprise that I was hungry.

Elizabeth came in and we hugged. "You look so elegant," I told her. "Did your husband make it back?"

She blushed and lowered her head. Then she lifted it and looked me straight in the eyes. "He's not here. He did not make it back, and so I accepted the gallant offer of my soldier to accompany me here to the dance. He has been most kind."

"Are you worried for your husband?"

She frowned. "I know I should be. I guess I'm worried every which way and trying not to think about it." She took a deep breath, forced a smile, and changed the subject. "Isn't this the most glorious dance?"

"You can say that after all the balls you must have attended in Philadelphia?"

"They seemed much more staid to me. There's a freedom here in Deadwood. I guess it must come from being out in this wilderness, but I feel like I am not judged the way I would be back East. A married woman going to a dance without her husband." She turned to the mirror and touched her face as if she did not recognize it. "Nor have I ever been as happy."

For a moment, I worried about Elizabeth—pregnant, alone, husband off who knows where—and then I thought, she's happy. And I'm happy too.

* * *

As I stepped out of the ladies' room, I saw Charlie talking with the mayor on the other side of the room. He looked up and across the room and spotted me. He came straight to me and asked if he might have the next dance.

I couldn't help myself but say what was on my mind. "Oh, Charlie, I said I would save it for you."

"Those are the sweetest words I've heard yet out of your lips. Have you changed the way you feel about me?"

"Not so considerably," I confessed.

"That statement can be taken two ways, and I dare not go into it with you right now. Rather, I will accept my good fortune and lead you to the floor." He took my arm and escorted me through the crowd. "Are you enjoying your dances?"

"Thank you, very much so. I have had many offers to entertainment. Two gentlemen proposed marriage, and one proposed something that I had to pretend not to hear."

Charlie roared with laughter. "Brigid, you are so refreshing."

The next dance was a beautiful Strauss waltz. Charlie identified it for me and I will always remember the sound of it, like a river flowing, a pulse that moved through the whole song. Even though my feet were worn, I danced like I had only stepped onto the floor. Charlie swirled me off my feet as we turned. At the end of it the band went right into "Auld Lang Syne."

I was suddenly lifted off my feet and twirled around by Charlie. Then he pulled me into his arms and kissed me. Caught in the joy of the moment, I kissed him back with my whole heart. The room disappeared and the music dimmed. I only felt the arms that held me and the mouth that embraced me. At midnight of the new year 1879, a small spot of time vanished, and in that moment I was held in the arms of Charlie Hunt.

When we separated from our kiss, the room was going wild around us. People banging pots and pans and kissing and yelling. Well-wishers around us hugged us and sang out "Happy New Year!"

Charlie grabbed me again and held me in his arms. He did not attempt to kiss me this time but looked down at me and asked, "Brigid, would you marry me?"

My heart leapt in my chest at the thought, but then I watched his mouth curve and his eyes crinkle and he was laughing at me. He was merely copying the other men who had danced with me that night. I pushed him away. I was furious. How dare he? Just when I was coming to trust him, he was back to his old habits. I flew away from him and lost myself in the crowd.

Men were grabbing at me and trying to embrace me. I could not stand to be there in that room any longer. I decided to take myself home.

There was nothing more I wanted to say to Charlie. Nothing would ever change the way he saw me. I would always be a servant girl to him, someone he could take advantage of and then discard. I wanted no part of his boorish behavior. His desire to court me might simply be a ruse to have his way with me, and it would come to no good. I saw clearly that he would never treat me with the respect I deserved.

As I made my way toward the door, the mayor and a group of men began to push the sporting women off the dance floor, and the women did not take it well. I saw Nellie elbow a man in the stomach. A battle ensued, and I tried to slip out the door and avoid the scuffle. I made it to the foyer and found my boots. I got them on and hooked them and found my wrap. I carefully slipped my new very worn shoes into the pockets.

Nellie and her friends were now in the foyer with me, and the scream-ing and cries were quite loud and profane. The pans that had been banged together to bring in the New Year were now being applied to the backsides of the women.

The women were shrieking profanities and the men returning some of them; I was astounded at some of the words I heard. I saw Nellie slug a man, and he fell backward into another. I felt like cheering for her. What right did these men have to turn out hardworking women?

I backed away from the melee and turned to step out into the night when I felt someone grab my arm.

As I turned, I was struck on the side of the head. I opened my mouth but no sound came out. The night turned very dark, and I felt my knees give out. I was enfolded in black.

Before I passed out, I heard a man's voice say in my ear, "Leave it alone. Lily is dead. So might you be soon."

20

For a moment I thought I was back in Ireland, lying on the floor of the hut we had called home, hungry and cold. The cold pinched my sides and filled my nostrils. Like pinpricks, it nipped and bruised me. I was shivering so hard that my teeth clattered in my mouth, my head clanged like an old bell. The hard ground beneath me smelled dank, like an old well.

The smell must have brought the memory of home to me, and for a moment I hoped to open my eyes and see my dear mother. But when I tried to open my eyes, I realized they were covered with something. The blackness was deeper than a peat bog. As I struggled I could feel that my hands were tied behind me. I stopped thrashing and tried to think clearly.

I had been at the dance.

Midnight had struck.

The end of the dance was all I could remember well and then my thoughts faded. I tried to figure out where I was by listening hard, but I could hear little. Only a dripping sound. From this I figured that I was not outside, and wherever I was, the temperature was not below freezing if the water was still running.

As I came to my senses, I remembered the end of the dance, Charlie's mean-spirited proposal, the pushing and shoving of the women in the entryway, and finally the blow to my head. But it was the whispering in my ear that hit me the hardest, and that I feared. *Dead. Lily. Leave it be.* A man's voice, that's all I could be sure of, warning me off my questions. I had been left for dead in this cold, dark place.

Fear grew in me like a bubble swelling in my chest. I could not breathe. Pulling on my hands, I twisted at the ropes that bound me, but to no avail. My hands were torn and bleeding from ripping at my bindings. I was secured tightly. I tried to stand and found that I was tied to something. I felt behind myself on the ground with my hands. I was tied to a metal bar that laid along the ground.

Calming myself, I thought logically about my predicament. The only thing for it was to get free. I might be someplace where no one would ever find me. I had to get loose before the man who had tied me came back, or I died in my ropes. The thought of dying made me shiver harder.

For an odd moment, I wanted to weep for my new dress. The lovely garment would be ruined I was sure. The only lovely dress I would ever have. Then, at the thought of my situation and my concern for my dress, I started to laugh. The sound of it shocked me. For all the world, I was behaving like a crazy woman wailing in the dark, like a lonely bird calling over a watery slough. I stopped myself.

The dripping sound echoed. Death, if it found me, would be hard. Starvation or exposure. The room felt cold enough to weaken me. That at least would be faster than starvation.

With these thoughts in my mind, I tore at my bindings again and found that my wrists suffered. I needed to be methodical. I felt with my hand along the metal bar. I could move my binding along it and so I had some movement if I crawled. Then the binding hit something on the bar. It was a sharp piece of metal driven into the ground.

As I picture this in my mind, it came to me that I was tied to some kind of track, like for a train only smaller. A track for a mining car? Possibly. This made some sense. It would explain the coldness. Billy had told me that there were many deserted mining tunnels under the town. I might have been left in one.

But this sharp tie on the railing might mean my freedom. I rubbed the rope against it, doing it slowly and steadily. I did not want to wear myself out. I worked for long stretches but from time to time took a rest to relieve the pressure on my arms and hands.

During those moments I thought of who might have done this to me. Although I did not want to face it, I came to the horrible conclusion it might well be Charlie. He had been trying to persuade me to desist from my inquiries into Lily's death. He was the last person with me. He saw me flee to the entryway. Few would question his solicitation in helping an ailing woman out of the dance hall.

Yet I hated to think he might have done this to me. Yes, he would tease me, but to actually hurt me didn't seem his way.

At the moment, it mattered little who had done this to me. All I need think about was how I would get out of this mess.

I sawed away at the rope. My hands lost feeling. My feet were freezing. My breath came in labored gulps, and I was forced to stop for longer and longer periods as my body could not bear the pain. I could no longer feel my hands on the end of my arms. As I rubbed, I cut off the blood to them and they were growing cold. My fingers had puffed up like little sausages.

I couldn't tell if I was getting anywhere—my fingers were too numb to check the rope and feel if it was fraying. I sank into a pile on the floor and felt tears push at the back of my eyelids. I would not cry. If I cried I would weaken, and if I weakened I might not live. I determined I would make my way out of this hole and continue my investigation. I had not come all this way to America to die in a stinking mining pit.

Breathing slowly, I gave myself a talking-to. I had much to be thankful for at this moment. I was strong from all the housework I had done. I was young and in good health. I was determined. Nothing mattered but freeing myself—before I died or before someone came back to do me more harm. My mother had taught me perseverance and I would make her proud. As much as I had loved my mother, I was not ready to join her.

I started in again on the sawing. The rhythm of it soothed me. My hands were past hurting. I feared to think of the wounds on my wrists. I would rub for fifty times and then I'd pause for ten breaths. Counting helped. And I prayed to the Virgin Mary. I asked her to aid me in my time of need.

Finally I prayed to St. Brigid. She would help me, I was sure. As I breathed her name out into the cold air of my prison, I felt a loosening. One of the bindings had been cut through and I could feel it falling away from my hand. This renewed me. I kept on with the other one, rubbing harder. After what seemed like hours it too came loose, and I could roll away from the railing.

As the circulation rushed into my hands, the pain rushed right behind.

My hands pounded like two drums. Carefully, I moved my arms until they were in front of me. I could go nowhere until I could see, and I wouldn't be able to do that until my hands were fit to untie my blindfold.

Suddenly I heard a noise like a footstep. I rolled back toward the railing and tried to put my hands as they had been. Maybe my attacker had come to check on me and would leave again as soon as he saw me lying still. Maybe he would lean over me and I would be able to hit him with my wounded hands and flee.

I listened for the sound to repeat. When I heard it again, I held my breath and knew it to be footsteps, but not of a man. A beast of some sort. And rather small. My air came out in a whistle of relief. Rats did not scare me.

I rolled onto my back and attempted to move my hands up toward my face but was only able to heave them onto my belly, hardly able to touch or to feel, let alone manage to untie a knot. I began to rub them against each other in an attempt to get the circulation going.

Quietly I sang a little ditty to scare the animal away and to keep myself company. "My true love wore a ribbon of brightest green . . ." My mother sang this song as she stirred our dinner. My mother sang whatever she was doing. She said that song kept the evils at bay and let the Lord find you more easily.

Shaking my hands in time to my song, I could feel life slowly flowing back into them. The pins and needles were leaving, and I was gaining more strength. When I next lifted my arms, they reached up to my face and felt for what was over my eyes.

My hands were not yet up to the work. Turning the back of my head, I could feel the knot in a kind of fabric. As my hands came to life, I tried them from time to time. Finally I was able to work the blind loose and pulled it from my face. My eyes blinked open and I pulled in my breath.

The surprise was that I still could not see. Wherever I was, was as black as pitch. I must have been brought down in the pit with a lantern. I sat and held myself. It would do no good to stay here. Yet I feared moving and falling into yet another deeper pit. I decided I must crawl and feel my way slowly.

On my hands and knees I moved forward a couple of body lengths until I hit a wall made of stone. Which way to move? I decided to head toward the dripping water. I followed the wall and came to a rough open-ing, flanked by wood beams. As I stuck my head through it, I saw a hint of light down the end of a long tunnel. This light seemed more miraculous than the changing of water to wine, and I drank deeply of its sight.

I stood slowly, keeping one hand on the wall and feeling forward care-fully with my foot. With each step, the light strengthened until I could make out the opening it came through. Another rough doorway, and this time when I poked my head through I could see the space I was stepping into, the bottom of a pit with a ladder attached to the side of it. I stepped to the bottom and found I couldn't reach up to the last rung of the ladder. It was half again my height above my head.

I looked down at my hands, ringed with blood bracelets, and won-dered if they would be able to pull me up the ladder. I had to try.

As I stepped back to see how I would get to the bottom of the ladder, I saw the holes where the other ladder had once been. Whoever had carried me down here had pulled the lower part of the ladder up behind him.

Like water pouring down my neck, I soaked in the realization that he had wanted me dead. He had intended me dead. My abduction had been deliberately planned and, if not for my determination, he might have got-ten his wish.

I would not die.

I would climb out of here if I had to dig my own footholds.

I would find out who killed Lily and avenge myself.

I needed to give myself a foothold from whence I could clamber up to the ladder. I sat at the bottom of the pit and took off my boot. Using the heel of it, I dug away at the hard-packed dirt wall about three feet off the ground. After countless minutes of agonizing work, I managed to form a lengthwise crease in the wall that might gain me a toehold. I wouldn't need much.

I put my boot back on, scrambled to my feet, and stepped as far back as I could from the ladder and ran at the wall. The toehold worked, but my hand missed the lowest rung. I tried again, and again I failed. On the third attempt I snagged it with my fingers. My hand felt wrenched from its socket and, as I tried to swing my other hand up, I slipped off.

I landed with a thud on the dirt floor. Tiredness seeped through me.

Hunger stabbed me. I did not know how much longer I would have the strength to make this attempt. One of the next few tries had best be successful. I could not think further.

Flexing my arms and wrists, I warmed them for their task. I made a few easy runs at the foothold, practicing planting my foot just so. I took off my coat and dropped it to the floor. It would be there for me if I didn't make it out of this pit, and if I did I would not need it so badly.

Sending up one more prayer to St. Brigid, I aimed myself at the ladder. In my mind's eye I could see it happening. The easy jump, the hands holding tight to the ladder, the making my way to the rungs until I could ascend as one should —with hands and feet.

I ran at the ladder. The foot was well planted and I flew up to the bottom rung, catching it in both hands. With my feet, I scrambled up the wall while I flung my right hand up and managed to catch the next rung. I wrapped my arm tight around it and brought my left hand up to it. Up again went my right hand and caught the next rung. My knee found the bottom rung and I was secured.

For a few moments I simply clung to the ladder and let tears leak out of my eyes, not so much crying as releasing my fears. Then I crawled up the ladder. The wooden cover for the pit was half off and I could peek up above it. I looked into what appeared to be a warehouse. Boxes and shovels and picks were arranged along the sides of the structure. Relief flooded me as I saw no one was in the room. Quietly, I stepped up off the ladder and crept silently to a door on the far side of the warehouse. I did not want to have come so far only to give myself away.

When I looked out the door, I saw I was down in the Badlands again. Bright light flooded in, and for a moment I was near to blind from it. As my eyes accustomed themselves, I could see the life on the street. Near to midday, I figured. People walked the streets, and I could step out into them and leave this place.

What a sight I must look, but stranger creatures than I roamed the streets at every hour of the day and night. What cared I for people's opinions? I was alive.

Stepping out into the street with the full noon sun shining down on me, I noticed my dress. Ripped in the sleeves, the flounces in ruins, it looked like an old curtain someone had hung on me. I smoothed it out as best I could and walked toward my brother's house. I would buy myself a new dress, maybe even today, and I would buy one that was even more beautiful. I would spare nothing to show whoever had done this to me that I was not vanquished.

Wrapping my arms around myself, I ran. People did stare at me, but I paid them no mind. Let me get home, I thought, let me be safe before whoever did this to me finds me again.

Then an even worse fear hit me. What if I was not safe in that house? What if neither Billy nor Paddy were there? I was hungry and cold and tired and weak. I needed help.

I nearly sat down on the street and wept. No place could be a safe haven to me. If only Seamus would come back and help me fight this battle. Had he known what he was leaving me to when he escaped? I realized that I was too exhausted and scared to make any sense.

Stepping into the doorway of a shop, I drew myself together. There was one place I knew I would be safe, where I could trust someone. I would go there and try to find my way out of this deeper hole I had fallen into.

21

"May I help you, my daughter?"

The gentle voice pulled me from my thoughts, and I looked up into the kind face of Father Lonegran. He was dressed all in his dark priest clothes, and his round, white face glowed above the dark vestments like a moon rising over the hills. A comforting sight indeed. I had been sitting in a pew at the back of the church with my hands folded in front of me, shaking from cold and from fright, and waiting for just such a heavenly vision.

"I don't know what to do," I said honestly.

He looked me over and said, "You need to put a few more clothes on and get some warm tea into you. Then we'll talk."

He took me by the arm and led me out of the church. We entered a small house next door with a darkened room that served as kitchen, parlor, and dining room. He mumbled to me that a priest's needs were few.

A round table was placed in front of a window with two chairs pulled up to it. A fire was going in the woodstove against the wall. Father Lonegran put on a kettle of water. Then he left the room and returned with a large wool sweater that he draped over my shoulders.

"Sit," he ordered in a gentle but firm voice and pushed me toward a rocking chair facing the fire.

He bustled around his room and brought over a plate of bread and butter. A teapot sat waiting on a small table he had placed between the two of us.

"My housekeeper isn't here today. But she made the bread yesterday. It's quite good. Please try some."

As I reached out to butter the bread, he caught sight of my wrists.

"Good gracious, what has happened to you, young lady?"

147

The kettle whistled at that moment and we both jumped. "Let me get you some tea first." He poured water into the teapot.

"This is no good," he mumbled to himself as he fussed about me. When the tea was ready, he poured me a cupful and watched me take a sip.

When the warmth of the tea entered me, I felt I would swoon. "It happened at the ball . . ."

"That is why the dress . . . I see, I see," he said thoughtfully.

"Someone hit me on the head and I passed out. Then I was left at the bottom of a mining shaft under the town, trussed up like a chicken."

"Oh, dear, this is too much. For someone like you." My story was too much for him to sit through, for he bobbed up and paced around me.

"Go on," he urged.

So I told him all I knew—of how my brother had been blamed for Lily's death, and how a man had grabbed me at the ball and warned me off of trying to find out who had really killed her, how I woke up to find myself in complete darkness. At the end, his round face had a pinched look and his hands were worrying each other. For myself, I felt done in. The warmth, the food, the comfort were all making me cave in on myself like an old mine shaft when the timbers have rotted through.

✻　✻　✻

After Father Lonegran had heard my story, he took charge. He sent a boy over to tell Padraic and Billy that I had been found and to ask them to bring me a change of clothes. Then he put me to bed in his featherbed with a big comforter and pillows with crisp cotton covers and a hot water bottle at my feet, and I slept for hours.

When I woke, the light had almost faded from the sky and the house was very quiet. Then I heard a knocking. Footsteps moved through the house, the front door opened, and I heard Padraic's voice.

"I must see her," he said outside the door.

"I will go and fetch her. You sit down and mind the fire. She's had a time of it."

After a moment, the door squeaked open and Father Lonegran's round face peeked into the room. I lifted up my head and smiled at him.

"Awake, are we? Here, I've brought you some warm clothes, and if you feel up to it, there's someone to see you." Then he left me.

In this small bed, I felt as warm and safe as I had felt in my life. Jesus smiled down on me from the far wall. His brown eyes were soft and forgiving, but a thin smile sat on his face. The world-weariness of his features made me feel closer to him.

Throwing the covers aside, I pushed myself out of the bed and dressed in my old working clothes. But I put the priest's sweater back on, a talisman of my stay with him.

When I stepped out into the small living area, Padraic leapt up from his chair and rushed to me, grabbing me by the arms. "You're all right, are you, Brigid? I couldn't stand it if anything were to happen to you."

"I'm fine, Padraic." I looked him in the eyes.

"Tell me what happened to you."

We sat and I told my story again, Father Lonegran nodding and prompting me as I went. At the end Padraic shook his head. "This is too much. I never dreamt you were in such grave danger. You must leave here, Brigid."

"Where would I go? We need to finish with the claim." I took his hand and calmed him. "Tell me what happened at the ball after I was taken. When did you discover my disappearance?"

Padraic rubbed his face as if to clear his mind. He sat forward and warmed his hands by the fire. "You must give up this search for Lily's killer. I could kick myself for not keeping you in my sight. The last I saw you, you were dancing with Charlie Hunt. You looked like you were enjoying yourself. He stopped.

I remembered that moment.

"Then I went in to supper and looked about for you but did not find you anywhere in the room. It must have been close to half an hour after midnight struck. I did not think that much of it until Hunt came running up to me. By this time, it was close to one o'clock in the morning. Such a state he was in. Said that you had had words and gone off. He claimed to have gone back to our house but found it dark and empty. Even after pounding on the door, he got no answer. Hunt begged us to help him find you. We rounded up Billy to help look for you. The night had turned cold and Mr. Hunt was much worried about you."

"We first gave a thorough look of the hall and then put on our coats and followed him out into the night." Padraic hung his head. "We've been at it ever since. It's been a long night. I don't know where they are now, but I'll get word to them that you are all right."

"Hunt might have been the one to have tied me up and left me." I uttered my most horrible thought.

Padraic nodded his head. "Oh, aye, I suppose it could have been him, he had the time, but I do not like to think of it. I'd hate to be doing business with the likes of such a man."

"We must do something about your wrists," Father Lonegran interrupted, putting more water on to boil.

He brought out some clean rags and a basin of water. Padraic placed himself opposite me with the bowl of hot water on his knees. He washed my wrists gently and cleaned them, then he wrapped each one in a neat bandage and fastened it securely with a pin.

"You'll come home with me now?" Padraic held both of my hands in his as if they were small birds and he was nestling them.

That night Billy and Padraic cosseted me, making sure I was warm and comfortable. Paddy slept on the couch down in the parlor and I kept my door open. Sometimes I could hear him tossing from one side to the other. Toward morning, he began snoring and it lulled me back to sleep, the sound deep and rhythmic like the ocean waves I had been born near.

I was forever grateful for these two good men, the closest thing I had to family.

The next day, Padraic was in the way much of the time, insisting on doing all the chores for me. He even tried his hand at making some bread. He turned out a rather heavy loaf, but he was proud of it.

Later in the day, he heated some water on the stove and had a look at my wrists. They were healing fine.

"You might be left with a fine white line on your pretty wrists."

"It could have been so much worse."

He put a hand to my lips. "Sh-sh-sh, Brigid. Don't think it. It's over. Naught will happen to you again."

Billy seemed almost shy around me, could barely meet my eyes. He brought me a piece of chocolate from the store, and I heated us some milk and we had hot chocolate in the late afternoon, all sitting around the fire.

As we were drinking it, there was a knock at the door. Billy jumped up to answer it and came back to tell us that Charlie Hunt would like to see me.

"I do not want to see him," I said.

"You're safe enough here with us two," Padraic told me.

"He looked all night and day for you, Brigid. Can you not let him see your face so he's reassured?" Billy asked.

"I am not ready to see anyone. Tell him I'm resting. I don't care what you tell him, simply make him go away."

Billy shook his head at me and went back to the door with my message.

He returned moments later and stood in front of me to deliver Charlie's reply. "He said to say he understands. He would like to see you as soon as you feel ready to see anyone. Send a boy with a note to tell him when you are better. He also said how glad he is that you are alive and feeling well. Then he gave me this to give you." Billy handed me a long package of newspaper.

I unrolled it and there was a flower, a lovely red rose with a few glossy leaves. However had he come to find such a rarity here in Deadwood in the middle of the winter? I lifted it to my nose and smelled. The sweet scent it gave off was all the more intoxicating because it should have been impossible to hold such a thing. The scent was almost as intoxicating as the thought of Charlie Hunt actually caring for me enough to search the night through and then bring me this rare gift. The stem was not long and the petals a faded red with a dark orange center, but I fetched a cup of water for it to serve as a vase.

A card was tucked into the newspaper. I opened it and read:

To my wild Irish rose.
Thank goodness you are found.
Charlie

Billy gave a chuckle as he looked at the flower in its white cup. "He means to have you, doesn't he?"

"It's nothing to you, I hope," I answered, joking with him.

"After we've got our money for the claim, I don't give a care what you do with him. Although I will say I think you'd be better off with one of your own and not that stuffed shirt."

22

January 3, 1879

Padraic was my shadow, staying with me in the house. He was quiet and easy to be with. We talked of what we might do when we sold the claim. He had a mind to go farther west and start a business in one of the new towns that were springing up on the prairies. The first thing I wanted to do was see my brother again, then we would make plans to bring the rest of the family to America.

"Who knows, I might set myself up in business too."

"And what would you sell?" Paddy asked.

I didn't have to think long. "Books," I said. "I'd love to have a whole store full of books."

He laughed. "Are you sure you'd make any money? I can see you reading them all."

"I would indeed—the better to sell them."

"Even I would buy a book from you."

This was high praise, for I was not sure Paddy could read a word.

By the third day of the new year, I felt that I was recovered enough to go out on the town. I had determined to see the sheriff and tell him what I knew, how I had been threatened for trying to find out the truth of Lily's death. If he was the smart gentleman he should be, he might be able to help us all. I was somewhat surprised the sheriff hadn't come to hear my story.

After the noon meal, Padraic and I argued while clearing the table.

"I'm going out today," I told him, knowing full well that it would raise some comment.

"That's fine. Will do you good. I'll go along with you, if you don't mind."

I held a stack of dishes and looked directly at him so that I might see his expression. "I'm going to see the sheriff."

He tightened his eyes until they were thin lines sunk into his face. He looked as if he were facing into a dust storm off the prairies. "He's a horse's ass and there's no one in this town who will say different."

"So you say."

"Let me tell you a story." This was Padraic's way. I had learned it well in my past few days with him. Everything brought out a story in him. "Sheriff Manning had heard that the treasurer, a little fella name of Brigham, was doing something shady with the town's funds, so he went to look over the records. When he got to Brigham's office, he found the man opening the safe as if ready to make off with the money. Brigham slammed the safe door into Manning and Manning pulled his gun and held it a foot away from the fellow's head. Only the fact that the gun failed to fire saved the man's life."

"Was Brigham guilty?"

"Well, yes, in fact he was. But Manning would have given him no chance to prove otherwise."

I wiped the table clear of our crumbs and pushed the chairs in. "Charlie has spoken well of him."

"Charlie has money. Money speaks louder than a tornado in this place."

"I mean to see him."

Padraic smiled and shrugged his shoulders as if to say, this is no surprise. "And I mean to go along with you."

"You may do that, Paddy."

"I won't see the man, but know that I will be waiting outside his office for you if you have need of me."

*　*　*

For most of the walk, we did not speak. I had some hope that I could reason with the sheriff and that when he had heard of my abduction, he would realize that whoever had killed Lily was still in town and meant to do me harm. This would pull him off Seamus's tail, and we could send word to call him back to Deadwood to help us negotiate the claim. I was to the point where I didn't care so much if they found out who killed Lily; I simply wanted the attention diverted from Seamus so we could conclude the sale of the claim and leave this wretched place.

"It's too bad we're not dealing with Bullock," Padraic finally said as we crossed the street. I held his arm as we walked. He steered me around a big mud puddle the warmer weather had caused.

"Bullock?"

"Seth Bullock was the sheriff before Manning took over. Now there was a man. As smart as they come."

"I suppose you've got some story to tell on him."

"There's a good one, to be sure." He launched into it. "The miners over at the Aurora Mine weren't happy about the money they were paid and they decided to sit it out. They moved into the tunnel, set up a stove right under an air shaft to keep themselves warm, and declared they would not budge until the management agreed to their demands. The owners brought in the cavalry and a cannon from Fort Meade, and it looked like blood would be spilled before the dispute was settled. Then Bullock showed up."

"The hero to save the day?"

"He was indeed. He was carrying a small brown box and grinning from ear to ear. He climbed up the mountain to the air shaft and dumped in the contents of the package—asafetida—which smells worse than skunk spray. Those miners couldn't get out of the shaft fast enough."

We reached the town's offices on, appropriately enough, Deadwood Street. The building was built right over a small creek called City Creek, which emptied into the Whitewood. Padraic said he had some supplies to get and he would meet me back in a quarter of an hour. I stood on the front steps of the Deadwood City Hall and wished I did not feel so alone. But I knew that I had to learn to count on myself if I was to get ahead in this world the way I was determined to.

❋   ❋   ❋

An older woman ushered me into the sheriff's office, and after a moment he looked up from his big roll-top desk and turned his wooden swivel chair around. He looked me up and down and then said, "Please sit, Miss Reardon."

I gave him the same perusal. When he had come to our house, he had seemed imposing, but here in the quiet sanctum of his office he seemed like a clerk poring over his papers. A pained expression sat on his face as if he already doubted all I had to say and would only suffer to listen to me because it was his job.

"What might I do for you?" he asked.

"I'm here to talk to you about an incident that I feel absolves my brother from having anything to do with Lily's death."

"Really?"

He was wearing wool pants tucked into tall boots and a vest buttoned over a large stomach. On the dark vest was pinned his sheriff's badge, a large silver star set in a gold background.

"That's an impressive badge you're wearing."

"Made by Mr. Gillette from our very own city of Deadwood. Given to me in honor of my actions in this office."

"And well deserved, I'm sure."

He nodded his head in recognition of the compliment.

"I've come to you for your help. Both for my brother's sake and my own."

"I'd be obliged to help you, miss."

"I have looked into Lily's death, having, as you must understand, a difficult time believing my good brother had anything to do with it."

"I fear I have no such problem."

I continued. "I have discovered a number of men who were interested in Lily."

"All for the same reason, I imagine."

"Be that as it may. Since I have checked into the matter, I feel like I have tumbled into a wild bee's nest. I have been shot at on one occasion. The French dressmaker can affirm this. And then, three nights ago, I was abducted from the New Year's Eve ball."

"What can you tell me of the man who stole you away?"

I wished I had more to tell him. "I'm afraid not enough. I heard his voice in a whisper and then I was knocked out. When I came to, I had been left alone in a mining shaft, tied to a metal rail."

He pursed his lips, then asked a question. "Did you get paid as much as Lily usually got for her charms?"

At first I thought I had not heard him right. When I listened to his question again in my mind, my blood boiled. That he could think that of me showed the narrowness of his mind. I shot out of my chair and stood shaking. "How dare you, sir!"

"Easily. You're your brother's sister. What more do I need to know? You've even bewitched Charlie Hunt. But then he always did have the taste for the sporting woman."

Taking myself in hand, I spoke loud and clear. I would not lose my temper to such an evil man. "I'll have you know that I'm no sporting woman, not that it should concern you. What you should be concerned about is that there is a man out there, roaming your streets, who has killed Lily and tried to do the same to me. He is not my brother. That should be obvious. I will let it be known that we have had this conversation, and it will be upon your head if anything happens to me."

He seemed unmoved by my words. I did not know what more I could say to him so I turned to go.

"I saw you came here with Padraic."

I had turned to the door, but I answered him. "Yes, he was kind enough to accompany me."

"I'll tell you this. If I weren't so dad-blamed sure that Seamus had killed Lily, I'd be looking at Padraic for the crime."

He had caught me. I turned and asked, "Why would you do that?"

"He's got a terrible temper. Doesn't take much for him to go off half-cocked. I've seen him in a fight or two when the spirit took him."

"He doesn't have much good to say of you either, sir." I turned on my heels, slamming the door behind me.

❋   ❋   ❋

I stood in the shelter of the door, wondering where Padraic was. The anger was still boiling up in me from the conversation. I thought of going back into the sheriff's office and slapping his slack-jawed face. I thought of taking his badge and sticking that sharp pin right into his chest. Then suddenly the anger dissipated and I felt sickened by what he had assumed of me. Was there no hope for a woman in this town?

I heard my name said and lifted my head, thinking to see Padraic.

Charlie Hunt came dashing across the street toward me. My first reaction was to retreat back into City Hall, but I would not take the chance of running into the sheriff. My second was to step toward him. Being pulled between these two actions, I stood quite still, poised on the top step as if on the brink of a precipice.

"You are out and about." He stood below me on the sidewalk and gave a small bow, taking off his hat.

"I appear to be, as do you."

"Brigid, are you really, truly fine?"

"I am."

"I cannot forgive myself for what I did to you that night, so I would not dream of asking you to forgive me, but I hope shortly you will not think of me too unkindly."

"What are you going on about?"

"I was teasing you about marriage, and yet again, I wasn't."

"Please, let's not talk about it here in the street."

"You are, as ever, right. When might I see you?"

"I believe we will meet soon to discuss the claim."

"That is not what I mean."

"For the time being, Mr. Hunt, let us get through this business before we move on to anything else."

"So there is a chance that we will move on?" he asked with what I took was hope in his voice.

"I cannot say. I am still not sure that you weren't behind my abduction."

"Lord, Brigid, how can you say that to me? Why, I went mad looking for you. Ask anyone. Ask Padraic."

"What should you ask me?" Padraic stood on the sidewalk next to Charlie Hunt.

"Tell her that I couldn't have abducted her."

"I would like to, but I didn't see you until a good half an hour later."

"Well, someone did. I will find someone who will tell you that I was searching for you at the ball."

"I look forward to hearing from them," I said.

Close to our house, Padraic asked me how my visit with the sheriff had gone.

I answered, "I fear I have now much the same opinion of Sheriff John Manning as you do."

23

"I'm glad for the chance to talk to this Charlie Hunt," Billy said as he pulled on his boots. "Seamus has done all the talking before, and I'll be happy to speak my mind."

"You have so much to tell him?" Paddy asked with a twinkle in his eye.

For my part, I had decided I would keep rather quiet at the meeting but listen hard. We had all agreed that Padraic would do the talking; even Billy knew that Paddy was a more considered speaker. But I had also told myself that I would speak up if need be. There was no sense in being dumb when you aren't deaf.

I dressed with care for our meeting. I wore my old black skirt with a new waist I had ordered. I pulled my hair back more severely than I usually did and pinned it tight to my head, wanting to appear, as much as possible, a practical businesswoman. I wore the locket that Padraic had given me, and I noted that he was pleased to see it on me.

Both Padraic and Billy had shined themselves up, but not like they had for the ball. They both were wearing their heavy boots with wool pants tucked into them and heavy wool shirts. They were clean and tidy looking, but they also looked like mining men. I was sure they hadn't done it consciously, but they would certainly stand out against Mr. Charlie Hunt's debonair look as the working men they were.

We had arranged to meet at seven at the Grand Central Hotel where Charlie was lodging.

As we walked over, I could tell that Billy was nervous. He went on and on about the other big mining claims in the area, the enormous amount of gold that was being pulled out of them, the money to be made. The Homestake was one he kept mentioning.

"I'd like a piece of that in exchange for our claim," he said, kicking at a clod of dirt that had formed in the mud.

"Oh, aye, that would be fine," Padraic responded.

"Hearst and Higgins bought that mine about the time we come to the Hills. That was in late '77, I think. Wasn't it?"

"As I recall."

"Remember, Paddy, they paid over a hundred thousand for that claim. Can you imagine? They shipped in a huge mill to work it and went into production right about this time last year. Since then, I've heard, they're pulling out about forty thousand dollars' worth of gold bullion in one month's time. Wouldn't I like a piece of that pie?"

"Our claim isn't on level with the Homestake, Billy." Padraic tried to calm him down.

"You can't be too sure about these things. I think the ore sample might surprise everyone. I've been finding some pretty good veins in the latest shaft we've dug."

While Padraic had been attending to me, Billy had been out at the claim nearly every day. Some days were awfully raw with just a trace of snow, but he said once he went underground it didn't really matter what the weather was like outside. He called himself "a rat digging in his burrow." His hands would not come clean, no matter how much scrubbing with lye soap he did.

I thought of Charlie Hunt's soft, clean hands—hands that I was sure had never done a day's worth of physical labor. For once I would see him at work, and negotiating the deal together would give me a chance to judge his worth, what kind of man he truly was out in the world.

*　*　*

Reaching the hotel front, we scraped the mud from our boots and walked into the lobby. A splendid place it was. Dark paneled walls with lovely paper cuttings festooned from the picture board. The floor had a runner of dark flowered carpet leading right up to the registration desk.

Directly we were shown into a small room where a fire was blazing.

Two men sat facing it, sitting on a long burgundy couch. There were a pair of antlers over the fireplace, which gave the room the feel of a man's study in a private home.

The two men stood as we entered and came toward us. Charlie looked comfortable in a light vest over a heavy wool shirt. He was dressed more informally than I had ever seen him, and I wondered if he had done it to make us feel more comfortable.

"Allow me to introduce you all to Professor Underwood. He's come out from Chicago to oversee the ore sample."

The professor was a strange, bony man who looked to be in his mid-forties. His face was splotchy, probably from the heat of the fire, and his hands were knobby and long.

We all shook hands and Charlie showed us to the fire.

"It's a cold evening," he remarked. "Gentlemen, may I offer you something to drink? The professor and I did not wait your arrival but are imbibing some excellent Century whiskey. Please join us." He sounded ever the grand host as he offered the men some libations.

Paddy and Billy agreed to this, and Charlie poured them each a tumbler full.

"I would not mind a taste of this fine liquor you are offering," I said. I had heard that a small amount of liquor can often calm the heart, and I felt like I could use such a drink in me that night.

Charlie raised his eyebrows.

"Brigid?" asked Paddy.

Billy turned his head to look at me.

Their surprise decided me. "Yes, please," I said.

"May I pour in a small amount of water?" Charlie asked.

"If you think that would add to my enjoyment of it, by all means," I said.

Charlie handed me a lovely cut-glass tumbler with a golden liquor mixed with a splash of water. I smelled it and the scent made me catch my breath. I would need to be careful with this beverage. But I did not want to start the evening left out by all the men.

We all held our glasses up to each other, said "Cheers" or "*Slainte*" and then took a swallow. I was glad I had smelled it and was prepared for the strength of it. The drink reminded me of a horrible remedy my mother's mother had given us for the croup. I let the liquid sit in my mouth for a moment, and when it was more diluted, I slipped it down my throat. The liquor burned but had a rich sweet aftertaste. I took another small sip and smiled.

"And I have with me some good cigars." He brought out a dark wooden box and offered it around, coming first to me. "Miss Reardon, do you smoke also?"

"No, thank you kindly, Mr. Hunt."

They all poked a big cigar in their mouths and lit up. The air plumed with their smoke, and the smell was rich and strong. I remembered the smell from cleaning Mr. Hunt's den in St. Paul. I could see that Billy and Paddy were relaxing and enjoying themselves. I reminded myself not to get too relaxed. We were here to get as much money as we could out of our claim, and unfortunately, Charlie and his man meant to do the opposite.

"We have some business to go over, gentlemen and miss." Charlie saved a smile for me and flourished a small bow in my direction.

Charlie sat next to Professor Underwood on the couch and said, "I think we all want the same thing—a fair price for your claim—and to that end I have asked Professor Underwood to oversee the extraction of the ore sample. He has had much expertise in this area. Correct, Professor?"

"Oh, yes, I would say, certainly so. Why I've been up to British Columbia, down to South America. Wherever there's gold and other valuable minerals to be found, I have worked, calculating the worth of many a mine. I consider myself well educated as a mining engineer, and I dare say I know this business as well as anyone." He seemed to swell as he spoke, his chest coming out a bit higher in his clothes, and he arranged his tie just to make sure we had time to take all his glory in. And yet, for all that, he seemed a nervous fellow to me, fidgeting and almost shaking when speaking. I wondered if he was really up to the job.

"Have you been here to Deadwood before, Professor Underwood?" I asked, curious if he would know his way around this rough-and-tumble place.

"No, my dear lady. I have not previously had the pleasure. But I think the mining here is just in its infancy. I have great hopes for this town.

Indeed, I gave a fine interview with the *Journal* in Rapid City, so that people might know that I have arrived in the area. I am sure there's a great deal of work in this town for an educated mining engineer like myself."

The men discussed how they would go about getting the ore sample. They decided that they would all ride into the claim the next day. The professor was vehement that he would gather the ore samples by himself and keep the bag with him at all times, bringing them back to be tested in St. Paul.

"Swindles have been known to happen," he declared.

Billy stirred in his chair. Paddy spoke, "We just want what we're due for our claim. We're not saying it's going to be another Homestake, but it's been good to us, and we think if a mill were brought in and it was worked as it should be, it would produce well for many years to come."

"That's certainly my wish and my father's wish also," Charlie lifted his glass again in a toast.

"Just the same, I will keep this sample to myself, and I want no one else's hands on it. I must have this agreed upon," the professor stated.

Slipping into our mother tongue, Billy whispered to Paddy, "He looks like a large turkey, sticking out his chest."

Not wanting to encourage him, I stifled my laugh. I drank a bit more of my whiskey to keep them company, then decided that I had had enough of the burning liquor. The men, on the other hand, kept helping themselves to more.

"Before we go on to more pleasantries, I have a question." I wanted to ask it before the men got too comfortable.

Charlie looked my way and said, "Miss Reardon, please continue."

"It strikes me that you are taking all these precautions to guarantee that your ore sample is not tampered with, but what guarantees do we have on our side that you will let us know truly what the results of it are? Might you not undercut the amount of gold in it and pay us less for our claim?"

All the men turned my way.

"What do you suggest?"

"That we, at the same time, send in a similar sample to be tested and we compare the results."

Paddy clapped his hands. "Just the thing."

Billy stamped his feet. "Our Brigid has a head on her shoulders, she does."

"Of course, if you would like, dear Brigid, but who would pay for this testing?" Charlie asked.

I knew our resources were limited. "We will pay for half of it, if you will cover the rest."

Charlie thought and then nodded. "I think that could be arranged."

After that, the talk went on for a while of other things, and I kept half an ear to it but felt the liquor had made me sleepy and the fire had warmed me through to my toes. Also, I was very aware of Charlie Hunt sitting across the room, watching me.

24

The next morning broke bitter cold. I rubbed a circle clear on the window and stared out at the streets of Deadwood. Frost covered every surface like a sugar coating in a bakery shop. The smoke from the chimneys rose straight up to the sky in the still and frigid air.

We had agreed to meet at noon with Charlie and the professor. I dressed in my new dungarees, and I put on one of Padraic's flannel shirts. I did not look very ladylike, but fashion was the last thing I needed to worry about.

The cold was a bit of a blessing as it would make the going easier, for the mud would be frozen.

Billy and Paddy had gone off to gather up some equipment and fetch the horses when I heard a pounding at the door. They said they would return in an hour's time, so I knew it was not them. For a moment I thought of disappearing into my room, but I knew if I wanted to get on with my life and make something of it, I couldn't shy away from it. I wondered if this fear I felt would stay with me—like a constant, whining pet—the rest of my life.

When I peered through the window, I saw Elizabeth outside our door, stamping her small feet to keep warm. She had obviously run over from next door and had only thrown a shawl over her head. I hurried to let her into the warmth of our house.

"What happened to you? Tell me." She rushed into the house, took me by the arms, and looked me in the face. She seemed reassured by what she saw. "Tell."

"Hello, Elizabeth," I said. "You look well today." And indeed she did. I wondered if she had had news of her husband. Or perhaps the pregnancy had moved into the phase where women glow. Her usually drawn face seemed fuller and more vital.

"Oh, thank goodness you are all right. So what did happen? I've heard horrible rumors." She pulled the shawl down around her shoulders.

"That is what this town is built on, isn't it?"

"Yes, I expect so."

I brought her into the main room and settled her in front of the fire. I had a teakettle warming on the stove and went to fetch some of the tea that Ching Lee had sent to me. When I had everything ready for tea and was seated next to her, I told her what had happened.

Her mouth grew into an *o* and her eyes widened. At the end of my tale, she clapped her hand over her mouth, then burst out with, "I cannot bear to think of you like that. The first I knew something was amiss was when Charlie came running up and asked the man I was with if he had seen you. My friend knew who he was talking about, you are so unmistakable with your dark curly hair and lovely blue eyes. Also, I had mentioned you to him, even pointed you out as you were dancing with Paddy."

This might be the proof that Charlie had had nothing to do with my abduction. Better proof than any other I could have, as it had come unrequested. "When did Charlie talk to you, Elizabeth?"

"'Tis hard to remember. But not long after the revelry of New Year's. Maybe five or ten minutes later."

"You're sure of this."

Her eyes grew wide at my asking and she nodded her head vigorously as though to further assure me. "Yes."

"And then what happened?" I stood up to check on the teakettle, even knowing that it would not boil when I watched it.

"Charlie continued to look for you. I saw him asking several other people. Then we went in to the supper and I assumed he had found you." She bent her head down and confessed, "I'm afraid I thought no more of it. It never occurred to me that something frightful could happen to you in the midst of such festivity."

"Well, as you now know, he had not found me. But I am most grateful for that information. I feared that Charlie might have had something to do with what happened to me. Now I am assured that he did not."

"Oh, I would think not. There was never such a man so desperate to find you. He seemed quite distraught. Who could have done this to you and why?" A horrible thought occurred to her and she pressed her hand to her mouth. "You are all right, aren't you, Brigid? No man has taken advantage of you?"

"No. Nothing like that happened." I remembered my conversation with the sheriff. "I think whoever abducted me did not want me dead. For if he had, and I assume it was a man who did this vile thing, I fear he would have killed me at once. Why leave me alive?"

Elizabeth pulled in her breath in a loud intake of air and fluttered her hands as if to push something away. Finally, when she had regained herself enough to speak she asked, "Why indeed?"

"All I can guess is that he wants me to stop asking questions about Lily's death. That he doesn't want me to discover who really killed her."

"What are you going to do? You must be careful at all times and never be alone. This town is hard enough as it is on a woman."

"I will do what I've been doing, taking care at all times to be with someone I can trust."

"If you ever need to come over and stay with me when the men are gone, please do it, Brigid. I'd love to have the company."

"Thank you, Elizabeth." The teakettle boiled, whistling as steam poured from its spout. I put the fragrant tea into a pot and let it steep by the fire.

She thought for a moment. "That Charlie Hunt, he is quite a handsome man. I've heard he will come into a family fortune. How do you know him?"

"I worked for his family."

Elizabeth shook her head. "That is unfortunate." Then she added, "But not insurmountable."

"I think he wants to court me." I had not wanted to talk of this, but since I had told no one, it had been burning inside of me for some time, and I found the words spilling out of my mouth. "He seems in earnest."

"What can be the harm of it?"

"I think there could be great harm if my name were linked with his in an unsavory fashion."

"Since I've come west, I care less what other people think of me. I was quite ruled by that back in Philadelphia. Take my husband. He was thought to be a great catch. So I married him. And look where it got me. I think one must listen to one's heart, at least from time to time."

"And how is your young lieutenant?"

Her face turned crimson and she smiled with her eyes lowered. "He is truly gallant. He came over this morning to make sure that I had enough firewood in the house. So, of course, I had to offer him something to eat. He stayed quite a little while. Now, back in Philadelphia that would have been quite unseemly, but here in Deadwood, who's to know or care?"

"And your husband?"

Her eye dropped, her face grew long. "He is late returning now at least a good month. I've had no news."

I would not press her on this. "How have you been feeling?"

She pressed a hand to her waist. "I cannot tighten the corset around me the way I used to be able to. Soon, I fear, I will have to stop wearing it. I must admit, it will be a relief."

There was a pause in our conversation, an unusual occurrence with Elizabeth. She appeared to be thinking about the two men in her life. Finally she asked, "What did you and Mr. Hunt disagree on when you left the dance?"

"Oh, a small matter. He was teasing me in what I found quite a mean way."

"Oh, but I know how that can be when you're beginning to know someone. Sometimes you don't know when to take them seriously and when not."

I poured us both cups of tea and then sat and stirred my own.

Elizabeth tasted hers and said, "This is very nice tea. It tastes like some kind of exotic flower."

"Yes, that's what I thought too. Ching Lee, the laundryman, gave it to me."

"Oh, I bring my laundry to him also. I think he does a very nice job. Except once he did lose a nightgown of mine. He's a striking man with his brooding eyes and dark looks, don't you think?"

"Yes. Did you see he was at the dance?"

"I noticed him with the other celestials. When midnight was announced, he bowed and took leave of them all. Actually, I was quite surprised any of them were there. There has been some friction in the community about them."

"So Ching Lee left at midnight?"

"On the button. Right before the fight with the sporting women broke out in the vestibule."

"That's when I was accosted. How did you happen to notice him?"

Elizabeth sipped her tea. "Well, it was funny, but he seemed in a hurry. Quite out of character. You don't suspect him of anything, do you? Surely he didn't know Lily?"

"Yes, he most certainly did."

25

We rode single file through the woods, on our way to the claim. Billy led the way, with Professor Underwood right behind him, Charlie Hunt followed, then myself, and finally Padraic brought up the rear, as always keeping an eye on me.

The snow was thick in the mountains, but Billy assured us all that the trail to the claim was passable. As most of Professor Underwood's work would take place underground, it did not matter tremendously that the ground was covered with at least half a foot of snow.

However, the snow made the task of being a bystander more difficult. At the last minute I had put on one of Padraic's woolen vests and I was happy for its warmth. I tucked my mittened hands into the soft coat of the horse as we rode. It mattered little what anyone thought of the way I looked. We were on this outing to get work done, not socialize.

I watched Charlie Hunt in front of me and noted that he sat his horse quite well. I remembered dancing with him and wondered what would happen between us once the claim was settled. One often wants what one shouldn't have, and as this was acting on me, so too must it be affecting Charlie.

He turned to look at me. I smiled and then bent over my horse's neck and whispered in its ear. I whispered in Irish, for that was the first language I spoke to horses.

* * *

As soon as we arrived at the claim, Padraic built a fire. They had dug out two new shafts since last I'd been there. The shafts went straight down to where they thought the ore vein ran through the claim and from both,

Billy told us, they had been happy with the quality of ore they had found.

"Why, we took out a piece of ore from that one," he pointed to the one where the windlass was still set up, "ground it up, panned the gold out of it, and Jaysus, if we didn't have a dollar or two worth. Isn't that right, Paddy?"

"It's true."

Billy took over with the professor, leading him toward the one shaft that was large enough to climb down into. Padraic had told me that Billy turned part burrowing animal when he mined. I suspected that Padraic did not actually like going down in the shaft, while Billy was as comfortable as could be.

Professor Underwood, while constantly assuring us that he was on top of everything, made me wonder. He was not much of a rider and once or twice had looked like he might slide off his horse. He had not dressed as he should have for the snow and the cold, certainly not for the riding and going underground. He had on a long coat and a muffler, which while it might have kept him warm, was constantly coming untied and getting in his way. He insisted on carrying his collection bag, or as he called it his "ore sack," with him everywhere.

When Billy led him to the first of the shafts, the professor peered into it as if he were afraid of what he might see. Billy jumped ahead of him and disappeared down the shaft. Underwood was long in following suit. The last sight I had of him was his white face peering out from the hole.

That left Charlie, Padraic, and me gathered around the fire. Padraic pulled up some logs that were the right size for stools, and we all sat down on them and held our hands out to the blaze.

"Good thing it's not snowing today," Charlie said.

"Oh, aye," Padraic answered.

I often thought that Padraic played the Irish idiot with Charlie, acting as if he did not know much, putting on the accent stronger than it ever was when he was with Billy and myself. Padraic seemed to have a store of confidence running in a heavy lode inside himself.

"How long will it take the professor to get what he needs?" I asked.

"I'm not really sure. He said it usually takes several days. Today he might not gather much of a sample but begin to see the way the ore runs through the ground. He had me up late last night telling me of various mines he had worked."

I left off querying him about the professor. He would do the job he did and we would all know the results soon enough.

"Would you both care for some tea?" I asked.

"Grand," said Padraic.

"Yes, please," said Charlie.

I walked back to my horse and got down the teakettle. We would all need a hot drink soon.

"Have you ever been down in a shaft?" I asked Charlie.

"No, I don't care for dark, tight places. They make me feel squeezed."

"I know what you mean."

I could see it pass across his face, his remembering that I had been tied up in such a place. "Brigid."

"It's fine. Don't think about it."

The water boiled and I brewed the tea. Charlie had wandered over to the shaft hole and then back again. He seemed restless. There was little for us to do. They had been down in the mine shaft for more than an hour, and none of us knew how long it would take.

We sat around the fire and drank the tea together, but it was not done with much socializing. We three seemed awkward around each other. If I had been alone with either of the men, we would have talked constantly, but I was very conscious of a strain between the two men.

When I handed Charlie Hunt a second mug of tea, he flashed me a wide smile and said, "Thanks for this, Miss Reardon. Nice of you to come with us on this expedition."

For a brief moment, I imagined myself going back to St. Paul on Charlie Hunt's arm, welcomed into the home where I had emptied out the chamber pots. How strange that would be. As we sat by the fire, drinking our tea quietly, I dreamed of the days that might come.

26

After that first day I did not go with the men when they returned to the mine. I found I served little purpose there, and it was frustrating to be so near to Charlie and yet able to say so little. I knew that the sampling of the ore would take only another two days at most.

At first Paddy fussed about my staying behind, but I explained that someone needed to see to the housework and the cooking, and since both he and Billy looked forward to warm meals when they arrived home, he agreed. But he gave me conditions: no one except Elizabeth was to come into the house; I was not to go out unless I was accompanied by Elizabeth or Father Lonegran.

To pass the time and keep my mind off my brother's absence, I had borrowed several books from Elizabeth. I was reading Louisa May Alcott's book *Little Women*. I sat enthralled by Jo, who worked so hard to have a life of her own. I must do that myself, I determined. Somehow I was sure that the life I wanted was not to be found in Deadwood.

Seeing the women in Deadwood run shops had given me an idea, one that was slowly growing in my mind. I saw myself in a handsome suit, opening the door to a small bookstore. Imagine a life filled with books. As these small towns grew, they would need books and stationery supplies. With the money from the claim, maybe I could set myself up in this business.

The snows were coming down steadily every day. Not huge storms, but a consistent few inches added to the blanket. An impressive landscape of white covered the land. Every day the horses would stamp a new path out to the mine until finally Paddy and Billy came home, three days after the sampling had started, and told me they were done.

"He seemed excited, the old scarecrow, didn't he?" Billy slapped Paddy on the back.

"He did indeed."

"So Charlie Hunt and the professor are heading to Cheyenne to-morrow to catch the train, then on from there to St. Paul to take the ore sample back to be analyzed," Paddy told me. "We've found someone to take our sample on the same trip. An engineer we've worked with before when we were staking our claim. He's from Cork and I'd trust him with my life."

"How long will all this take?" I asked, interested in when we would settle on the mine, also wondering when Charlie would return.

"About two weeks, I think. It can be analyzed right there in St. Paul. Our man thought he could return when they did. He's taking another claim's sample out at the same time. The professor and Charlie will travel with the ore sample, returning with the results. And, we can hope, a fair offer for our stake."

"Two weeks. I suppose it would take that long."

"That's if the weather holds. This snow could strand them at many places along the way."

I stood by the window and watched the snow fluttering down. The mounds shone in the dark, reminding me of the phosphorescence I had seen in the ocean, the glowing in the deep, the beauty hidden in darkness, and I wondered what would come of the ore that had been taken from the earth. Would it prove of worth? Would it shine with gold?

※　※　※

Charlie came to see me the next morning before he went off to Cheyenne. The snow had stopped and the sun reflected off it like a thousand gaslights in a theater. I hoped that his travel would go smoothly.

I answered the door and he doffed his hat at me. He stood as tall as I remembered, and I found myself happy to see him. He brought with him all the good memories I had of his home and family. Surely he was to be trusted.

I smiled and stepped out onto the porch with him, closing the door behind me. Paddy and Billy had both decided to stay home from the mine.

Paddy was whittling on the sofa while Billy played a game of solitaire. Neither of them needed to be party to my conversation with Charlie.

"I wanted to say goodbye to you."

"You will be gone two weeks, I've heard."

"I'm hoping no more than that." He took my hand. "When I'm back, I'd like to court you in earnest."

"I would like that also."

"May I bring you back something from the States?"

"Just yourself would be more than gift enough."

"Foolish to ask a woman what she wants as a gift. I should know better. I'll surprise you."

"I turn eighteen on the second of February," I blurted out, and it surprised me to see what a child I still was, wanting everyone to know when my birthday was.

"I swear I will be back here by then, even if I have to walk through snowdrifts ten feet high."

His skin seemed rosy from the sun, and I yearned to reach out and touch his cheek.

"Take care, Charlie," I said.

"I will, Brigid."

"I'll pray for your safe return."

"I know there's no one God would be more willing to listen to than you."

"I may have been named for a saint, but I'm not one myself."

"I'm glad to hear it." Before I could move back to the door he had claimed me. Both hands on my shoulders and a kiss placed right on my mouth. Goodbye whispered in my ear. And then he pulled away with a more formal goodbye said out into the thin cold air of winter, where the sound of it hung long after he had turned and gone down the steps and walked off into the streets of Deadwood.

✽   ✽   ✽

The waiting was hard on all of us. Lily's death stayed in my mind but—as we might all be leaving soon—I wasn't sure I would ever clear my brother's

name. If the claim's ore was found rich in gold, we would be leaving Deadwood and could find Seamus in Cheyenne. However, if I chose to enter
Charlie's life, who knows where I might end up?

Paddy still watched over me. He stayed close to the house, whittled,
cut wood, tended the fires, and kept me company. Often, I read to him
because he did not know how. I taught him to write his name and how
to write out the numbers up to ten. I read to him from another book I
borrowed from Elizabeth, *The Adventures of Tom Sawyer,* and we laughed
together at how Tom got all the boys to paint the fence. Paddy said if he
would have known there were such good stories in books, then he would
have learned to read sooner in his life.

Billy, however, could not stay in the house and remain calm. He
needed to move. He went out every day and many times did not return
until late in the evening, if he returned at all. The smell on him was awful
sometimes, as if he had been dropped in a vat of brew. Paddy worried that
he was gambling and spending all his money.

"He's counting on this big sum of money from the sale of the claim
something fierce. If this sale were not to happen, I hate to think what he
would do."

The last week in January, Paddy surprised me by informing me we
were going out celebrating that night. We had been sitting comfortably
in front of the fire and it was getting late. I had actually been thinking of
getting ready for bed.

"Celebrating what?"

"Don't you know that it's the New Year?"

"Are you daft?"

"I don't believe so."

"Whatever are you on about, Paddy?"

He laughed and explained, "The Chinese apparently have a different
calendar from us. Their New Year moves around a bit, but I've heard that
it's to be celebrated tonight. You haven't lived until you've seen and heard
a Chinese New Year. Last year they put on quite an affair, and it promises
to be even bigger this year."

"What do they do?" I asked, thrilled at the idea.

"There will be a parade with a large dragon and wonderful costumes by the celestials. Lots of noise and strange music. And then there will be fireworks."

"In the snow?"

"They've probably cleared the streets."

"When do we go?"

"They stay up all night to celebrate, but I think the parade will be in another hour or so. Dress warmly. And stay close to me."

❋　❋　❋

I wore my men's boots with wool socks, long underwear under my skirts, a woolen vest over my dress, and then my wrap and a scarf around my neck. Paddy insisted that I put on a buffalo skin hat that he had recently bought, which fit over my chignon and was not unbecoming in a rough sort of way.

We walked out into a still and brilliant night, but already loud bangs and noises were drifting up the streets from the Chinese settlement. As we drew closer to the crowds, I noticed red lanterns hanging from the door-ways of many shops and homes. Then a man with a queue leaned out his doorway and held out a long string of fireworks tied to the end of a pole. A little boy dressed in loose pants and a padded vest ran out with a lit stick and set fire to the string. The red firecrackers danced and jumped, bursting open in a series of loud bangs in the cold air.

I grabbed Paddy's arm and we laughed as we steered between the fireworks.

The parade was starting from the joss house at 558 Main Street, which served, Paddy told me, as a general meeting hall for the Chinese. Men slept there until they found places to stay, and they had even held a trial there of one of their own kind.

Banners hung down the front of the building with Chinese writing on them. In the streets around us celestials and other citizens of Deadwood mingled. Children were making snowballs, throwing them at each other and at some of the men lining up for the parade.

"So many people," I commented to Paddy as we watched the scene.

"The Chinese have come here from all over the hills to celebrate."

I heard the Chinese around us greeting each other in their language.

The sound was nothing like English but had some of the softness of Irish. I made out they were saying, "*Gung hay fat choy.*"

Then the other would respond, "*La choy.*"

A band gathered at the front of the house, and at the stroke of midnight they let out a mighty blast. At this signal everyone who was in possession of a firecracker set it off and any man who was carrying a firearm shot it off into the air. The noise was infernal and echoed throughout the hills until I was sure that we had woken everyone in the territory.

The band started to move forward, and then I saw the dragon. This wonderful creature had many feet and a large gold face with red eyes and a huge mouth that opened and closed as it cavorted down the street. Men walking alongside it were waving red streamers and a man was in front of it, teasing it with some sort of ball.

The band was playing a spritely and oddly tuned music that tinkled in the air like wrapping paper being crumpled by hand.

I moved forward to see the dragon more closely, watching it dance down the street, and I followed for a while to watch the wonderful creature. The movement had such energy that I almost believed the dragon was alive. What must the children think of this spectacle? I wondered and looked around to see their faces wide with a mixture of fear and amazement.

I twirled around but could not find Paddy anywhere near me. I grew frantic as I continued to search for him. The parade swept down the street and all the while the fireworks exploded in the air with red paper flying out from their centers like so much blood on the snow.

Suddenly, a pair of hands grabbed me and pulled me into a doorway.

"Why are you out walking alone at night?" a man's quiet voice asked close to my ear.

He was dressed in padded clothes with his shaved head bent forward. I turned to face him in a doorway, afraid of what he might want from me. When I saw who it was, I wanted to run but he still had hold of me.

I tried to keep my voice from shaking. It would do no good to let him know that I was afraid. "Mr. Lee."

"Miss Brigid," he said. Ching Lee was staring at me. He let loose of me.

"Happy New Year," I managed to say.

"Have you been watching the parade?" he asked.

"Yes, and I'm with Paddy."

He looked around, then said, "He does not appear to be close by."

"I think we've been separated."

"It's too cold for you to be outside alone like this. Please, step into my house." His hand closed around my arm again and he moved me a few steps down the street. He was insistent. "Please. I will take care of you."

I looked around for Paddy as Ching Lee pulled me toward a door with a red lantern hanging under the eaves. He opened the door and escorted me into the house. Inside it was warm and the air was rich with incense. His children ran to greet me, and his wife rose from the game she was playing with another woman.

She bowed to me and I bowed back as best I could. She said, "*Gung hay fat choy.*"

Ching Lee translated, "She says Happy New Year."

I answered, "*La choy,*" as I had heard others do. Her face broke into a big smile. Ching Lee seemed pleased. "You have said 'Good luck' to her."

I looked around the room. Paper cutouts hung in the windows and small narcissus flowers were blooming out of bowls of water and stones. A small shrine was set up on a table and had red streamers around it.

Ching Lee brought me to a chair and had me sit. His wife gave me a bowl of tea and some small dumplings. They were delicious, hot and sweet.

"I will go get your Paddy for you. Wait with my wife. You will be safe here."

The two women looked up from their game. They talked to me, but in their language, and all I could do was smile.

Ching Lee's wife held up a small ivory piece with carvings on it. "Mahjong," she said.

"Mahjong," I copied her.

Both the women laughed, then they went back to their game. I watched them and drank my tea. I was warm and sleepy and wondered that I had been afraid of Ching Lee.

When Ching Lee returned with Paddy, I felt he was someone I could trust. He had taken me into his home, with his wife in attendance, and then returned me to the safety of my friends.

On the other hand, Paddy looked quite fearful. He scolded me but seemed immensely happy to have found me.

As we were leaving, I still couldn't help asking Ching Lee, "When you left the dance on our New Year's Eve, where did you go?"

"I went home to my wife." He looked at me. "You must stop suspecting me of something I have not done. I mean you no harm. You and I want much the same. We want our families to be safe and our lives to be peaceful. We work hard for our money and we try to spend it wisely. In Chinese we say, 'The large of mind see the truth in all faith, the small of mind see only the difference.'"

February second was a midwinter day, dark and dreary, but I smiled at the sight of it because it was my eighteenth birthday. I had always looked forward to my birthday because it was the day, my father had told me, that we Irish once called *Imbolc,* the first day of spring.

"How happy we were to see you that morning when you arrived," my father would tell me and tickle me under my chin. But, more important, he said, it was a very holy day for it was St. Brigid's Day. There was nothing for it but my father must have me named after the saint.

"For she is the saint of healing and poetry," he told me. "And you're a poem if ever I saw one."

I shook myself away from my memories of my homeland and my family and turned to face the day, wondering if anyone would notice that I was another year older. As I went to stir the fire, a knock came at the door and I hurried to answer it.

A young boy handed me a note and I thanked him, expecting him to go away, but he stood watching me.

"Do you need something?" I asked him.

"I'm to wait for an answer. That's what the gentleman said."

The note bore my name. I tore it open and found an invitation to dinner from Charlie. He had gotten in early that morning and asked for the pleasure of my company.

"Tell the gentleman yes," I said to the boy.

That night, as I was leaving, Paddy had a word with me. "Set up a meeting for us all, and if you have any chance to glean information, it might be very helpful. We will know what we're walking into."

"I will see how the evening goes."

"Try to find out what they intend to do."

"I promise I will try."

Paddy helped me on with my wrapper and for a moment I felt his arms tighten around me and his breath upon my neck. "Best wishes to you on this day of your birth," he said close in my ear and then let me go.

*　*　*

"I had them set up a private dining room for us, my dear," Charlie told me as he greeted me at the door of the hotel. He was waiting in the lobby for my arrival and stepped out into the snow to greet me. He took me by the arm and ushered me into the hotel.

"That sounds lovely," I said.

"Brigid, you do look older and more elegant than ever." He complimented me before he even saw what I was wearing. I hoped he would not be disappointed. All I had to wear was my old best dress, which he might recognize as his mother's.

"Thank you, and I hope that I am also wiser."

"Too much wisdom in a woman cannot be good."

"Certainly not for a man who wants to have his way."

He laughed and showed his fine teeth. Every time I saw him, he grew in comeliness and stature. He never wore the same clothes more than once. He had on a handsome black vest and a shirt clean and white as a new drift of snow.

Continuing to hold my arm, he led me to the stairs. I assumed we were going up to the private dining room. We went up one flight and then he ushered me into a large room with a fireplace blazing away and a small table set right in front of it with two carved wooden chairs. Three tall windows overlooked the street, draped with velvet curtains of a deep burgundy color. The feeling in the room was one of warmth and elegance.

I turned toward the other end of the room and saw through a doorway a bed and realized that I was in fact being asked to dine in Charlie's bedroom suite.

"Charlie," his first name slipped out quite naturally. I continued, "Is this quite proper?" I asked. My eyes swept the room again and then up to his face.

He took both my hands and faced me directly. "I don't know and I don't care. I'm sick to death of proper. After all, I can't ask you out for a walk and take you up into the deep woods of the Black Hills. There's certainly too much snow for that. Or that I fancy the idea of spending the evening with Paddy and Billy and talking business with you all. Or we might have done as we did last time and eat a nice formal meal in front of the crowd that gathers in the restaurant and be able to say hardly anything and have everyone talking about us for days afterwards. I wanted you alone and to myself. I wanted to be able to talk with you about whatever I felt like tonight. I wanted to celebrate your birthday in the only privacy I could allow. Please forgive me if I do you a disservice, but I have set up this dinner for the two of us, privately in my chambers because I thought it would suit us the best."

"You argue well. Have you had thoughts of going into law?" I stepped nearer to the fire and removed my wrapper. Charlie took it from me.

"Yes, as a matter of fact. If I can only get this mining business settled for my father, I might well pursue such a course." He ushered me to the table and pulled out a chair for me.

"Well, I too am thinking of my future. I might set myself up in a bookstore."

He looked at me with surprise. "Surely not here in Deadwood. I doubt that one in five men can read."

"No, maybe back in St. Paul. Or, who knows, maybe out west. I hear San Francisco is becoming a much cultured town."

I noticed next to my plate a large present wrapped in gold foil with a big white bow on top.

"May I pour you some champagne?" Charlie asked me.

I nodded and he handed me a glass flute full of bubbles. We held the stems and clinked the rims together and they made a fine high ringing note.

"To many more years of your life, and to the hope that I might share them with you, dear Brigid."

We drank. The champagne felt like I was drinking sea foam and then the aftertaste of it was like a fine ripe peach. All in all, I liked it very much.

"Now, it is my turn." I said. We both lifted our glasses up again and clicked them together. I launched into my toast. "To settling the claim agreement and getting on with our lives."

"Hear, hear," Charlie said. "That will happen in the next day or two. It all looks quite good. I left before Underwood. They had no need for me, and he and the gentleman with your ore sample should be here in the next day or two."

"I'm glad to hear that." I drank another sip of the bubbly and felt it fizz in my nose. "May I tell Paddy and Billy that all is going well?"

"I don't see it can hurt."

We sat by the fire, sipping champagne. My thoughts went naturally to Charlie's family, and I asked, "How are your mother and father and sister?"

"They are all very well. Father had a cold that laid him up in bed for a day or two, but he was fine when I left. Mother misses your attendance. Dorry is doing well with her lessons. She's always a bit shy around me, but she was persuaded to recite a long poem to me one night at dinner. Part of that one by Longfellow. 'Hiawatha,' I think it's called."

"And how are all the servants?" I would not forget them. Agnes, especially, had been so good to me.

"They are well. Aggy tries to force food down me when I'm home. She seems to think I'm dwindling away." He laughed. "And of course Bigsby bows and sends his love."

The image of Bigsby having anything to do with love made me laugh. "Charlie, you are a tease. No wonder Dorry is shy with you."

"No, no. I do it only to make you laugh. I love the sound of your laughter, like a brook, a singing brook. Mother agrees. She mentioned that she loved the joy you showed in living."

I blushed from the simple compliment. "You have talked of me to her?"

"Yes." Charlie bent his head. "Of course I have mentioned you. In fact, she helped me pick out this gift for you. She sends her best wishes."

"She knows that you are giving me a gift? What does she think of that?"

"All she has said on the matter is that I should be generous and kind to you. She thinks you a bright and spirited young woman. I think that you remind her of herself when she was your age."

"You are presumptuous. Your mother is so much above me."

"Only in age. And you must remember when I say that, that I love my mother very well." He lifted up the package. "Finish that glass of champagne so I might fill your glass again, and then I will give you this gift."

I gulped down the rest of the drink and handed him my glass, being as obedient as I had ever been in his presence. In exchange he handed over the lovely gold-wrapped box large enough to hold a garment. I carefully undid the bow and eased the package out of the paper, folding it carefully, wanting to save it all. Then I opened the box and found nestled in fine white tissue paper a lovely paisley shawl, burgundy with a gold band running through it so that it looked like it was shot with gold.

"Oh," I said with great wit and again, "oh, Charlie."

While words failed me, my hands went to work and pulled the shawl out of its wrappings and twirled it over my head, wrapping it around my shoulders. My dark best dress was transformed. With the shawl adorning my shoulders, I felt as well dressed as any woman I had ever seen. The shawl was so beautiful, easily one that his mother might have worn, and she was certainly the most elegant woman I had known.

"Yes, that color becomes you," he said from his seat where he watched me with pleasure.

"This is too much," I started.

"Not enough," he assured me.

"I can't possibly . . ."

"You must."

"But . . ."

"For my mother's sake."

"You fight most unfairly."

"Yes, I do."

"I will remember that."

"I hope you will."

I stood and twirled around in front of the fire to show him the full effect. "How does it look?"

"Fine on such a lovely model."

We made it through dinner, eating slowly and leisurely, course by course, drinking a red wine with the main course of pheasant and potatoes, and finally dessert was brought in, a lovely white cake with flowers decorated in the frosting, a single candle burning in the center of it.

"Blow it out and you'll get your wish."

"You've made it too easy," I laughed at him.

"I mean it to be easy."

I thought for a moment of all I wanted. I looked at Charlie, wished in my mind that I might find true love, and then I blew at the candle. The light flickered for a moment, then burned brightly again. Quickly I blew again and it went out. We both laughed, and then he grabbed my hand and pulled me to his lap.

"Let me feed it to you," he asked and then kissed me.

The kiss lasted a good long while. I felt like I had already had the cake, so sweet it tasted on my lips.

After the kiss, he cut me a piece of the cake and fed it to me, patting my lips between each bite. I laughed and laughed, giddy with the closeness of him.

One more glass of champagne followed, and then Charlie asked if he might show me the view from his bedroom.

"What view is there from the bedroom windows that you cannot see out these windows?" I asked, wondering how he would handle this question.

"A bit of the mountains." He answered very seriously and led me into his room. I followed. He took me to the street-side window and pointed up through the streets, and indeed there was a gap in the building through which a glimpse of the hilltops could be seen. He stood behind me as I peered out at it.

"The snow gleams in the moonlight," I said.

"Yes," he replied. Then I felt his arms wrap around my waist and come up under my arms. "But not nearly as brightly as your radiant skin." He kissed me on the neck right below my ear.

I said nothing, but stood feeling his breath on my neck. I did not move, surprised that I wanted him to kiss me again. I wanted to turn in his arms and kiss him back twice as full and as hard as he had embraced me.

Then I remembered myself. While I was intrigued by the thought of being Charlie Hunt's wife, I wasn't sure that was what he intended, as much as he might talk of courting me, as much as he might insist that I was an equal to his mother. "I think I must go now, Charlie."

He turned me in his arms and looked down into my face. "Stay just a little while longer."

Before I could answer, he kissed me full on the mouth, which stopped me from adding to my argument. The only thing I appeared to like better than arguing with Charlie Hunt was kissing him. I noticed that we were slowly moving backward into the room.

Suddenly, I was pushed back and fell upon the bed. Charlie stretched out next to me. "Brigid, I think I'm falling in love with you."

I had never had a man say such words to me. I so wanted to believe him, that he might love me, that he might be capable of such a thing. But one small spot in my mind continued to think, and I realized that giving in to him might not be the smart thing to do. I also knew that if I let him kiss me one more time, I was lost.

So I asked the only question I could think of that might bring our movements to a halt before it was too late to stop them. "But I must know: what were your dealings with Lily?" I sat up and looked down at him.

Charlie sat up next to me. "What about her? She's dead and buried these past four weeks."

"Certainly I know that, but what I would like to discuss is what you were to her or, rather, what she was to you."

"Not what you think."

"What do you mean?"

He looked quite uncomfortable. "Well, to be frank, I did not pay her for her pleasures."

"What?" I was more shocked than I thought I could be. "You did not pay her to be with you?"

"No, I did pay her. But I did not sleep with her."

I sat on the edge of the bed. "What are you telling me?"

"This does not make you happy?"

I tested my feelings. I had seen Lily. I knew how lovely she was. "I'm not sure I believe you."

He looked distressed. "Brigid, you must understand."

"I will try."

"It happened before I knew you."

"I realize that."

"I was trying to buy the claim, and I did not trust your brother and Paddy."

"What has that to do with Lily?"

"I knew that she was friendly with Seamus, and I thought I might get some information from her. So I hired her to find out what they were doing with the claim, if they were salting it."

"What is salting, exactly?"

"Adding gold illegally to the ore so that it makes it look like the claim is worth more than it is."

I stood up. He had been snooping about and had hired Lily to spy for him. Pretty low to ask my brother's fiancée for such information. That explained what he had said to his father the night I had overheard them talking about the claim.

"I see."

He tried to pull me back down onto the bed with him, but I resisted.

"What do you see?" He suddenly got angry in a way that I had never seen him do before. "You do not seem to ever believe anything I say, Brigid."

I tried to disagree, but he continued.

"No, hear me out." He took me by the shoulders and forced his face close to mine. "First, you must check to be sure I didn't abduct you and tie you up in a mine shaft, that I did not kill Lily, and now that I did not sleep with her. Even before this all, at my parents' house, you had to ask the other servants about my previous engagement. I know because Aggy told me. What must I do so that you will trust me?"

"But I am the one who is in a vulnerable position. What would you doubt about me? Is there any matter in which I might trick you?" I pulled away from him, angry that he did not see my situation better.

"Yes, there is. For one, you might be in league with your brother and his friends to get the most money out of me for the mine. For another, you might trick me about your very feelings for me, your affection. You could be going along with me now, having dinner with me, leading me on, so that

I would think more favorably about the mining deal. Or maybe you will even take it further. Marry me for my money."

"That you could think that . . ." I stomped my foot.

I gathered up my wrapper and left the room. I swept down the darkened hallway and then tripped down the grand stairway into the entrance. Before I went outside, the doorman helped me into my wrapper and held the door for me. The night had turned colder and a sniveling wind wound through the streets. I ran for home.

Charlie did not follow me, and I must admit part of myself was disappointed. What would I have become if I had stayed? A streel like many of the women in Deadwood—or a wife?

28

The day after my birthday, the sky was close and heavy with steel-gray clouds above us like the lid of a cast-iron pan. This lid rested on the high hills that surrounded the town and gave the sense that we were truly closed in.

Elizabeth had complained to me that "February, while technically being the shortest month of the year, here in the territories lasts forever." Already I knew what she was talking about. The month, while barely started, seemed interminable, with the same cold, steely days we had had most of January. I found that I had grown bone tired of this winter.

"I'm off to work at the claim today," Billy announced as the three of us sat around the table and ate warm oatbread and coffee.

I longed for a bit of sweetness, some jam to put on our bread, but we were very low on gold at the moment. If Billy went to the claim, we might be able to shop for some food supplies. Besides, I was all for getting him out of the house. He had been nothing but a nuisance and a bother the past two weeks.

"I don't know about that," said Paddy. "Myself I don't care for the look of the sky this morning."

"The great weather foreseer. Looks the same as it has looked the past fortnight, Paddy."

"I'd lay odds that we'll be in a storm before nightfall."

"And I will be home before that happens," Billy assured him.

Billy was in a queer mood these days—waiting did not suit him at all. I had told them that Charlie had been quite positive about the claim settlement and that we would probably hear from the Hunts today or tomorrow. Professor Underwood was still on his way and so was the man with our ore sample.

"I'd like to pull a bit more gold out of the earth before we sell it. Lord knows, we could use it."

"Be off with you, then," Paddy agreed. "But go now and do not stay out too late. You'll have to camp there if it gets too bad."

I cleared off the table and was washing the dishes when Billy left.

Paddy came up behind me and said, "I'm off to run to the hardware store. Can I get you anything, Brigid?"

I kept working away at the dishes. The water cooled so fast I had to work quickly. "Paddy, thanks, but I'm fine."

"Did you have a good birthday?" he asked.

I turned and faced him. He had a solemn, rather distant look on his face as if he were asking the question merely out of politeness.

"Fine enough. Did your family make a fuss about the birthdays?"

"No, not much of one. There was never enough to go around in the ordinary run of things, so a birthday was nothing but another day. How was it with your family?"

"Much the same. My mother would try to add a festive note, even during the hard times."

"But you had a fine meal then, last night? I heard you come in not so late."

"It was a very nice meal indeed, but I think we'll all be glad when this transaction is done."

"Is Mr. Hunt serious about you?" He looked me straight in the face.

"Who's to know."

"Do you believe him?"

I looked to Paddy. "Do you?"

His face dropped. Then he said, "I might not be the man to ask." His words trailed off, and without another word he left the room.

I watched him go, my hands in the cooling dishwater, wondering who had caused the ache in my heart—Charlie or the look in Paddy's eyes.

*   *   *

As soon as he was out the door, I whisked off my apron and went to put on my wrapper and new shawl. I hoped that if I questioned Nellie today I would know the truth about Charlie. But before I could step out the door, I heard a knocking. Elizabeth peeked her head in.

When I invited her in, she held a hand over her stomach and burst into tears. "I don't know what to do," she said through her tears.

I pulled her to a chair and made her sit quietly by the fire, rubbing her shoulders. "Cry for a bit longer. It will pull the sadness out of you."

She did as she was told, and when she came out of her sobbing, she said, "I need your advice, Brigid."

"I can give that, and freely too."

She rubbed her face with a handkerchief and gave me a small smile. "My husband has still not returned and it's over a month now he has been gone. I can ignore his absence no longer. The first week I thought I would see him any day. The second week I enjoyed being on my own because of the attention I was receiving, the third week I tried to put it out of my mind, but now I'm past the fourth week, and I'm afraid this child grows bigger in me with every day. What if my husband never comes home? I can't have this child all by myself. What am I to do?"

"Do you have money?"

"Yes, enough for another month or so. He left me with enough for a few weeks, but I had held some by for myself that he did not know about."

"What do you want to do?"

Without hesitation, she said, "I want to go home. This is not the life I want out here in the frontier and certainly not the life I want for my child. I want to go back to Philadelphia."

"What about your soldier friend?"

"He is a nice man, but he's not my husband. I can't be here by myself anymore. If my husband loves me, he can come back to Philadelphia to be with me."

"Sounds to me like you are fair finished with this life."

"Might I do that? Desert my husband?"

"Is it possible that he has deserted you? Or maybe is even dead?" I only said to her what I knew she must be thinking.

"Yes, you are right. He might be dead, and if he is, I will be sorry and I will miss him, but no matter what, I want to go back to the States."

"Then you shall," I told her.

"Really? You think I can manage the trip on my own?"

"I do."

"Oh, but Brigid, you are nearly as brave as a man. You can shoot a gun and ride a horse. I know nothing of such things."

"There is a good man who drives the coach who helped me from Cheyenne. I'll give you his name and you find out when he's driving. He will watch over you and help you get to the train."

She lifted her face up to me and smiled at the thought of the train. "I know I could manage the train. I will only pack what I really need. I will leave you my books, Brigid. I know you will take care of them."

For a moment, I thought again of my idea for a bookstore. Maybe Elizabeth's small cache of books might be the start of my own store. Then I thought of Charlie Hunt and all that he might be promising me. If his promise led to marriage, I would have it all: wealth, honor, respect, and hopefully my own family safe around me. I would never want for anything again.

But there were other towns farther west that Paddy had talked of—Cheyenne, Portland, and the famed San Francisco, which was called the Paris of the West. What might life be like out there—for a woman of some means and some ambition?

Elizabeth, sheltered woman that she might be, was making a good decision for her life and the child she carried. I wondered what decision I might make.

*   *   *

When I stepped out the door, the cold of the air shocked me. Each breath felt like it was filled with shards of ice. I had to think that Paddy was right about the weather—there did feel to be a difference in the air, an ominous feeling that something would break over our heads soon.

The only place I knew to look for Nellie was the Gem. The theater was quiet so early in the morning, but there were still women promenading themselves in scanty clothing past the few available men. I went up to one of them, a tall woman with a wart on her nose, bright red lips, and eyes nearly as red, and asked her if she could direct me to Nellie.

"She's not working today," she said and stared at me, taking in my new scarf with jealous eyes.

"Does she have a room here?"

"Nah, them rooms above they're only working rooms, you know what I mean?" She gave a sharp little laugh and cocked her hip. She was so accustomed to flirting that she even did it with me. Or perhaps she was simply trying to make me uncomfortable.

"Do you know where I might find her?"

"Did ya try Billy's place? She's often over there when she's not working. He's her fancy man."

"I am aware of that, but she's not there this morning."

"Well, then she camps down to the Grand Central on her days off sometimes. You might try that."

I left the Gem and walked two streets down to the hotel. When I asked for her at the desk, I realized I did not know her last name. I tried anyway, "Please, sir. I'm looking for Nellie."

The older gentleman behind the desk looked over his eyeglasses at me, cleared his throat, and then said, "She's up in the top floor toward the back. Room number 333."

I nodded and followed his hand wave to the stairs, climbing till I got to Nellie's floor. When I stood in front of her door, I hesitated. I was sure she would be found sleeping. After all, it was her day off and she usually stayed up all hours of the night. She might not be in the best of moods when I talked to her, but I must do it. Stepping forward, I faced the wooden door.

I knocked. At first there was no sound. I knocked again. A rustle of bedclothes. I knocked with more force. A hard object, I guessed a shoe, hit the inside of the door. Then I said her name, "Nellie, it's Brigid."

A bed creaked. What if she were not alone? But it was too late for me to leave. I heard footsteps on the floor. Then the door opened and Nellie stood before me in a silk kimono-style wrapper. Her hair was down and her face had the remnants of makeup smeared on it. She stepped out into the hallway with me, pulling the door shut behind her, and this confirmed my notion that someone was in her bed.

She shook her head as if to clear it and asked, "Brigid, what brings you out so early in the morning?"

"Nellie, I am sorry to wake you. And when you hear what I have to ask, you might think me a fool."

"Out with it. I've got a better place to be than standing here in the blasted cold hallway." She lifted one foot up and then the other as I spoke to her, the floor must have been that cold.

"Charlie told me that he paid Lily, but that he didn't sleep with her." I spoke as fast as I could, hoping to get the words out before I froze up. "Is that true? Would you know if that's true?"

Nellie's eyes opened wider and a smile played on her face. "He told you that, did he?"

"Yes."

"Why?"

"Because I wanted to know what kind of man he was."

"Why?"

"Because he has declared his intentions toward me."

"Good for you, lovey. He's not a bad man. Truth be told, Lily did mention something of the likes of that to me. Said he was an odd bird. Don't get me wrong, though, she liked him fine. Paid her money and asked her questions and left her same as he found her."

"Asked her questions about the claim?"

"I guess that was it. You know, what Seamus might have planned or some such matter." She shook her head and then talked close to my face. "You listen to me, Brigid, you marry that man before you do anything with him. This is your chance, girl. Don't waste it."

She looked toward the closed door, then whispered, "How's my Billy boy?"

"Fine. He's gone off to work at the claim today."

"Good for him. A little work won't hurt him none."

Knowing how close Nellie and Billy were, I asked her, "Did you ever tell Billy about Lily and Charlie? I mean, the fact that she talked to him about the claim?"

She thought for a moment and then nodded her head. "I did, in fact. I think I mentioned Charlie's questions to Billy."

"When was this?"

"Christmas Eve. That's why I didn't stay the night. Got him all upset. He didn't like the idea one bit of Charlie asking around about them. Sent him off the deep end, it did indeed. I left shortly thereafter."

"How mad was he?" I asked.

"You know Billy, he has a dark cloud inside him."

29

The air had turned sharper and bits of ice were flying in the strong wind that rushed through the streets of Deadwood. The bitterness of it swept against me, biting at my face. The sky was coming on darker, and yet it was only near to midday. Even to me, unused to this weather, it felt like a fearsome storm might be coming our way.

I thought to go home, but I wanted to tell Charlie what I had just heard. Truth be told, I wanted to see him again and reassure myself that he had not turned against me after last night. I wrapped my scarf over my head and walked down to his hotel.

At the desk I asked the tall gentleman if Mr. Hunt was in his room. He looked up from his ledger and scanned me from head to toe, then scooped back his dark hair and pushed it behind his ears. I was coming to know the demeanor of hotel clerks.

"I beg your pardon," he said in a snooty voice that meant in fact he did not.

I repeated my question. He glanced back at the row of keys that hung from hooks under boxes behind him. "I don't believe so."

"Are you sure?"

"As sure as I may be."

"May I go up and look?"

"Be my guest."

I walked up the stairs and then down the corridor to Charlie's room. I knocked on the door and waited to hear footsteps, then knocked again. Nothing. I leaned back against the door. I was buzzing with this new information and wanted to do something, to tell someone.

A door opened down the hallway and Professor Underwood came out without seeing me. He turned his back to me and locked his door, singing a small tuneless song under his breath.

I called to him, "Professor. You have arrived."

He spun around and then smiled when he saw me—or showed what passed for a smile on his thin face.

"Oh, Miss Reardon, I must show you," he exclaimed, rubbing his hands together. "I must show you what I have brought back with me from St. Paul. Come and see, come and see." He turned back to his door and quickly opened it again. Then he motioned me into his room.

I walked in and saw that he was in a smaller suite than Charlie, a single bed with a window that overlooked the back alleyway. On his bureau was an object wrapped in brown paper, and he lifted that up carefully. He removed the paper gently and handed the object to me. There was a kind of reverence in the way he handled the thing that made me wonder what it was.

A small bar of gold lay in my hand, so shiny as to appear painted, and much heavier than I would have thought it, to look at it.

"What is this lovely thing worth?" I asked the professor.

"You are holding a bar that weighs nearly a pound. It is worth three hundred and twenty dollars."

He took it back from me and returned it to its wrappings. "This means that the claim is very much worth Mr. Hunt's time and energy. We had hoped and assumed that the claim would prove valuable, but the ore is much richer than expected."

"Wonderful news indeed!" I told him because I knew he wanted to hear my excitement. Then I asked him, "Do you know where Mr. Hunt is?"

"I thought he was on his way over to your house. He wanted to talk to Billy. Did you not see him?"

This surprised me. I would have thought that he would talk to Padraic or myself. "Why Billy?"

"I'm really not sure, and he wouldn't tell me what business it was. I assured him that everything had been on the up and up with the ore sample. He simply nodded his head. He can be close-mouthed when he chooses. Yes, Mr. Hunt is quite pleased with the prospect of the claim, I can tell you."

I needed to get to the two of them. I had my own questions to ask Billy, and I certainly wanted someone there with me when I did.

❋ ❋ ❋

I had hoped Charlie would be waiting for me at the house, but no one was there when I arrived. The door had been left standing open, and the sight of a small drift of snow in the house scared me.

Where had Paddy gone? And Charlie? Had they ridden out to the claim? I could at least check at the livery stable. They might be able to tell me if Charlie had taken out his horse.

If need be, I decided I would ride out to the claim myself.

I pulled on a pair of dungarees under my dress and a woolen sweater of Paddy's. The buffalo hat was nowhere to be found so I wrapped my scarf around my head. I put on my heavy boots, then pulled Billy's vest over everything.

I left the house, closing the door tightly behind me and stood on the front step for a moment. Then I went back in. After retrieving the derringer, I checked that it carried bullets in its belly and tucked it into the pocket of my jacket.

As I walked toward the livery stable, the snow sifted down on me. So light and gentle, yet I noticed it was piling up on the sides of the road. I avoided the fresh manure steaming on top of the snow as I turned into the door of the stables.

A heavily whiskered man was feeding hay to the horses.

I asked him if Charlie Hunt had taken out his horse.

"Yup. Not so awful long ago. 'Bout half an hour or so. I told him not good weather to be travelin' in."

"I'd like to take out Gertie."

"I'd not advise it. This snow's goin' pile up something fierce."

"I won't be gone long," I assured him. "And our claim is not so very far."

"See that you're not. There's no guarantee this sky won't fall right down on top of you."

He brought out Gertie, and she shook herself all over when the saddle was placed on her back.

"If anything happens to this horse, it's your money that pays for it," he said as he gave me a hand up on the horse.

"Yes, sir."

As I rode out of town, I stuck my hand into the pocket of Billy's vest and felt a wad of cloth. I pulled it out carefully, expecting to see a nugget of gold. It would be just like Billy to have tucked some gold into his pocket. I did see a flash of gold, but not in the form I had expected.

Instead, a ring.

A gold ring.

I looked on the inside of the ring and saw two initials engraved there: Seamus and Lily's.

My heart froze in my chest. How had the ring come to be in Billy's vest? As I realized what must have happened, I drove the horse onward into the woods.

❊　❊　❊

The forest was dark and deep. The branches of the trees bowed under the weight of the snow blankets they carried. The silence followed us down the trail. The slight depression of recent hoof prints could be seen, the snow filling them up quickly.

On the trail alone, my thoughts worried over what I had learned. Billy knew about Lily's relationship with Charlie; he had been drinking and angry; and most incriminating of all, he had the ring in his pocket.

As my thoughts raced, I prodded the horse along, and sweet creature that she was, she caught my mood and picked up her speed.

I was sore anxious about what I might find at the claim. I resolved to say nothing to Billy, but simply get Charlie away and then tell him all that I had learned. Charlie would surely know what to do.

I ran into no other rider on the trail, on account of the weather I was sure. Finally I rode past the turnoff to the Walker claim and knew I was within earshot of ours. Slowing my horse down, I came to the turnoff from the trail down into the valley.

Pulling up my horse, I listened. All I heard was a thudding noise. Billy working at the claim, I thought.

When I clucked my tongue, the horse stepped out. The poor thing was probably as cold as I was.

Slowly, through the snow, we moved forward.

I stopped when I heard two voices rising up through the snow and trees, shouting.

30

"I mean to have her," a man roared from deep in the valley. I was sure the voice was that of Charlie.

I shivered from cold and from fear. My father had taught me if you were afraid in your heart, pray to God to be with you.

Quietly, I let the horse move forward at its own slow pace. The snow muffled the sound of its hooves hitting the dirt path. The wind whistled through the trees. Above it all, I could hear the voices of two men.

Billy's voice rang out. "I will not lie for you again. And you will not have Brigid. You have taken enough, God damn ye, and enough is enough!"

Through the bare tree branches, I made out a fire burning. The flames glowed bright orange in this whitened world. I tried to see through the snow's fine net and find the men.

Someone was sitting on their haunches near the fire. I could tell by the red cap that it was Billy himself. He was rocking slowly back and forth.

Then I saw another form standing by the fire with his back toward me. Tall and straight. I made it to be Charlie. I didn't see Paddy anyplace and I had hoped to find him there.

He spoke to Billy. "I'll have her. There is nothing you can do to stop me and I have everything in my power to stop you. This deal for the claim will not go through unless you keep your part of the bargain."

At these words, I stopped. What could have brought this argument on? I dismounted and tied up Gertie. Keeping myself in the shadows of the fir trees, I crept closer to the men.

Billy stood up and moved away from the fire.

But Charlie would not let him go. He strode up to Billy and pushed him in the chest. "You're deep in this, Billy. Don't you think of backing out now. Lily's death was as much your doing as it was my own."

I stopped and sank down into the snow.

"We did what we set out to do," Charlie roared. I had never heard him raise his voice like that before. "We drove Seamus out of town and left the claim in your hands. All has worked out as planned. You will get what you want, more money than you'll know what to do with, you stupid Mick."

Billy finally answered him. "Once we sell the claim to you, we're leaving, and Brigid is coming with us. You're not to have her. She was never part of the bargain."

"She is the cherry on top of the pudding. She's a pretty little thing, and I've made up my mind to have her."

"So that is the way it is?" Billy asked.

"All you have to do is tell Brigid that Lily never slept with me," Charlie explained. "She's ready to believe it. She might already. Nellie already told her as much this morning. Brigid might not even ask you anything about it. But if she does, you know what you must say."

Nellie. How did he know what Nellie had told me? Then I remembered the closed door to her room, the way she moved me away from the door when she told me to get Charlie to marry me before sleeping with him. Everything was falling into horrible place.

Charlie had been in her bed. When I left him last night, he had sought another woman out, one who would serve two needs for him: one who would sleep with him for money and lie for him for the same.

While I was standing outside the hotel room door, Charlie had been lounging in the warmth of Nellie's bed, listening to me.

The snow fell as slowly as a feather. I felt my body wanted to fall with it. The cold came into my heart and I shivered as if I would never stop.

The two men were standing between the fire and the mouth of the new mine shaft. Billy shouted, "I will tell Brigid how you have been with every pretty woman here in Deadwood. Lily included. I will warn her that this will not stop, even if you do marry her, which I doubt would ever happen. Why would you marry her when you can have her when you want? Buy her like any other woman?"

Charlie moved in toward Billy. "You will tell her what I ask of you or

I will tell everyone that you killed Lily. My man will swear to it. You are in no position to try to bargain with me."

Billy spat at Charlie. "The devil spits on your soul. I hate the day I met you. I will tell her the truth—that it was you who killed our Lily."

At these words, Charlie jumped at him and the two men locked arms. They were fighting on the cleared ground in front of the new mine shaft. The snow scraped to dirt beneath their boots. I could hear the sound of their breathing, harsh like horses pulling heavy loads.

I stood up and felt in my pocket for the derringer.

Charlie was much bigger than Billy, but Billy was fast. He pulled away from Charlie and then danced around him, landing punches when he could. Like a gnat, he buzzed around Charlie and stung him. Charlie connected less often, but when he did, he did damage. Billy's face was bleeding and Charlie was getting the better of him.

Suddenly Billy ran to the entrance of the mine. Charlie followed. Billy reached down and grabbed a pickax that was leaning by the opening. He held it out and motioned Charlie away with it. But Charlie moved in on him again. Billy was forced to defend himself and swung the ax at Charlie's head. Charlie caught a glancing blow and went down.

Billy backed off, unwilling to finish Charlie off. He held the ax dangling from his one arm and breathed hard in the cold air.

When I stepped forward, Billy lifted his head and saw me.

❋   ❋   ❋

In the time it took Billy to recognize me, Charlie pushed himself up in a fury and ran at Billy. Billy said my name and then Charlie pushed him hard in the chest.

Billy flew backwards, falling into the mine opening. He fell into the mouth of the earth as if his body were parting the waters of an ocean. The darkness swallowed him up. A scream and then a thud and then silence. He was gone.

I was alone with Charlie Hunt.

"Brigid." He said my name softly as if I were a shy animal he wanted to call in.

I had the derringer hidden in the folds of my skirt. I stood my ground.

"Mr. Hunt," I answered.

"It was Billy who killed Lily. His idea entirely. He wanted to get rid of Seamus, for Seamus was opposed to selling the mine." He spoke quickly.

I did not say anything. Let Charlie pour out the words like waves pounding a far shore— they meant nothing to me. I believed him not at all.

"I had to stop him before he did more killing. He was talking of harming you, and I would never let that happen."

I nodded.

Charlie started walking toward me. "You know I would never let anything happen to you. When he put you in the mine shaft, I went nearly mad trying to find you. He wouldn't tell me where you were."

I felt sick deep inside of me. I needed to get to Billy. Somehow I must get past Charlie. He continued to walk up the hill toward me.

"Let us leave this place now. Billy's dead, I'm sure, and we need never think of this again. We can say that it was an accident, and in many ways it was. I want to take you home. Back to my parents' house and marry you as soon as possible."

In some old part of me, I wanted to do what he suggested. I wanted to go back in time to his parents' house so that I would never become the woman I now was. But it was not possible, any more than I could make the snow fall up into the sky.

I could not feel my face. I looked at Charlie. If I felt anything for him, it was a deep and abiding hatred.

He was within two body lengths of me. With a rush, he could be upon me. He would push me down the shaft just as he had done to Billy. I knew I could wait no longer. With a sure hand, I lifted the derringer and sighted as Paddy had shown me. Charlie yelled at me to stop.

I pulled the trigger. My shot found its mark in the cold winter air.

Charlie fell.

Blood stained the snow.

He gasped and writhed on the ground, his body arching from the pain.

I had shot a hole in his leg, which was my intention. I was surprised I had succeeded. He would stay put for a while, I hoped.

Not looking at him, I made my way to the mine shaft.

Behind me, I heard him calling my name. His voice came out in a whimper. I would not help him.

Down into the dark shaft I went without even the help of the head-lamp, going hand over hand on the ladder strapped to the side of the shaft. The light fell in a narrow stream, and at the bottom of the shaft I could see Billy's white face upturned to the sky.

I stepped down next to him and touched him. He groaned and I was careful not to move him.

"Billy, I'm here."

"Oh Brigid. I've done you such wrong."

"Don't think of that now, Billy. Tell me what to do. What do you need? What can I do for you?"

"I'm hurt deep inside. I'm no good anymore." I could see his face and blood came to his tongue. I knew he spoke the truth.

"Billy, lie still. Save yourself. I'll go get Paddy."

He reached for me. "No, please don't leave me here, Brigid. Stay with me. Like St. Brigid, you'll see that I make it to heaven. Please hear my confession."

I shushed him, but he would not stop talking.

"You know the saying . . . there are three oaths you must believe: that of a woman giving birth, that of man without land, and the oath of a dead man. I am the last, Brigid, hear me out."

I held his hand and squeezed it.

"Charlie killed Lily. He did it before anyone even knew he was back in town. He figured that Seamus would be blamed. With Seamus out of the way, Paddy and I could sell the claim to him." Billy paused to get his breath and I heard a rattle in his throat. "I did not stop him. I watched and I did nothing to stop him. Sure, she was a streel, but all in all Seamus loved her. I must confess, I wanted the money."

I bowed my head. For money she was killed.

"I found the ring," I said.

"Yes, I took it from her hand. I did not want Charlie to have it." Billy went on. "I did not want Charlie to have you, either. Which is why I put you in the mining shaft. To scare you and put you on your guard. I wanted you to think Charlie had done it. But I would not have left you there, Brigid. I only meant to put the fear into you. You must believe me."

"I do, Billy. I do."

"I could not let Charlie have you. I knew he would treat you badly, and you have been like a sister to me."

Suddenly, his face froze and he gasped, "God help me." His head turned violently to the side and a sound crept up his throat like wind blowing through a mine shaft. Blood threaded its way out of his mouth and he lay motionless.

Death settled heavy in the darkness and I felt weary of it. In the silence, I asked Billy to forgive me for the part I had played in his dying.

The gloom of the shaft grew around me, and I knew I had to leave him there. I stood and made the sign of the cross over him. I prayed his soul to heaven to be with all the saints and angels.

I climbed up out of the shaft in time to see Charlie struggling onto his horse, his leg hanging useless as he pulled himself up onto the saddle. He did not look back. He clung to the saddle and urged the horse to ride off up the hill. When he reached my horse, Gertie, he untied her and took her with him. The trail of blood he left behind glittered in the snow. Soon it would be covered with white.

The snow drew the world in tight around me. My derringer was loaded and close at hand in my pocket. I faced the path that led out of the claim and watched the snow fall.

The fire warmed me through and I sat staring at the flames dancing as if to some unheard music, a jig, a reel, some haunting tune that accompanied Billy on his journey away from this world and into the next.

*　*　*

After time had passed, I saw a horse and rider moving through the trees. The fire had sunk low and I was feeling very sleepy. The thought of lying down in the snow had come to me.

I felt no fear. What would come, would come.

But as I watched the rider come near, I recognized a face I loved, and hope poured through me.

Paddy called my name as he rode down the hill. "The man at the livery told me you had taken a horse. I came as quick as I could."

When I said nothing but looked up at him with tears running from my eyes, he leapt down from his horse and came to me.

"Is it as bad as that?" he asked, standing over me.

I nodded.

"Billy? Is he all right?" he asked.

I shook my head.

"What has happened here?" he asked, looking around.

I could not say.

He knelt down next to me and opened his arms, saying, "Brigid, my own."

I moved into the warmth of his arms, and all I could say was, "Paddy, I prayed you would come."

31

For the day or two after Billy's death, I was good for nothing at all. I lay abed and slept and wept when not sleeping. Paddy brought me broth and told me more stories of his childhood, the happy ones. I told him briefly what had happened. He asked me no questions.

On the third day, I knew it was time to get up when the sun made its way to my window. Late afternoon, I finally rose from my bed, cleaned myself as best I could, and dressed. Paddy was out of the house for the moment, and when he came back, he found me sitting up in a chair near to the fire.

"It's good to see you up."

"When is the funeral for Billy?"

"The morrow." Paddy took off his jacket and sat down on the couch near me. "The priest is seeing to it. I've bought Billy a plot in the graveyard. Will you be well enough to go?"

"I will be well enough. I would not miss it. Have you heard news of Charlie?"

"He's left town. He was in a bad way. His kneecap was shattered. I don't know how they managed to move him, but I think they were afraid if he stayed, he would never walk again."

I tried to push the thought of Charlie from my mind. "No loss."

"Can you talk of it more, Brigid?" He reached out and took my hand.

So holding tight to his hand, I told him all that had happened: how I had talked to Nellie, how I had found the ring, the fight between Billy and Charlie, the fall, the shot. I even told him that I knew Charlie had been with Nellie.

"And so you shot him?" Paddy asked.

"I did. Not for what he did to me, but for Lily and Seamus and Billy."

"That wound will probably be all the punishment he will get, for no one will believe us that he killed Lily. And who knows what will come of our claim now."

"I know. I think we must use Billy's death to save my brother," I said. "If it is all right with you, I think we should let it be known that Billy killed Lily so Seamus will be free of the crime."

Paddy bowed his head. "I hate to do it, but you might be right. He had his hand in it too. If not for his silence, some of this wouldn't have happened. God forgive us."

I squeezed his hand. "I think he will."

❋   ❋   ❋

The following day Elizabeth left Deadwood. I helped her pack and walked with her to the stagecoach. Her books had been moved to our house, and she told me to rent out their house to someone and watch over it, in case her husband ever returned. She hugged me and I felt a deep sorrow at the thought of her leaving. There were not many women to be friends with in Deadwood. But then I didn't expect to stay much longer in the town myself.

The day of the funeral was cold and dark. We were a very small gathering—Father Lonegran, Paddy, Nellie, and myself. We said the prayers and listened to the Word, and then I threw a wee bit of gold dust down into the dirt on the coffin. I knew Billy would hate to leave it all behind.

Three days later, I heard the rumor going round town that Billy had killed Lily, and the sheriff talked to Paddy to confirm it. The wanted posters of Seamus came down from the storefronts.

Not long after, a letter arrived from Seamus, just a page of simple words, but I was never so happy to see his scrawl. He told us to sell the claim, however we could, and come to meet him in Cheyenne.

That night I was fixing dinner and Paddy said he must talk with me. "Oh, aye, I hate to tell you this but Nellie was found dead this morning."

"Paddy, never. What happened to her?"

"What I've been hearing is that she took the opium and it was too much for her."

I sat with the news. I knew that she had loved Billy. She must have heard the news that he had killed her friend Lily. And so another death.

They followed on each other so fast. Like links in a necklace, they were connected.

I fell to weeping and Paddy pulled me into his lap. "She was only a streel, my Brigid."

"But that's what makes me weep, that you too can say it so. Only a streel, a woman made to earn her living in a hard way like that. What if it were me? What if I too must become a streel?"

"I would never let that come to be. Do not think it."

"Paddy, what's to become of us?"

He touched my cheek to wipe a tear away. At his touch, I calmed. He said nothing and that felt right. We had not yet come to the time to say the words that might one day pass between us. I leaned against his chest and heard the comfort of his great heart beating there.

32

There was no fire and there was no whiskey and there were no cigars being smoked. There was no sense of camaraderie or joy. In fact, a somber feeling hung in the room. This was a business transaction. So it was on St. Patrick's Day, we went again to the Grand Central Hotel where we had once met before to discuss selling the Green Isle claim, but this time it was only Padraic and I, and we were talking to Mr. Hunt, Charlie's father, and Professor Underwood.

Before he left after Billy's accident, the professor had given us the gold bar made from the ore sample, and the money from that had tided Paddy and me over well until the meeting. Paddy had also gone out to the claim and continued to pull gold from the ground. I feared that Seamus had been right all along and that we would have more money if we held on to the claim and worked it ourselves, but I was sick to death of it, and so was Paddy.

In preparation for this meeting, I had ordered my first dress from the French woman—a lovely dark blue, it had a full skirt with flounces all down the back. I had cut Paddy's hair, shaved his face, and dressed him like a gentleman. He looked quiet and dignified; his dark, thick hair swept back from his face.

I held his arm as we entered the room. Mr. Hunt rose and bowed. The professor stood also and nodded his head. We all sat and Mr. Hunt pulled out some papers.

He looked over the papers through his small glasses and then lifted his head. There was to be no small talk. "We are ready to offer you two, as the remaining owners of the claim, thirty thousand dollars for the claim and all the rights that go with it," Mr. Hunt said in his solemn voice.

This was twice again as much as we had originally hoped to gain from the sale of the claim. But that was in another lifetime. The claim had gone up in price.

Mr. Hunt was addressing himself to Paddy and turned his head quickly when I began to speak.

"That is not an untoward offer, Mr. Hunt, and if it had been made several months ago, we might have accepted it. But claims are going for more money now, and much has passed between us and your family. Therefore, I feel I must ask for fifty thousand dollars."

Possibly I had an unfair advantage. I had worked in his household for almost a year. I had watched the amounts of money that were spent on keeping the family in style. I knew what this man could afford and I knew what we needed.

He blanched. "Fifty thousand dollars. Why, that's unheard of."

I continued. "What is unheard of is the manner in which your son went about guaranteeing the sale of the claim to your company."

"My son, what do you know?" Mr. Hunt spit out at me.

I could tell he was holding himself back.

"My son has little freedom these days. The leg turned gangrenous on the train ride home. We were barely able to save his life. He lost the leg; he has lost his health and nearly lost his mind."

Neither Paddy nor I answered anything to this statement.

There was silence in the room for a few moments and then Mr. Hunt cleared his throat. "I can offer you forty."

Somehow I stayed firm. "Fifty."

He bowed his head and repeated after me, "Fifty."

The numbers were written in to the papers, and we all signed them. I looked on as Paddy took the pen and paper and signed his name to it, *Padraic Hennessy.* He had been working on his signature for some weeks now. He was beginning to be able to read, and it delighted him to read the headlines in the paper aloud to me.

Mr. Hunt told us the money would be made available to us from whatever bank we would choose. We explained that we wanted it waiting for us in Cheyenne and that we would pick it up there in the weeks to come.

After the papers were in order, we all stood.

Mr. Hunt would not look at me. He did not offer me his hand. I held my head up high and took Paddy's arm, making ready to leave the room.

Finally, Mr. Hunt raised his head and said, "My son has not forgotten you."

"But I will forget him."

I felt the pressure of Paddy's hand on my arm. We walked out into the clear sunlight of the Black Hills in spring.

Author's Note

I am of Irish descent. A year after my mother's death I decided to find out where in Ireland my ancestors came from and why they emigrated to the United States. I was able to ascertain that my father's family, the Logues, were from Donegal and my mother's, the Kirwins, from Galway. In my research I was even able to find which ships two of my great-great-grandparents came over on in 1849.

While I can't say exactly why the Logues and the Kirwins left their homeland, after reading many stories of the potato famine, I'm quite sure they were pushed out by English landowners and forced by poverty to follow the promise of a better life in America. When I think of what they did, leaving all they knew behind—their family, their friends, their language—and arriving on a new continent, then making their way halfway across this unknown land, I'm astounded. I feel like the equivalent for me would be to take a spaceship to Mars and try to settle there.

Some years ago I wrote a book about my grandmother, *Halfway Home: A Granddaughter's Biography,* which told how she grew up in the far western part of Minnesota near the South Dakota border. A sense of not telling the whole story of such Irish immigrants never left me. I wanted to write more about what the Irish diaspora found when they came to this new land, so I set out to create a new character from my family history. My great-grandfather married a Reardon, and Brigid is an important saint in the Irish Catholic hierarchy—thus the name for my main character, Brigid Reardon, in *The Streel.* My brother, James Kirwin Logue, was called Jamie, but often we used the Gaelic form of his name, Seamus. Jamie died when he was only sixteen, and it was nice to honor him as Brigid's dearly loved brother.

I'm lucky to live with a wonderful writer, Pete Hautman. For a time Pete was somewhat addicted to poker, and the closest legal place to play it was Deadwood, South Dakota. We took several trips there, and while he lost and won money, I wandered around the town and soaked up the history from its early mining days. As a flatlander, I was fascinated by the Black Hills, a small mountain range, and Deadwood, an old mining town set in a deep valley. I was amazed to learn from reading menus from the 1870s that oysters had been shipped to its fancy restaurants from the West Coast. In its heyday the town was a wild and exciting place where almost anything could happen. When Brigid Reardon sprang to life, demanding her story be written, I knew where she would end up in this first tale.

My research for *The Streel* included studying maps, newspaper clippings and photographs, and other books written about this place and time. The James J. Hill House served as the model for the Hunt house in St. Paul. In Deadwood I read old diaries from women living in this frontier town; I imagined hearing their voices as they wrote about their daily lives. I even found an old book of Irish Gaelic prayers and translated many of them, with the blessing of an Irish priest from the University of Notre Dame.

So here are my thanks. First to Pete, for giving me all the space and support I needed to dive headlong into this book. To my two sisters, Robin and Dodie, for reading anything I hand them. For the Minnesota Historical Society Press, especially Ann Regan, Deborah Miller, and Jean Brookins, who in the early 1990s gave me a grant to write the history of my grandmother. And to all my ancestors, for the courage to come to this foreign land and make their way.

My gratitude also goes to all the librarians and researchers who helped me, finding just the right book that would give me the nugget of information I needed.

I am most thankful for the new home I've found at the University of Minnesota Press and quite grateful to work with Erik Anderson and the rest of the crew.

Go raibh maith agaibh.

Mary Logue is the author of thirteen mystery novels, including the Claire Watkins mystery series, and five volumes of poetry, several nonfiction books, and many young adult, middle grade, and children's books. She has received a Minnesota Book Award, a Wisconsin Outstanding Achievement award, and several Minnesota State Arts Board awards. Her picture book *Sleep Like a Tiger* won a Charlotte Zolotow honor, a Caldecott honor, and a Best Picture Book award in Japan. Her writing has been published in the *New York Times,* the *Star Tribune,* and the *Village Voice,* and she has taught writing at the University of Minnesota and Hamline University. She lives with writer Pete Hautman in Golden Valley, Minnesota, and Stockholm, Wisconsin.